SIERRA SUNRISE
A Mojave Adventure

Randall G Doughty

SierraSunriseComment@gmail.com

Copyright © 2022 Randall G Doughty

All rights reserved.

ISBN: **9798849461694**

110722

DEDICATION

This book is dedicated to my father, for he inspired this story.
"Write the book you'd like to read," he advised, so I did.
To my wife and children, whose help and patience made this book possible.

DISCLAIMER

This is a work of fiction. Unless otherwise indicated, all the names, characters, businesses, places, events, and incidents in this book are either the product of the author's imagination or used in a fictitious manner.

CHAPTER 1

There may be no more thrilling or inspiring sight in North America than standing high on the slopes of the Sierra Nevada Mountains and watching the red dawn rush at you from the east like a great silent ocean wave, flowing over hill and rock and sandy plain, to crash against the foothills below, shadows, scurrying before it like doomed children, fleeing from the light.

The cabin built by the Strider family was perched high on a shelf of land that was front row and center to this daily morning spectacle, a recurring reminder of the glory of creation.

All the days of the boy's life that he could remember had begun and ended in the same way. Mornings began with the familiar rattle of the firebox door being closed and latched on the heavy cast iron cookstove, a signal to roll over and pull the covers up over his head, where he would try to climb back down inside whatever dream he had just emerged from. Those moments of stolen sleep between the clank of metal and his mother's welcome call to the family to muster at the kitchen table for breakfast were the sweetest of the night. He knew that shortly there would begin a lullaby of clicks and clacks and scrapes from pans and skillets and spoons as his mother transformed the air of the kitchen into a feast of smells with her cooking, hot biscuits from the oven, fried ham, potatoes and eggs from the skillet, the sharp odor of glowing oakwood fueling the stove, and the spicy smell of burning coal oil from the soot-stained lantern forever hanging above the kitchen table.

Time for him was marked by the comfortable monotony of a full belly and the endless ramblings of a frontier boy loosed on the unexplored wilds of mountains and woods. There was enough discipline to make him respectful and enough love to make him thoughtful, and evenings spent in the comfort of his family led to nights of untroubled sleep. At this point in the boy's life, his world was small enough that he loved every person in it, for its isolation was as complete as an island floating through space. There was nothing his father could not do, no problem that his mother couldn't solve, and his vocabulary didn't yet include words like hate, fear, or sorrow.

For some reason, the sounds of this morning were different. He sensed it from the unnatural rhythm the wood chamber door made being closed by an unfamiliar hand, which failed to account for the worn hinges, forcing a second attempt before the latch would seat.

As the cobwebs of sleep slowly fell away, he noticed the patient smokey lantern light, warmed by the kitchen stove, drifting across the floor, sitting on the foot of his bed, and climbing the roughhewn log wall of his bedroom, clinging there faithfully as it did every morning waiting for him to rise.

"You awake in there boy?" came his father's subdued voice from the kitchen.

"Yessir," came the immediate reply.

"Get a move on then."

"Yessir."

It came back to him then. He had slept fully clothed except for his boots to be ready to go this morning. He now noticed his shirt twisted up around his chest and britches almost sideways, socks hopelessly lost in the folds of his quilts from his unusual, fitful, rolling sleep. In the cool shadows of morning, he stood, yanked, and pulled everything back into place as best he could. He grabbed a pair of socks, and the boots made for him by his mother from leather tanned from the hide of a mountain lion, shot while attacking the Appaloosa mare and her new foal by his father. He hurried into the kitchen, almost knocking over a chair that had strayed from its place beneath the kitchen table.

"Better take up a knot on that buffalo you're leadin over there son," his father said, peering back over his shoulder. "You know, the one it looks like you slept with last night!"

"Yessir, no buffalo, just me," the boy replied, looking down at the hopeless state of his clothes.

"I'da swore," said the man. "Here, this will iron you out," and he handed the boy a cup of hot black coffee. "I made a pot to get us started this morning."

The boy accepted the cup, which was a surprise, and he stood a little taller as a man would who was preparing to embark upon an important mission, wrinkled clothes and all. He couldn't recall another morning entering the kitchen and seeing his father standing at the cook stove with his mother nowhere in sight.

The man was tall for an Indian and lean due in part to the unlikely remnants of Scandinavian blood brought to America in some unknown past by a Viking explorer. How it made its way into a family of Native Americans residing in Arizona was a mystery of little consequence except when occasionally a child was born with bright blue eyes. The elders of the tribe many generations back had determined that it was the result of the mother drinking excessive amounts of the blue-green water that flowed through their valley at the bottom of the great canyon where the tribe's village had stood for generations beyond memory. The boy had the same lanky stature as his father, and both bore dark brown eyes that showed black except when seen in bright sunlight.

On the table sat a pan of cold biscuits and fried salt pork that the boy recognized as leftovers from yesterday morning's breakfast, likely put there by his absent mother.

They both sat down, and hands went into the pan and came back with the makings of cold, greasy biscuit sandwiches. In moments they were both going at them with the enthusiasm of a couple of hound dogs who had just remembered they were starving.

"Where's Momma?" the boy asked between bites.

"She went back to bed," said the man, glancing down the hall to see if the bedroom door was still closed.

"What did she say about me coming with?" asked the boy.

"Plenty," replied the man.

"Was she mad then?" his son asked, knowing that mad was a relative term when it came to his mother.

"Some, I guess," said the man.

The boy finished his first biscuit and lifted his cup to his lips, anticipating his first real taste of coffee, unpolluted with half a glass of cow's milk. He sipped, then rushed to the cook stove with pursed lips in a panic and spat a mouth full of coffee grounds into the ash pan. The man looked up as the boy hawked loudly and spat again, then returned to his seat, and frowned down into his cup.

"I wish she'd stayed up long enough to make the coffee," the boy offered.

Sierra Sunrise

The man raised his eyebrows and peered into his own cup, then grunted a reluctant agreement, for he was aware of his disability when it came to making coffee.

They each had another sandwich, then the man folded in the excess of dishcloth that lined the biscuit pan and tied the opposing corners making a bundle of the leavings. He stood and reached up to turn down the wick on the kitchen lantern, then carried the bundle to the door leading outside and set it down in favor of the chipped earthen bowl that his wife used to make up the dog's food, then opened the door.

The boy walked barefoot past him, carrying his coffee cup, and ceremoniously tipped it over and poured a clotted stream of brown liquid into the dirt. Expressionless, he turned again and started back inside.

The man stood curiously watching his son's small demonstration, and just before the boy stepped back in, he pushed the door shut. He waited with his hand on the door handle until he saw the boy start dancing on the frosty boards of the porch before reopening it.

"I like my coffee strong," he offered as the boy stepped quickly back inside.

"Yessir, strong enough to walk and carry a poleaxe!" the boy retorted.

The cold thin light of morning pouring in through the open doorway allowed the boy to slip on his socks and boots. Then they each located their blanket coats and hats on wall hooks and donned them, tying the waist straps tight and flipping up the tall collars against the chilled wind that was sure to be coming down from the mountain. Winter stayed long this high up the Sierra, even though it was almost May and spring was just around the corner.

On the porch, they were greeted by Juliet, the family's rawboned bluetick gyp, swinging her tail like a hickory branch back and forth so hard that her hind feet wouldn't stay put. She accompanied the man on all his hunts, and in between, she followed the children on their adventures, both with equal enthusiasm. She slept beneath the porch treads in straw during the winter and upon them in the otherwise and never failed to greet anyone exiting the kitchen door. The man dropped the leavings from last night's supper onto the planks, and the dog scarfed them up in two huffs and looked up for more, her red tongue dripping saliva, hung slack to one side as she grinned up at them.

The man looked from the dog to the boy as if comparing their common traits, and when his son gave him a look, he handed him the bowl and told him to grab the packet of food and close the door.

Patchy snow, crusty from being warmed by the sun, then refrozen in the dark, crunched beneath their feet as they made their way to the barn. They entered, leaving the doors swung wide for the dim light filtering in through the tall pines.

The boy slipped the halter over his father's big Appaloosa mare's face and then backed her from the stall, speaking softly, for she could get spooky in the early morning shadows. Her name was Sogalikas (sugar-making moon), the Indian word for the first full moon of April, as she had been born beneath its soft glow.

"Easy Sugar," the boy cooed as he pushed back on the reins.

The man had won the horse from a Nez Perce tracker, who wouldn't entertain selling the animal, but was unable to refuse a bet of a hundred dollars against the mare that he could put a rifle bullet through a Prince Albert tobacco tin at a hundred and fifty paces. The tracker, being long of leg, lit out at a dead run and covered some two hundred yards before stopping to hang the can upside down on the limb of a big red oak tree. Sporting a broad smile, and thinking himself clever for outsmarting the man, the tracker returned, only to be disappointed after watching the can fly over the oak tree at the first shot. The man gave the Indian the hundred dollars anyway, explaining that the Nez Perce are well known for breeding Appaloosa and tracking, but not so much for their gambling skills. In the recollection of all who knew the man, he had never lost this bet.

The boy walked his father's horse into the patch of dim light framed by the doorway and dropped the reins to the ground, anchoring her there while he flipped a cold saddle blanket up over her spotted rump and settled it on her back. After he rubbed it down smooth with his hands, he went to the saddle rack and hooked the right stirrup of his father's heavy leather saddle over the horn before swinging it with difficulty up onto her back.

By now, the man had lead ropes on the two tall blond mules that the boy's younger siblings had christened Rachel and Leah, having just learned the sister's names from a Bible story taught to them by their mother the day that he had led them home. He walked them over to a feed trough nailed to the wall and drew two hands of grain from a gunny sack to buy their patience while he rigged them up. He squared the thick pad on Rachel's back and then lifted a sawbuck saddle up on top of it. He reached under, pulled the front cinch strap up, fitted its latigo through the D-ring on the sawbuck tree, pulled it tight and knotted it, then did the same on the rear cinch, pulling it a bit more snuggly than he had the front. He pulled the breaching strap under the mule's tail, attached the flank strap and quarter strap to the tree, tested each adjusting strap for placement, and then did it all again on Leah. Finally, he hung two large canvas pack panniers on the sides of the X frames of each saddle and loaded in the supplies they had gathered the day before.

The boy saddled his own four-year-old filly named Dotty, sired by his father's Mustang stud, purchased in California after the Great War, and the daughter of the Appaloosa mare. Sadly, the man had been forced to put the Mustang down two years ago after a rabid coyote had attacked it. The horse kicked the coyote to death, but not before he was bitten. You could still just make out the faded letters of the name 'Cisco' painted on the crude cross the children had insisted on making to mark the horse's final resting place.

They led both horses and mules from the barn, and while the boy closed and dropped the latch on the unpainted doors, the man tied the lead rope from each mule to a saddle string on their horses.

The red face of the morning sun was just high enough to be seen creeping above the eastern horizon across the Mojave, and like the waning moon, it cast faint shadows but shared no warmth. The sky had lightened enough to snuff out the few remaining stars and replaced them with a dark, icy blue already fading at the edges. The pale-yellow moon seemed to be hurrying toward the western horizon, having been caught napping by the sun.

The man took a moment to look out across the Mojave basin because at this height, on a clear day, you could see what your weather would likely be six to eight hours in the future.

"Looks like we might be in for a storm by sundown," he told his son, still looking in the direction of the Rockies.

As they both mounted, the man's Mexican wife stepped out onto the porch, wrapped in a long shawl she had made during his many absences. Her hair was jet black in this light, but under bright sunshine, he knew that a hint of red shone through it. He also knew that behind the soft fair face and coal black eyes lurked flint hard convictions gilded in iron. Whenever possible, he simply yielded to her wishes, this was just one of those rare times when he could not, and he fully expected to rue this day.

Side by side, man and boy, horse and horse, mule and mule stopped and waited in the woman's shadow cast by the thin watery light that had followed with her through the open kitchen doorway. It was an awkward moment for them all as she offered her final display of dissatisfied submission, the man continued to practice his silent tolerance, and the boy focused on finding neutral ground somewhere in the waning darkness.

Nervously, the boy glanced from one to the other of his parents until the man finally broke the spell by lifting his reins, causing their horses to step out as if tied together with a string. The woman touched the boy's knee as he rode by, and their dark eyes met, but neither spoke.

The man didn't look back, but the boy stole a guilty glance over his shoulder just before they turned from the wagon lane to enter the tree line and lost sight of the house. The woman still stood in the same attitude she was in before and unknown to the boy, continued there until long after they had ridden out of sight.

Although they were still on familiar ground, the boy was filled with a sense of adventure at being on an official assignment for the U.S. Government. He knew that his job on this trip was to watch and learn to track, but secretly he just hoped to unravel some of the mystery surrounding his stoic and often absent Poppa.

Dotty easily picked her way through the timber beneath the shadowy boughs of the tall pine trees, and in the dim light of morning, they eased off the plateau of level ground where their house and barn were built and entered a world that was familiar but still foreign to the boy.

The man's name was William Strider. William had been the next name in a great book of names used by the head of the Indian Boarding School to drive the first wedge between young Native American children and their culture. In their wisdom, the Bureau of Indian Affairs began sending all the children controlled on reservations to these schools to speed their assimilation into what they now considered a civilized America. As a boy of eight, he had no idea what the name meant but was too young and obedient to refuse it. Later in life, he found it beneficial to use this white name in place of his Indian one in order to survive in this new world. William had known Indians who refused to bend to this climate, and to the man, they had been broken or now lived lives of solitary exile. His father was numbered among this second group.

Strider was a name that he did understand, given to him when he was ten by a withered tribal ancient for his heads up, eyes forward, mile-eating pace on display as he walked back into the village. She had sat watching the trail day by day through cloudy eyes, waiting for a different child missing some forty years hence.

"The child lost comes striding home," she had rasped.

She didn't seem to know or care that this was not the child of her intention, but William, ending a ninety-mile trek having rendered a final judgment on his captors and escaped to return home.

William's son was named to honor him, with the addition of Miguel as a middle name, given to the boy by his Mexican mother and chosen for having been borne by one of the seven archangels and the one closest to God.

There were two other children, Raphael and Gabriella, twins born five years after Miguel, who had thirteen years at his last birthday. Their mother had used her own great book to name the two little ones. The small boy inherited his mother's black eyes, but the girl's eyes were bright blue-green. When William saw their unusual aqua color, he remarked that this certainly disproved the elder's theory because his wife had never stepped foot into the canyon where he was born.

The trail took the man and boy down the mountain toward the western Mojave Desert. Here, total desolation slowly morphed on the rising ground into tortured vegetation, coaxed into life by renegade rain showers that had been bullied over the Sierras by Pacific storms, only to die pointless deaths in the alkali sands below.

The boy had not traveled more than a few miles from home in his life but was free to range within that boundary even with his brother and sister in tow. This freedom was a gift from his father, without the approval of Maria, his mother, who ascribed life only to the accidental absence of death, which she believed was forever actively seeking to correct the error. A view well earned by her early encounters with death as a child in Mexico.

The man had traversed these trails many times over the years in fulfilling the final morbid promise made by stymied rescuers, who had broken all previous promises by downgrading their mission to the level of body retrieval. This happened after newspapers stopped reporting their progress, and the family, if any, had lost all faith in prayers and miracles. Some officials, anxious to wash their hands of the responsibility, would calculate how much it would be worth to be rid of a disappointing and otherwise uncomfortable situation and post a finder's fee amount in a notice to be circulated amongst men like Will Strider, Indians or other mountain riff-raff who were not allowed to ride to rescue but only to recover bodies.

Occasionally, someone would have a reason for the confirmation of life or death and offer up a reward on top of the fee. These were the occasions that Will Strider looked forward to. A standard finder's fee was a hundred dollars, but it was only collected when a body was stumbled upon entirely by fate while looking for someone more worthy of attention, for his position, wealth, or notoriety.

This country, desert, and mountains connected the United States to Mexico, and though it was hazardous, it had become the most likely corridor between the two countries. Most who made the journey were men, some were criminals, and a few were innocents simply trying to escape a life that had treated them harshly. Somewhere along the way, each made the calculation that the distance they had traveled was too great to risk a return and instead preferred to continue on and leave it to God to judge their motives. It had occurred to the man over time that in these situations, the dread and horror of death usually turns out to be a kindness meted out by God.

They rode in silence for some hours, descending through pines and cedars, following trails and switchbacks used more often by deer than men on horseback until they reached a north-south fork. The man steered south with the boy and two mules following. Before long, they pulled up at a fast-running rivulet and dismounted. The ground had gradually become less vertical and more horizontal, and the terrain became a series of canyons and ridges as they rode along the base of the mountains above the desert.

The boy stepped down and held his reins, and they watched the horses drink the cold clear water. Once the horses were satisfied, they led them across the creek and allowed the mules to drink.

"What are you thinkin?" asked the man.

"About Momma, I guess," said the boy.

"That's good; I was thinkin about her too."

"Why do you suppose she got mad like that?" asked the boy.

"She's the she-wolf losing one of her pups," said the man.

"I ain't no pup!"

"To her, you are."

"What I was thinking too," continued the boy, "was, do you think you can teach me about tracking people?"

"Let me ask you," said the man, "do you think you could teach a rock to whistle?"

"No, sir, I don't believe I could," replied the boy.

"Would that be because you ain't a good enough whistler or because the rock just ain't interested in learnin?"

"Well, sir, if I'm to tell the strict truth, I couldn't lay it all off on the rock."

"Yes, I've heard you whistle," chuckled the man. "All I'm sayin is that the measure ain't in the teachin; it's in the learnin."

"Yessir."

"How do you figure where to set your traps when you go after rabbits and possums and the like?" asked the man.

"Well, sir, I can see where they've been, and I just figure where they are apt to go."

"Same as me," said the man.

"Then, do you suppose I'm ready?"

"Don't worry, I'll have you whistlin in no time," smiled the man.

"Ah, Poppa," the boy grinned.

They both remounted their horses, and after jerking on the lead ropes to redirect the mule's attention back to the journey, they struck out again. Juliet, whom they hadn't seen since entering the timber at the house, caught them up at the stream and drank, then sat watching to see what they would do next. When their direction was plain, she lit out through the trees, preferring the pine needles to the bare track of the trail, and continued to scout ahead for whatever reason dogs scout ahead, and they saw only glimpses of her when she checked their location to ensure they hadn't gotten themselves lost.

With his father choosing the path and his horse following the pack mule's rump, the boy was left to appreciate the lay of the country that he hadn't witnessed before today. He found that to look right was to look up, for one's eyes couldn't help but follow the terrain as it rose beyond sight into the misty heights. To the left were thick pine trees with an occasional vista down steep ravines that led out across the ruined landscape of the Mojave.

They came to the edge of a wide canyon; instead of stopping to survey the way ahead, the man, the horse, and the mule's rump disappeared into the scrub, which hid a deer track no more than a foot wide, leading diagonally down a sandy bank some thirty feet to the bottom.

Grabbing the pommel and saddle horn with both hands, the boy felt the air rush out of his lungs and had to clench to control his bladder as his horse made the turn down. For a second, it seemed they were standing in midair until gravity finally returned, and he could feel the horse's feet still touching the ground. All he could do was slip the reins as the horse's head dropped following the angle of the track. About halfway down and better composed, the boy questioned Dot's good sense at having followed the mule virtually over a cliff with no thought of balking. The man sat smiling at the bottom, one hand on the cantle as he twisted back to watch them descend.

"Steep, ain't it?" the man called up. He was proud to know that his son trusted him enough to follow.

"Yessir," said the boy. "You might warn me next time, though, if we are apt to have to fly!"

The man smiled as he raised his reins and returned to the trail. He knew that his decision was correct in bringing the boy on this trek, despite his wife's misgivings. The test to come would be when their hunt was concluded, and the truth about life and death was revealed. Although she had offered it most reluctantly, his wife's main argument was her firm belief that unburied bodies are vessels for vindictive spirits with a grudge against the living. She agreed with his argument that the dead deserve a place in the earth to rest until the rapture comes, but her apprehension was for the time between discovery and that rest. It was little comfort to her that he prayed their forgiveness for his handling before placing the evidence of their existence into a canvas bag for transport. He was tempted, but to date, had resisted the urge to tell his wife that if the danger from spirits was proportionate to the number of body parts found, then the threat is usually much diminished.

The trail followed the canyon bottom down toward the desert. Still, at the first opportunity, the man urged his horse up and out of the other side of the deep gorge, as many a critter, including men, have lost their lives to flash floods that originate miles away and send a wall of water down these ravines under sunny skies. The first rule of camping in this country was to find high ground, no matter how inviting the flat sandy bottom of an arroyo might be.

Their trek continued to skirt the mountains but edged ever eastward, following the irresistible terrain formed by gravity over the millennia. The closer to the desert floor they came, the shorter everything grew, including the cedars and pines.

The boy yawned as the warm sunshine bore down through the colder air clinging to the heights above, making it seem like spring come early, and warmth rising out of the desert brought the pleasant odor of creosote bushes up into these lowland canyons. They rode into the afternoon, and the boy urged his horse up beside his father when the way widened.

"Poppa?"

"Yes, son."

"How do we go about this, finding people, I mean?"

"Well, you can pretty much forget what you know about tracking animals, as they live in a place as long as they can feed themselves and only move when they can't. On the other hand, a man starts at a place and has in his mind a place that he wants to get to, and he usually ain't particularly smart about how he gets there. So, if you know where he was going, you just put yourself between there and where he started to find him. Of course, you must allow that a lost fellow might go off his nut somewhere along the way and wander off a cliff, or climb up a tree, or dig a hole and get down into it."

This gave Miguel something to ponder as they picked their way toward the desert floor.

They rode on, and at the next shady spot with a clearing, they got down, dropped their reins to the ground, and loosened the cinch straps to let the horses blow. Then they tied the mule's lead ropes to the lower branches of a blackjack oak to let them browse. The man pulled the package wrapped in a dishcloth from his saddle bag, sat cross-legged on the ground, and began unwrapping bread and cold meat. The boy brought an army canteen of water and sat beside him, and they went to work on the food.

Eating was something that they both took pretty seriously, so they didn't talk until the last scrap was accounted for and washed down from the canteen. The misty clouds from far above had begun to settle into the lower reaches and tumbled down through the canyons bringing a chill that hadn't been present when they stopped.

"It's gonna be an early night," the man observed, looking up through the pine trees where the cottony air was clinging to the upper branches like smoke.

The boy stood up, brushed the crumbs from his lap, and agreed, "Yeah, getting colder too!"

"We better rig up the tent," said the man. "It looks like this is where we are going to spend the night unless we want to ride til we're soaked."

They both walked to Rachel, lifted her pack panniers, unhitched the sawbuck, set it and the pad on the ground, and then led the mule from between them all. The man always kept a soft rawhide hobble buckled around the neck of each mule so that he didn't have to dig through a pannier to find one in a pinch; he knelt and placed the hobble on the mule's front legs, then loosed the lead rope and slapped her on the rump to graze, then they did the same to Leah.

They unsaddled the horses, set their hobbles, and let them join the mules to wander for the night.

The man raised the flap on one of the panniers and pulled out a folded bundle of canvas that had been seamed together with the zig-zag stitching of a sailmaker. It was a souvenir from the wreck of a small sailboat that had carried three men up the coast of Mexico into the Gulf of California and then on to the Colorado River delta, where the remains of that great river ends its journey from the Rocky Mountains. They had attempted to sail up into the river, and it was their bad luck that a summer flood had sent a wall of water across the delta, swamped their boat, and drowned the men. William Strider was the man hired to find them as they had stolen the boat and killed a man in the process. Criminals, considered dangerous, were the exception to the body retrieval restriction put on Indians and mountain men. It made little sense to the Government to risk soldiers or lawmen on tasks better suited to those with more primal instincts. Besides, there was an annoying amount of paperwork associated with the death of a soldier and little or none for those of lesser status.

When he found them, they were bloated and gull-pecked to the point of non-recognition. Their thin white cotton shirts and pants were stained and stretched to their limits trying to enforce a human form onto shapeless human flesh. The gaps between buttons were filled with colorless skin and hair, necks and faces one continuous mass. Two were together in the sand as if they had clung to one another even in death. The third's bottom half was lost beneath the boat gunnel, face to the sky, matching the hull, which was keel up, bow pointing inland as if it were cruising through a subterranean world with one of its mates attempting to abandon ship.

The mast had snapped at the deck and trailed behind, still supporting the sail and attached only by the backstay. As it turned out, the sail was the only extra payment that William Strider would collect for that journey, as the men, in his absence, were determined to be of no particular interest, and the man they had killed was wanted in Mexico for various crimes. Since they were all confirmed dead, the Mexican government had felt no obligation to make good on their original reward offer, and to that, there was no recourse. The only good decision he thought he had made was burying the three big men at the mouth of the Colorado river to avoid an odorous journey back to the mountains, having collected enough identifying evidence to prove a successful hunt.

The sail had paid back it's worth many times over as defense against the elements after it was rubbed with bee's wax and hand-sewed together to transform it into a three-sided tent.

The sail had been fifteen feet at the mast and twelve feet at the base, which was more than enough material for the man's wife to lace together a lean-to with triangle flaps on two sides that could be thrown up and over in warm weather or staked to the ground in cold. The top extended well past the front of the sides, providing extra shade and shelter, and it went all the way to the ground at the back. With the top staked to the ground at the rear and stretched tight with lines attached to two trees in front, and with the sides being generously long, they could be pulled outward and staked down to form water sheds to direct rainwater away from its center. If the opening was placed on the leeward side away from the wind, a fire could be maintained inside the shelter without the bother of smoke but benefitting from the heat even in the rain.

They set the tent up on a slope against a sandy bank, staked down the sides against the expected blow, and arranged their possibles inside, including the pack panniers, saddles, and other leather gear. With the horses and mules hobbled and managing for themselves, the man and boy built a small fire and sat feeding it sticks from the pile of wood that they had collected for the night. As predicted, the moisture-laden air pushed the thin vapor clouds down among the tree branches and obscured the land down the slope from their camp. The glow of sunshine through the wafting clouds first dimmed and then died as the cool sun topped the mountains behind them and turned its attention to the Pacific coast and the Baja peninsula. The glow of their fire took on new strength as the sun subsided, and a circle of light reached out through the moist air and got the attention of a group of trees across the small clearing where they had lunched just a few hours ago. Heavy fog collected on the limbs above and formed water droplets that tap, tapped on the canvas above their heads, then rolled down the sloping roof to mingle with the fallen pine needles covering the bank.

"Where are we going to?" asked the boy.

"Well, we have a family of lost pilgrims to find," replied the man.

"Alive ones or dead?" asked the boy, for he knew of the unwritten rules of rescue.

The man just looked at him, as it made no sense to waste words on speculation. The boy was used to this response, for he had learned long ago that his father took spells of rationing spoken words as though he had been allotted a precious few and intended not to run short.

They ate beans warmed over the fire in the can they came in, taking turns dipping in their spoons until the can was cool enough for the boy to lift and drain the last of the juice. The man pulled a strip of jerked deer meat from the pannier sitting between them and sawed it in half with his hunting knife, handing a piece to the boy. They spent the rest of the evening gnawing at the tough smokey meat, then sat sucking their teeth, staring into the fire.

Just before full dark, the dog arrived, wet, hungry, and cold, to take her usual place by the fire just inside the tent and began to lick her forepaws.

"Wherever have you been?" the man commented, looking the dog over and fishing in the pannier for a couple of the hard biscuits they had packed and tossed them to her.

The steam began rising from Juliet's thick wet hair and carried with it the pungent odor of dog into the tent.

"Juliet!" the boy scolded at the smell but received no sympathy from the dog.

They both rose to relieve themselves before turning in and stoked the fire with larger pieces of wood. They pushed their saddles to the back of the tent to use for pillows, then rolled up in their blankets and waited for sleep, each recalling the day in his own way.

Sometime during the night, the boy woke to see his father sitting by the fire, poking the coals, trying to ignite the new limbs he had just applied. In the glow of the infant flames, Miguel saw it was snowing.

The man found it difficult to sleep well when his wife was upset, particularly when the reason remained a mystery to him. He knew that all women are prone to occasional insanities, and he accepted this as neither good nor bad. Even so, her objection to his teaching his son the skills needed to locate bodies in the wilderness troubled him.

He had learned his skills as a Havasu boy living at the bottom of the Grand Canyon in Arizona. The Havasupai, 'The people of the blue-green waters,' had lived in and around the canyon for more than eight hundred years before the U.S. Government decided in 1880 to make their part of the canyon a reservation, this to make way for the mining companies to harvest the rich mineral deposits on their ancestral lands above.

When Theodore Roosevelt established the Grand Canyon National Park in 1919, he stated that visiting Americans shouldn't have to look at a bunch of ragged Indians and ordered that their movements be restricted to the bottom of their canyon. Losing their homes and grazing land on the rims forced the tribe into poverty, and many, including the man's family, escaped the reservation and fled to Mexico. Two years before this, William had been conscripted into the U.S. Marines to fight in World War I and was sent to Europe. William began the long ocean voyage home as his family warily made their way south.

When the troop ship docked at the port of New York City, he was thanked for his service to his country and given his back pay in cash along with his discharge papers. The one thing he managed to hang on to was the 1917 Enfield sniper rifle that he had carried during the war. It was issued to him after the military discovered that he had the steady hand of a marksman and clear eyes adept at estimating distance. With this gun's unique Galilean sights, with adjustable rear sight and optical front sight, he had gained a reputation for making impossibly long shots with unerring accuracy.

The last thing he was given was a piece of advice, 'Don't let the sun set on you inside these city limits.' Heeding the warning, he located the rail yard and got a seat on a troop train headed West. It amazed him that he had spent the last two years as a scout and sharpshooter in the worst hell he could imagine, fighting alongside men who now wouldn't even look him in the eye for fear of being associated with an Indian. He mistakenly assumed that the scars he had received in battle should have earned him at least some bit of respect, but upon returning to America, he realized nothing had changed. He would have no such illusions going forward.

He stayed on the train until it stopped at the Pacific Ocean in San Francisco, California, where he traded for a good horse and mule, then found a saddler and bought new rigs for them both. It took a couple of extra days, but he had the craftsmen design a unique rigid saddle scabbard to fit his unusual rifle where the latigos could be buckled together to form a shoulder strap when it was removed from the horse. That way, the gun was protected even when he was on foot. He spent the last of his money on ammunition and provisions, then found his way out of the city.

He planned to head into the mountains and work his way south and east until he had descended into Arizona, then on to Nogales, Mexico, to begin his search for his fugitive parents. Seeking to leave so-called civilization behind as fast as possible, he crossed the San Juaquin valley heading east toward the Sierra, then skirted the foothills south to Fresno. There he plunged into the wilderness, following paths left by men that he preferred to think had the same bent as he.

His way went upward until it led him over and through the teeth of the mountains, where he began his descent down the Nevada side. Here the trails and an endless series of canyons tempted him ever downward toward the desert, but he stayed high, blazing his own way, avoiding the steep ravines until he came to a sheer drop-off made by a landslide in the ancient past.

He had no choice but to descend the edge of the cut, looking for a way through, and when he found it, he was amazed at what was there—a broad expanse of level terrain covered by grassy meadows and tall trees. The young Marine had stumbled upon a sanctuary for a man in desperate need of one. He felt as if God had him in mind when untold years ago, he shook the earth, created this place, and left it for nature to tend, waiting for him to arrive.

He drank from the clear mountain stream originating hundreds of feet above, flowing down the sheer rock face of the scar left by the quake. Hard granite, born in the molten bowels of the earth, then pushed to the surface as the Pacific plate collided with North America, had even then contained the fault that would make this place possible. Snow melt, collecting in cracks and fissures above, made the mountain weep to form a perpetual pool that nourished the plateau.

Some believe that a series of unrelated and random events have created the world we know today; others ascribe all things to God. But maybe, like a single domino falling causes the next to move and then the next, perhaps God's part in this world is simply that he created a set of rules for the universe and then pushed the first domino, and only in that remote and distant action can he be blamed for all that has come after, especially the bad.

CHAPTER 2

Maria stood looking at the gap in the trees marking the departure point of her husband and young son from the tiny island of civilization they had carved from the vast wilderness of the Sierra Nevada.

She had been a teenage girl when she followed the man away from her small, ruined village in Mexico. An epidemic of Spanish flu had been delivered by a wagon full of pilgrims fleeing from that same disease. It had embedded in her a dreadful apprehension that time would never remove and was the basis of her fear for her son.

"Momma, what are you doing out here Momma?" It was Gabriella from the open kitchen doorway.

Her breath caught her up, and Maria turned and forced a smile back at her daughter.

"Nada mi bebita (Nothing, my baby)," she cooed, then stepped to the child and led her inside.

"It's cold in here Momma; why did you have the door open? Where's Willie and Poppa at Momma?"

"Hush and put some wood in the stove, and I will make us

breakfast."

The dark-haired, green-eyed wisp of a girl skipped to the stove, and with a bright red potholder knitted by her mother, she twisted and pulled the firebox door handle and dropped in several sticks of stove wood from the pile, then shut the door back with a clank.

"Go and get your brother up and put on some clothes," Maria commanded as she turned up the wick in the hanging lantern.

The girl once again skipped across the kitchen in her long cotton nightie and down the short hallway to her open bedroom door.

"Momma said to git up Raphe!" she yelled as she walked through the door.

For the first time, the woman felt the chill in the air that she hadn't noticed even while standing outside in her reverie of childhood memories. She pulled her shawl tighter to suppress a shiver that she couldn't contribute entirely to the cold.

She gathered and prepared the meal with a mother's practiced hand without consideration for the details of the process, all the while picturing her vulnerable young son's last glance before disappearing into the woods.

Raphael walked into the kitchen, stretching, yawning, and scratching, pulled a chair back from the table, and sat with a plop. His mother looked up and was brought back into the present as she marveled at the image of the male version of her daughter in front of her. Black hair askew, clothes a jumble, and mouth agape. Here sat the cloned opposite of her neat, prim, and dainty little girl. She shook her head, and smiled at the evidence of God's deliberate sense of humor, then turned back to her cooking.

By now, the warm kitchen air was a soup of delicious smells, and the familiar sounds of spoons clacking, pans rattling and dishes being set penetrated the boy's early morning stupor.

"Where's Poppa and Willie at?" the boy managed to get out around a huge gaping yawn.

"Never you mind about that; you just worry about yourself!" Gabriella commanded as she entered the room and took her catbird seat next to her mother's.

After the food was dealt and all seats were taken, and with Raphael shoveling eggs and potatoes into his mouth at an alarming rate, Gabriella paused to look up at her mother.

"Where'd Poppa and Willie go, Momma?"

The woman sighed, resigned herself to face her reality, and explained to the two children that Miguel was learning to help his father with his job of tracking for the Government. They would be gone for a week or more, and the twins would have to help her with the livestock, chickens, and chores around the place. They would have to pray for their safe return and be brave and good so that God would watch out for them all and not to worry.

"Are they going to find dead people, Momma?" Raphael wanted to know. He had formed his own notions about where his father went on his many trips away from the cabin from bits and pieces of conversations he had overheard between their father and mother.

"Shut up and eat your breakfast!" Gabriella demanded and gave him a stern look for having interrupted their mother.

"Gabby, don't be bossy; I said we must be nice to each other while your father and brother are away."

"Yes, ma'am," said the girl, but she gave the boy another hard look, just the same.

The boy simply waved her away with his fork as if she were a gnat and went back at his food.

"Gabriella, after breakfast, you can help me with the kitchen, and Raphael, you get your bucket and go collect the eggs. Let the hens out into the run for a while, but don't you dare forget to close that gate when you leave!"

"Yes, ma'am," the boy mumbled around a piece of ham he was trying to chew in two.

"Don't speak with your mouth full, Raphe!" the girl scolded, unable to contain her disgust for her idiot brother.

He gave her a greasy smile, displaying the gap from his missing front teeth, and continued chewing.

"We will come help you with the hay and milking," the woman continued, choosing not to waste more breath on the hopeless quest to stifle her relentless daughter.

When Raphael finished his food, he dropped his fork into his plate, drained his glass of milk, wiped his greasy hands on his pant legs, dragged his right sleeve across his mouth, and headed for the door.

All of this elicited an open-mouthed gasp from Gabby, and she moved to go after the boy, and but for her mother's hand on her arm, she would have chased him down and done who knows what to him for his offense to human decency. Instead, she sat back down, seething with disgust.

The kitchen door slammed, and they heard the rapid fire from the boy's finger guns as he slaughtered would-be assailants going across the way toward the hen house.

The woman and girl looked at each other, and unable to match Gabby's indignation; Maria laughed out loud.

This would be the first time they had all coped with the man's absence without the presence of Miguel to do the heavy lifting. His attempts to be the man of the house and his sober mimicry of his father's actions somehow reassured the others that they would all be able to handle whatever came up.

One such time when William had been gone for several weeks, two men had arrived unannounced, riding shabby horses and wearing greasy hunting frocks and leather pants that looked to be of Indian origin but without the Indians inside them. They had the long hair and beards of men more used to wilderness than civilized society, and both had quick eyes ever looking for opportunities.

Miguel was returning from running one of his trap lines and walked up behind the two as Maria confronted them at the front gate of the yard. He could tell that the conversation was winding down, with his mother insisting that the two continue on their way as there was nothing on this place that would be of interest to them. The larger man doing most of the talking seemed to be trying to ascertain whether any men were about, and if so, where they were.

His mother was keeping a tight grip on the Damascus barrel shotgun that had hung handy above the kitchen door, and Miguel knew that she was capable with the gun because he had seen her use it more than once on varmints and owls and the like that got after her chickens, but he wasn't sure if she would use it on a man, even one of these two.

The two younger kids were peering through the open kitchen doorway, each holding on to a door jam on opposite sides and leaning out enough to see what was going on at the gate. Both were scared, and shading their eyes against the sun, which shone high overhead.

William had always told Miguel that if there is trouble, a man just as soon walk up to it rather than try to walk around it. If you show that you are reluctant to face up to a man, you might just be loaning him backbone enough to do something he would otherwise back away from.

It had only taken Miguel a heartbeat to size up this situation. He dropped the bag of fresh hides that he was carrying, and like his father said, walked into the middle of it. His moccasin-shod feet were silent on the sandy lane, and horses and men alike were taken aback when he strode between them straight to the gate. Both horses shied as he pulled it open and stepped inside. He walked to his mother's side, took the shotgun from her without asking, and leveled it at the big man's head. Before anyone else could think of anything to say, Miguel, speaking in a low steady tone, told his mother, "Count to three."

The Men looked surprised but didn't offer to move until the woman abruptly said, "Three!" The two then turned to each other in alarm, yanked reins, and dug in heels, and in moments, the dust in the air was the only evidence that they had been there at all.

Something in the young boy's eyes and the sight of the bore of the ten-gauge double barrel shotgun had said more to the men than anything that had come from his mouth. The lesson for the boy was that he had a mother who was not one to be trifled with.

The two younger kids exploded from the kitchen door. Gabriella found her mother, buried her face in her apron, and shook with uncontrollable sobs.

"Oh, Momma, Momma, Momma!"

Raphael ran up and grabbed his older brother by the shoulders and beamed up at him with a broad smile.

"Would you have killed him, Willie? I bet you would have! You looked just like Daddy standing there!"

Maria reached over, put her arm around her oldest son's neck, and pulled them all four together.

"Gracias, mi hijo (Thank you, my son), we need never be afraid when you are with us."

Miguel didn't know why but suddenly his vision blurred, and he felt tears burning his eyes. He hugged his mother and buried his face in her shoulder.

**

When the two riders were well out of sight of the house, they slowed, then stopped.

"Well, Mr. Bodine, that went well!" the smaller man said sarcastically.

"At least now we know where Strider lives," the larger man replied, and they continued on their way but watched warily lest they stumble upon the man of their original intention.

CHAPTER 3

The circle of embers served only to highlight the dark stillness that had pushed its way past the faltering campfire to invade the closeness of the tent where the man and boy slept.

Miguel opened his eyes in the blackness and sat up to a face full of canvas that the snow had pushed down upon them in the night.

"Poppa?" the boy whispered, trying to get his bearings in the close confines that he couldn't quite reconcile.

"What the heck?" came the man's bewildered reply as he pushed up on the tent top until he heard the snow sluffing off to the sides.

The boy crawled from his covers to the mouth of the canvas cave and was met by a warm wet tongue that quickly washed his face and ears before he could duck under his arms to fend off the dog's friendly attack.

"Juliet, quit that!" he yelled.

He couldn't see it, but he knew the dog's hind quarters were dancing a jig from the whop, whop, whop of her tail against the stiff tent side. For the dog's part, she couldn't have been happier if the boy had just been raised from the dead and sang Hosannas.

The man quickly joined them in the faint light of the glowing ashes and had to push his way past the excited hound dog to get outside where he could stand. The dog followed him out, grinning and twisting with joy, looking up at him as if to say, "Look at what I done!"

"Well, Atlantic Ocean!" the man marveled when he looked around at what must have been over a foot of wet snow covering everything in sight.

The moon, a small dim lantern in the sky, cast barely enough light to cause a crystalline hue to echo off the land. Cedar trees, looking like smooth white pyramids, stood apart in the forest. Pines with limbs bent toward the earth, seemingly supporting wagons full of fluffy cotton waiting to be ginned.

"What happened?" the boy asked in awe as he slowly turned in the well of snow that came up to his thighs.

"God happened!" the man said as he kicked at the snow covering the wood they had piled outside the tent the night before.

The dog, unable to contain her enthusiasm, went at the pile of limbs as if it were a den full of badgers that had just insulted them all, slinging branches in every direction.

"Juliet!" the man said, with enough authority to get her attention and back her up against the snowbank that formed a wall around the mouth of the tent. Even with the rest of her subdued, her tail beat a steady rhythm on the snow.

The man managed to resurrect the fire and stacked most of the remaining wet limbs over the small pocket of flames for them to eventually dry and catch themselves alight.

The boy shouldered the rest of the snow from the tent top, standing inside the enclosure, leaving the canvas loose but high enough to let him manage their gear to the front. The man dug through the food pannier, looking for a quick, easy breakfast. It turned out to be hard biscuits and cold jerky since the wet fire was resisting his efforts.

"I can't wait to see you track somethin in this!" said the boy, motioning with his jerky toward the brightening snow.

All he got in return was a look that made him grin as he took a bite of biscuit.

"This might be a good time for you to meet somebody," the man mentioned in an offhand way.

The boy was caught in mid-bite and turned to his father without lowering his hand or the biscuit. He started to speak but found that he couldn't for the mouthful of bread still waiting to be chewed. He spat it on the ground, where the dog inhaled it before it could bounce and looked up at him in case there would be more.

"I didn't know anybody lived out here but us?" stated the surprised boy.

"There is," replied the man.

"Who is it then?" persisted the boy.

"Your grandpa."

"I didn't even know I had one," continued the boy.

"Everybody's got one, alive or dead."

"Is mine alive or dead?"

"Alive the last time I talked to him."

"At least there's that," the boy replied. "Is he Indian or Mexican?"

"He's Indian."

"Like us?"

"He's Indian, but he ain't like us. Besides, you are Mex-Indian because of your mother."

"Does that matter?"

"Not to a white man, and sure not to the folks we've gone lookin for."

The boy contemplated this news and considered asking why he hadn't met his grandfather before now, but knew that if his father didn't offer information up on his own, he wasn't likely to expand on the subject. Experience had taught him that the more questions you asked his father, the shorter the answers grew until you wound up talking to yourself.

It was late morning when they struck camp and coaxed the horses and mules out of a thicket where they had holed up against the heavy snow for the night. They led them one at a time, hopping where the snow had drifted too deep to walk until they all stood where the tent had been pitched as the only bare ground in sight.

After the horses were saddled and mules loaded, they started up again on the track they were following the day before, but soon they turned upland on a new trail leading to higher ground out of the deep snow.

"Does Grandpa know about me?" the boy asked across the mule his father was leading.

"He knows," said the man without looking back.

"Then he knows about Momma and the twins?"

"He knows."

"Does Momma know about him?"

After a few minutes without an answer, the boy said, "You're talking to yourself, Willie."

With the late start and terrible travel conditions, they continued the new path higher up the mountain without pausing until the sun tipped over the peaks above, and unleashed the evening shadows to slide down on their small caravan, then out across the desert.

Just before too dark to see, the boy noticed a light up ahead that could have been a lamp in a window or just the glow of a campfire reflecting through the timber. As they grew nearer, he could make out a dome-shaped structure that appeared to be made of wood but covered with sod. The light was a campfire, but the smoke rose through a hole in the roof of the building.

"What's that?" asked the boy as his father reined in and sat waiting for him to come alongside.

"That's your grandpa's wickiup," answered the man. "Better wait for him to call us in."

They sat for a few moments, and the boy caught the shape of a man standing only a few feet to his side. He turned with a start and gulped a breath of air that didn't seem to want to go all the way to the bottom, and he made a kind of squawking sound that amused the visitor, who smiled up at him with a toothy grin.

The boy glanced from the older man to his father and tried to sound an alarm to be sure that he was aware of their situation, but all he could muster were more of the squawking noises he had made before.

The long-haired Indian man dressed in buckskins of his own construction walked around to the front of the horses and gave the man a concerned look. He said something in a native tongue that the boy didn't understand, then turned and walked toward the wickiup. William and Maria had settled upon English as a compromise language to teach the children, but somehow, they could all speak a good deal of Spanish and none of their father's tongue.

The man smiled, clucked to his horse, and raised the reins to start her forward.

After sitting dumbfounded for a moment, the boy urged Dotty onward until he caught up with his father.

"Poppa?" the boy queried over at him.

The man looked at him, maintaining his amused air, "that is your grandpa," he offered.

"Well, what did he say?"

"He said it saddens him to learn that his grandson turned out to be an idjit."

The boy's jaw dropped, but he continued to follow on.

When they reached the wickiup, the old Indian motioned toward a corral constructed of tree limbs and branches laced together to form a fence, above which two inquisitive mules' heads watched the procession with great interest.

The man and boy dismounted and began stripping the gear from their horses and mules and placing it inside the wickiup entrance. Then they led all four animals to the corral, slipped the lock on the gate, and turned them in to commune with their curious cousins for the night.

The dog walked uninvited into the structure, sniffed the old Indian's face, and he sniffed hers seemingly for mutual recognition, then she curled up by the fire as if she were home.

When the man and boy returned from tending the animals and entered the unusual structure, the boy marveled at the intricate construction of his grandfather's home and the practical placement of everything around the stones that circled the firepit.

The old man muttered almost continuously in the tongue the boy couldn't understand, as if unspoken words had accumulated in his isolation and now flowed forth of their own volition without being sanctioned by their host.

A large flat clay comal about a foot across, charred black from roasting spices, chilies, tortillas, and meats, sat heating on a stone at the fire's edge. A skinned animal was hanging from one of the roof's supports that Miguel hoped was a goat but couldn't rule out the possibility that it was a big dog, as the head and feet were missing. The odors of cooking clung to everything like the smoky shadows of untold meals prepared over the years. Spoons, dippers, and bowls made from gourds sat on one sizeable flat stone slab that looked like the structure might have been built around it to be used as a table for cutting, preparing, and eating.

The old man sat cross-legged on what looked to be a deer skin by the fire, holding a bowl in which he was kneading lard into flour for tortillas.

"Father," acknowledged the man as he and the boy sat on skins that were either goat or dog, depending, that had been laid down for them.

"Son," the old man replied in English, still working the dough but looking only at the boy, who was transfixed by the unblinking liquid black eyes.

"What do you call that boy?" the old man asked loudly, lifting the bowl toward Miguel.

"Tell him your name, son."

"William Miguel Strider, sir."

The old man stopped working the flour and looked at the man to ensure he wasn't being tricked.

The man nodded his assurance to his father that he had heard correctly.

"Wy, I thought he was a dummy!" said the Indian, looking at the man.

"I ain't no dummy!" the boy defended.

"That's good to know!" grinned the old man looking back at the boy.

Miguel glanced at his father, who echoed the old man's smile.

"You're both just havin me on!" the boy said with indignation that his blood kin would treat him in such a manner.

The two older men laughed aloud, sharing the joke. The boy managed a sheepish smile.

"Momma said that Indians are funny people; guess I know what she meant now," the boy said under his breath.

When the joke was over, the old man stretched across the firepit and offered the boy a hand covered with lard and flour.

"Glad to meet you, William Miguel Strider," the Indian said with a warm smile.

The boy hesitated at the look of the hand but took it anyway and gave a firm shake.

"Glad to meet you, Grandpa."

The old man, still holding the boy's hand, looked at the man now and said with more emotion than intended, "He looks just like you when you was a boy!" Then he quickly released the hand and returned to forming the tortillas. "Got any coffee in them bags you brought?"

William got up, walked to the pack panniers, opened one, and began unloading its contents. A bag of coffee, a two-gallon tin of lard, a ten-pound sack of flour, a bag of sugar, and some quart jars of canned goods wrapped each in their own towel that Maria would question the absence of when she noticed them gone.

"Miguel, set these over with your grandpa's other supplies," William said to his son.

The boy looked around until he spotted several shelves made from split cedar logs up on stubbed-off limbs protruding from the wall at the other end of the structure, and moved the things that his father unloaded there except for the bag of coffee, which the man was opening. William took a canteen from the side of his saddle and a steeping pot from one of the other panniers and started to pour in the water.

"Whoa," said the old man. "I'll make that coffee."

The boy looked inquisitively at his grandfather.

"You ever tried to drink his coffee?" the old man blinked at him.

"Yessir," the boy grinned. "I surely have!"

It was now the man's turn to display a sheepish smile.

The boy thought that at least there was one thing that he liked about this old man, he didn't care who he embarrassed.

William sat the coffee makings near his father, then stood and motioned to his son.

"Let's go check the stock, and I will show you where we get water."

"Yessir," said the boy and rose, reluctant to leave his grandfather's company.

The moon, topping the mountains from the east, supplied enough light that they easily navigated the open distance between the hut and corral. Still, its thin glow only managed to deepen the blue-black shadows of the trees and bushes bordering the small clearing. A cold breeze floated down from the heights above, and in the distance across the desert came an occasional silent flicker of light from the receding spring storm. Standing in the shadow of the fence, the man put his elbows on top of the gate made from long thin aspen poles, and they looked over at the grazing animals, though both knew there was nothing new to see.

Miguel patiently waited to learn why his father had made up the excuse to bring him out here, and after a time, he did.

"You need to know something about your grandpa," said the man.

"Yessir?"

"Well, he don't live out here by himself just because he don't like people. I mean, generally, he don't like em', but that's because of the way him and his family have been treated, and too, he got a little sideways with the government a while back. He's gone to some trouble so that nobody knows where he lives, and we would like to help make sure it stays that way."

The boy thought of about ten questions all at once but didn't want to muddle things with his father offering up information without being threatened with a gun.

"I aimed to bring you here all along but didn't want your momma to know," William said.

"I figured," said the boy, "since we packed enough supplies to get us to Canada and back."

William smiled through the darkness at his clever son, though he could hardly see his face.

"It would be best if you just didn't say anything when we get home."

"No, sir," said the boy, another question forming in his mind.

"Good," said the man, "I'll show you where the spring is then."

The boy followed his father across the meadow toward a colony of aspens bordering a small stream defining the lower edge of his grandfather's clearing. The breeze combed the tops of the tall thin trees, making them move like black stage cutouts against the starry curtain of the sky. A few paces inside the tree line, they came upon a secluded pool that looked to be the origin of the mountain stream. Rippling water reflected the starlight as it danced over the smooth rocks, making sounds like a group of excited schoolchildren at the beginning of a fantastic journey.

"There is a trough in the corral," the man said, "and buckets are hanging on the fence. While we're here, it's your job to keep the stock watered."

"Yessir," the boy replied, then risking the question.

"Why don't you want Momma to know we came here?"

The man gave him a long, considered look, but in the end, he just turned and started walking back up the slope.

When they entered the smokey wickiup, the old Indian motioned them to sit, and with a narrow spatula shaped from wood, picked the last tortilla from the hot comal and placed it on the stone table.

"Eat or starve," he said and picked up the steeping pot beside the fire and poured three cups of coffee.

The boy took his and looked closely down into the dark brown liquid.

"Don't worry," said the old man. "I put all the grinds in your daddy's cup; that's how he likes it."

They all shared a grin, but then the man swirled his cup just to make sure, and this time the Indian and young boy laughed out loud.

They all slept that night on blankets arranged around the warm stones of the firepit, and when the light inside had dimmed, the boy lay looking up through the smoke hole in the ceiling. Through the diminishing haze wafting toward the heavens, he marked the slow rotation of the firmament dictated according to the silent turning of the earth.

He imagined all sorts of scenarios that might explain the problem between his mother and grandfather but dismissed them each, one after another, because they all required wrongdoing by one or the other. He felt his mother was incapable, and although he barely knew him, he couldn't make an evil deed stick to this humorous old Indian man. Finally, he decided it must be something to do with his mother's unyielding religious views. He smiled at the thought that maybe the old man had once offered her an indelicate part of a dog to eat, and she had taken offense at the offer, and he felt the same about her refusal. Whatever it was, Miguel decided he wouldn't worry more about it and drifted off, wondering what flavor Juliet might be anyway.

The following morning, they ate heartily of tortillas and whatever the mystery meat was and chased it down with more strong coffee.

The boy decided that if it was dog, then it was good enough that he wasn't going to complain, but at the first chance he was going to ask his father.

After breakfast, the boy said he would water the horses, got up, thanked his grandfather for the food, and left the two men alone in the wickiup.

"I think you got a good boy there," the old Indian offered after Miguel.

"I think so too," said the man.

"What are you up here huntin after this time?"

"A family of Mexicans that went missing about six weeks ago, according to some family that knew they were headed to California. A man and woman and a couple of kids. Most likely dead, one way or another."

"Don't them people know that there's bad forajidos (outlaws) out there just waitin for 'em?"

"Some of them don't have no choice when things are bad enough down there," meaning Mexico.

"You need one of my mules, then?"

"I need you if you can come. It's time that boy out there gets to know his family and I thought you might help me get him through this first hunt. I think it might be a bad one."

"They're all bad ones," said the Indian, "but a man does what he knows. I will go with you; I'd kinda like to get to know my family too."

CHAPTER 4

After Maria and Gabriella finished the dishes and wiped the table and stovetop clean, they donned their heavy coats and hats and stepped out onto the porch treads.

"Juliet?" the young girl sang, then remembered that the dog would be gone with her father, so she trailed on after her mother.

The sun was high in the east, and warmth, sliding down thin shafts of sunlight peeking through the tall pines, reached down to touch them gently on their face and shoulders as one walked and the other skipped to the barn.

"Gabby, go check on your brother, then both of you come help me with the hay," Maria said.

"Yes, ma'am," said the girl, and she dashed to the chicken coop while her mother opened the barn doors.

"Raphe, you better git out here; Momma said so!" the girl yelled through the cage wire.

From the open haymow door of the barn, the boy leaned out, holding on with one hand, and took aim down at the girl with his trusty finger gun and put two rounds through the back of her coat. A pow, pow loosed the bullets, then an elaborate twirl holstered the weapon.

"Next time, tell your momma not to send a mouse to do a cat's job," the boy whispered. Then, having satisfied his honor, he quietly pulled the loft door closed behind him, careful that the girl didn't see him.

Unaware of her fatal wounds, Gabby impatiently opened the coop gate and stomped inside to find her dim-witted brother. Looking into the roost without seeing the boy, she stormed out, slammed the gate, and walked determinedly to the barn. She entered in a huff, prepared to expose her brother's wanton defiance of their mother's orders.

"Momma!" yelled the girl, "Raphe ain't even in the chicken coop!"

Maria looked up, holding the wooden pitchfork she had just used to toss the hay Raphael had dropped down over into the milking stanchion.

"Come on and bring me the milk bucket," Maria told her daughter as she leaned the fork against the wall and opened the manger door for the jersey cow waiting to come inside.

Dismayed, Gabby walked across the barn, picked up the bucket, and carried it to her mother.

Maria took the one-legged stool from its place by the stanchion and sat balancing by leaning her head into the cow's flank, and began stripping milk into the bucket. The pet cow, the kids had named Mary Magdalene, stood patiently munching the loose hay. There was a patch of dark hair on the cow's flank where their mother placed her head, and the children claimed it was her black hair that had caused it. No one asked how the same dark spot got on the other side of the cow, however.

"Momma, Raphe wasn't even in the chicken coop like you told him, and I bet he never got them eggs, neither."

Maria looked up without losing her rhythm and said kindly to her daughter, "Raphael gathered the eggs like I asked him and was in the hay loft pitching down hay when I got here, so don't ride him so hard all the time."

"Yes, ma'am, but if you would leave me at him, I would teach that boy some manners!"

"Ok, but just so you know, I think I heard him take a couple of shots in your direction when you were yelling at him."

"Oh, Momma, you know that boy is just ridiculous with those play-like guns of his."

Maria smiled at the look on her daughter's face, then turned her attention back to her milking and preoccupation with her eldest son.

After the barn chores were done, the milk was strained, and the eggs put in the cooling box, the woman and her eight-year-old shadow began the daily work around the house.

Raphael was condemned to butter churn duty, the one job that he had and the one that he hated most. The job was well suited to the boy, for he never stood still and worked the dasher handle like a steam drill driving spikes on the Northern Pacific railroad, and he always finished in half the time as anyone else. Afterward, it took him ten minutes outside of running, yelling, and shooting to burn off the excess energy built up during his confinement.

This time he hadn't been gone more than a minute until the kitchen door burst open, and Raphael flew in, yelling and crying.

"Momma, wolves have got Mary Magdalene down, and they're killin her! Momma, come quick, they're killin her!"

Maria froze for just a moment looking in the direction of the door, then she grabbed her son and turned him every which way, looking for blood or wounds but finding none; she left him spinning in the middle of the kitchen floor and rushed to the door and snatched the shotgun from its pegs and ran outside.

She saw not wolves, but just as terrifying, three huge wild dogs. Two had the cow stretched out on the ground, one at the nose and the other at her tail, trying desperately to hold the terrified, struggling milk cow down while the third big cur slashed at her soft underbelly. Dodging hooves and trying to get a firm grip on the grass-filled gut, the third dog dashed in and out, growling and slobbering.

Maria was halfway to the split rail fence before the dog in the middle noticed and turned to face her with lips turned back in a menacing snarl, revealing bloody fangs in front of rheumy red eyes that locked on hers. At that moment, she recognized a manic hatred that she had never experienced before in her life. Momentum carried her forward, or fear would have stopped her in her tracks as the monster left the floundering cow to start toward her. The ugly cur approached the fence with the low crouching gait of a great cat preparing to spring. Unbridled hatred oozed from every pore of the wild beast, imagining the taste of the blood of this intruder. It was as if it had always hated her; even before it was born, it had hated her; even after it died from the blast of the ten-gauge shotgun that turned it almost inside out, she could still feel its hatred.

Like the roar of a cannon on a battlefield, the two barrels firing simultaneously echoed across the field and down through the canyons producing a thick, rolling white smoke that obscured the other two dogs and the struggling cow. What started as a game for these two had quickly turned deadly when their leader saw the struggling cow writhing on the ground. They had no problem abandoning their brother, who had been snarling and snapping at them all morning. Before the smoke cleared, they had melted into the timber on the far side of the field.

Maria collapsed at the base of the fence, leaned weakly against its rails, and looked down at the heavy gun that had surely fired itself, for she had no recollection of aiming or pulling the triggers. Before she knew it, the two young children who had followed bravely with her to the fight were both in her lap, crying, fearful that she might be hurt.

After a while, when she had petted them, and they had petted her, and all the tears were kissed away, and they sat holding each other through halting sobs, they helped each other rise to look back at the scene of the crime. The ferocious dog now lay grotesquely still where he had coiled for the final charge and where he had paid a villain's price for his treachery.

Mary Magdalene was up and standing, numbly looking at her assailant and far less battered than he, with a bloody nose and a flap of skin hanging from her tail and the marks from the killer forever tattooed on her ribs.

"We must get Mary to the barn where we can look at her and tend her wounds," said Maria almost to herself.

"But Momma," Gabriella cautioned, crying again, "What if the other wolves come back?"

"I don't think they will," Maria said. "I think that we took the fight out of them."

Raphael was standing looking over the fence at the dog that came so close to hurting his mother.

"That thing had to be crazy to come at you like that, Momma!" he said gravely.

"Not crazy, baby," Maria realized as she looked at her young son, "he was mad; mad with the hydrophobia!"

They all stood looking at the dead animal, contemplating the seriousness of what had just been said. Hydrophobia was one of the most feared scourges in these mountains. Never a year passed without new stories of the terrible disease taking the life of some man, child, or animal in the most horrific way. Once an outbreak began in an area, it could spread like wildfire through the animal population from the saliva of an infected creature through bites or simply by one being too closely exposed to the other.

"Gabriella, go to the house and bring me a pocket full of shells for the gun and some wooden matches. Raphe and I will start gathering brush to burn the dog where he lays. We must all be careful and not touch anything around it."

"Ok, Momma," said the girl tearfully, "but what about Mary?"

"We will worry about Mary later; right now, we must get rid of that dog before the varmints can get at it!"

The girl made a beeline for the house, and Maria and the boy walked around the fence line to the timber and began tossing fallen limbs over into the pasture.

After stacking the limbs around and over the dog as high as they could reach, they chased the befuddled milk cow out of the pasture and into the corral, where they determined that none of her wounds were bad enough to bother with. They filled the manger with hay, topped off the water trough to accommodate her extended confinement, and then went back and set the brush alight. The air was still, and the dirty brown smoke rose straight to the heavens, a sign Maria said that the dog hadn't always been bad and that the disease caused it to act in such a vile manner.

There was nothing more to do now, so they stood and watched the wood burn and listened to the dead branches pop and hiss, and they occasionally shifted their position when a puff of wind threatened to push the thick smoke toward them. When only glowing embers remained of the bonfire, the boy took the shotgun from its place against the fence, and they all tiredly made their way to the house.

Mary Magdalene needed to be milked, but Maria thought it best to let her go till morning and see how she acted when they could watch her for a while. She knew the cow would be uncomfortable, but she wasn't willing to risk contamination if the dog had actually been sick. After the panic of the occasion was several hours passed, the woman started having doubts about her diagnosis, having only seen the beast for a few moments before ending its life. It would be prudent to destroy the cow, but she was too valuable to them not to wait and at least see.

A good lye soap bath was called for, so Maria heated water on the stove while the children brought in the tin bathtub, and she scrubbed the two little ones until they glowed bright red; then, while they dressed for bed, she gave herself a thorough cleaning.

It was dusky dark before supper was ready, which was a simple affair. After they were fed, they left the dishes for morning and all piled into the woman's bed, where they lay staring into the darkness until sleep finally took them.

CHAPTER 5

Miguel walked to the corral under clear blue skies where the stars he had watched during the night were closing their eyes against the glare of the early morning sun struggling above the eastern horizon. A sea of white clouds had settled into the Mojave basin, stretching out like a slowly churning caldron, stirred by the warming air rising from the desert floor. The remains of the storm that had slid down from the heights to bury them in snow the day before now lay writhing in the moisture-killing wasteland below.

He located two wooden buckets and a yoke fashioned from an oak branch for carrying them near what looked like a crude canoe made from a hollowed-out log extending through both sides of the corral fence. He settled the yoke on his shoulders, hung the buckets from their rope bails onto the staff's carved ends, and headed to the spring.

The air was thinner up here than it was at home, and he was disappointed to find himself panting by the time he was halfway back up the slope with his first load, for he was used to running the canyons and ridges for hours with little effort while hunting and trapping in what he considered his private domain laid out for him by his father.

The trough was half full when he started, and it took him six trips before the last bucket filled it to overflowing. He hung the two pails on the fence where he had found them and slipped the yoke back through their bail handles. When he heard the two men coming, he was watching the satisfied look on the face of one of his grandfather's mules, who had found a branch protruding at just the right height from the fence to satisfy an annoying itch.

"Your grandpa is coming with us," said the man to the boy as he unlatched the pole gate. He dragged it from beneath the chins of the mules who had been watching as Miguel filled the water trough. They stood looking like a mute dance troop waiting for their turn on stage. The two horses stood apart, as if offended at having to spend the night with the likes of the four common mules.

The man took a lead rope from a branch on the fence where they had hung it the night before, fastened it to the nearest available mule's halter, and led it through the gate. He repeated this until he had all the mules handed off to his son and father, then went after the two uppity horses.

"Grandpa, how old was my poppa when you started teachin him how to hunt?" the boy asked the Indian over the back of one of the mules.

The old man seemed to be remembering back to get just the right answer from the past, then said, "Well, sir, I reckon he was just learnin to scratch left-handed when I started taking him out huntin." Without waiting for a reaction, the Indian stepped out, leading his two mules toward the wickiup.

The boy looked uncertainly down at his own left hand, flexing his fingers, then back up at his receding grandfather. He wasn't at all surprised to see the old man grinning.

"Indians!" the boy said, shaking his head.

They rigged up three of the mules with sawbucks and panniers; then, the old man pulled out the strangest-looking saddle the boy had ever seen and sat it on the fourth mule. At first glance, it looked like someone had tied a small wooden bench to a piece of a feather mattress. The back was wide, the front narrow, and the three slats on each side looked whittled from axe handles. The two top slats were curved to form a seat, and all of them extended through the front and rear bench legs and were secured with leather strips. The cinch straps and stirrups were made of rawhide leather and attached to the bottom slat on each side. After it was cinched to the mule, the Indian threw what appeared to be a sheep skin, wool side up, over the whole mess and called it done. The boy stood silent until his grandfather took a step back to admire his work.

"Why don't you just use a horse saddle?" the boy remarked.

"You know, boy, you look old enough to be about half as dumb as you are," muttered the old man. "Does that look like a horse to you?"

"No sir, right now it looks more like a camel!" the boy replied defiantly.

"You ever seen a camel?"

"No, sir."

"I thought maybe all you city boys rode around on camels and such like."

"No sir, I ain't never seen no city neither!"

"I guess maybe you don't know everything there is to know then, do you?"

"No, sir, I guess not."

"Well, I'm about to learn you somethin then. Go git one of your daddy's horses and bring it here."

"Yessir," said the boy, and met his father halfway from the corral and asked to have his own horse, Dotty.

The man looked to his father for a clue about what was going on, and the old Indian held up a hand, palm forward, signaling for the man's patience.

William handed the reins to the boy and stopped to watch what would happen next.

When the boy walked up to his grandfather, the old man said, "Now git up on her back."

Miguel reached under the horse's neck, threw the right rein over, and stepped up to her left side. He grabbed a handful of mane hair with his left hand, then with his right hand on her rump, he jumped and hung his belly over the horse's tall back, then swung his right leg over and sat up on the horse's bareback.

"Now scoot up on her shoulders and walk her around a bit."

The boy did as he was told, sliding forward until he was over his horse's front legs, then walked her in a circle back to his grandfather.

The Indian had uncinched the contraption on the mule's back, pulled it off, and sat it on the ground.

"Now git on this mule and do the same thing."

Miguel slid down, handed the horse's reins to the old man, and mounted the tall mule in the same manner as he had done the horse. As he was walking the same circle, he noticed that instead of feeling the mule's shoulders sliding smoothly forward and back like the horse, he found himself being lifted first to one side and then to the other as the mule's shoulders rose and fell. His jaw dropped as he realized his suggestion of using a horse saddle on his grandpa's mule had been absurd. It was clear that the saddle would wear a hole in the mule's shoulders in no time.

He stopped the mule, slid to the ground, and walked around to face his grandfather.

"I guess I am an idjit, Grandpa," he said apologetically.

"Well," said the old man, "I cured your daddy of it; I guess maybe you can be cured too," and he slapped the boy affectionately on the back of the head and began putting the feather bed saddle back on the mule.

"Are all mules built like this one?" the boy asked.

"They are," said the Indian. "They get it from their donkey daddy. If you ever ride one of them, you'll see for yourself."

William walked up, leading the Appaloosa, and said to the boy, "I told you he wasn't like us, didn't I?"

"Yessir, I guess you did," the boy said sheepishly. "Did we just eat a dog for breakfast?"

William flashed an amused smile but said nothing.

They saddled the horses and waited while the old man carried out some of his cooking utensils and supplies, including the clay comal from which he picked several dog hairs. He glanced suspiciously around for Juliet before placing everything carefully into his pack mule's pannier. They all mounted, and the Indian led the way across his clearing onto a path different from the one on which the man and boy had arrived the day before. Each of them led a pack mule, and the man brought up the rear as they descended through the pines on a line that took them south and east down the mountain.

Miguel amused himself by squinting his eyes and imagining a turban on his grandfather's head, balancing atop a camel's hump, swaying from side to side, and navigating through the sand dunes of Arabia.

The dog sat patiently by the trail just before it entered the timber, and having inspected and cleaned all the cooking utensils when the men left her alone in the wickiup, she was well prepared to go. As the small troop came across the clearing, she took the lead as if she knew exactly where they were going, for this wasn't the first time she had accompanied the old Indian and man on a search for corpses in the desert below.

**

Two grizzled mountain men sat their horses patiently watching the activity below from a promontory overlooking the old Indian's camp. The smaller of the two spat a string of brown tobacco juice onto the ground next to his horse and said, "Are you sure you want to get tangled up with these particular Indians?"

"All I'm sure of is that Will Strider owes us a debt, said the big man. He's got them government boys thinkin that he's the only tracker in these mountains, and I aim to do somethin about it."

"Well, all I'm sayin is, I know these boys, and I don't think they are the ones we want to git on the wrong side of. When it comes to trackin and shootin, if they ain't the best, they'll do till the best gits here."

"I ain't a scared of no man, Indian or white," said Bodine with a scowl.

"I guess you don't recall when that Strider kid put that ten gage in your face. I know I wasn't the only one whippin the hair off my horse tryin to git out of that boy's yard."

"That wasn't scared; that was bein smart! That kid could have blowed us in two with that cannon on accident."

"Well, all I'm sayin is, if you aimed to scare somebody, then I guess you got the job done."

"Don't get smart, Skinner, that gut eatin Indian is takin money out of your pocket too, you know!"

"I know, but what are we gonna do about it that don't set them two on our trail."

"Well, the way I figure it, if we run on to em' somewhere out in the scrub on accident, we might just ride along with them until we can git the jump and put a bullet in their brains," said Bodine.

"I guess it's that or me and you better find another line of work," replied Skinner.

"Come on; we'll trail them and bide our time till our chance comes."

They guided their horses from the promontory into the trees and down the mountain toward the old man's clearing at a leisurely pace to avoid getting too close to the party they meant to follow.

**

The old Indian kept his mule on a mile-eating pace down the steep mountain trail through the pine and cedar forest on a path that would lead the group onto the desert plain within a few hours. There were more than a few well-known trails across the Mojave to choose from, but experience had taught them which were the most likely candidates to be selected by which type of travelers. A group like the one they were looking for, carrying small children, was more likely to choose one or two over the rest for the terrain to be managed and the possibility of finding water during this winter season. If they were lucky, they would strike sign by cutting perpendicular across the trails until they hit the correct one without having to venture too far into the wasteland.

**

The two leather-clad followers stayed with the group until they reached the flats, left the trees, and entered the desert, making it more challenging to remain concealed. They turned south on an arc that would make them appear to be coming out of the desert when they met up with the group and avoid any thought that they had been following.

**

The wasted desert stretched before the two Indian men and half-Indian boy when they topped the last rise before descending into the basin. Saguaro cactus beckoned them onward, silent sentinels with raised arms and blank faces that failed to convey the true nature of the land they were ushering the small party into.

Miguel stole a look over his shoulder, back at the inviting mountains they were leaving; the image of his mother standing watch somewhere above tugged at his heart.

The old Indian stopped his mule on the crest of the ridge and waited for the man and boy to come alongside.

"Does the boy know what we're out here lookin for?" the old man asked his son.

"Well, we ain't talked much about it, but he knows what I do for a living."

"I swear, son, you'd starve to death before you'd say biscuit!"

"I know what we're lookin for, Grandpa," said the boy.

"Lookin' for ain't seein, have you ever been close to a dead human man?"

"No, sir, but I've seen my share of dead animals."

"Well," said the Indian, "I guess a dead man ain't no more than a dead animal that somebody washed his face, combed his hair, and put shoes on him anyways." The old man put a heel in the mule's flank, and they were away, down the slope leading to the desert floor.

CHAPTER 6

Maria carried another fresh basket of wash to the clothesline, set it down, and then picked the short pocket apron that held her wooden clothes pins from the pile. As she tied its strings behind her back, she heard Raphael burst forth from the house's back door, running at full speed, followed closely by his sister grabbing savagely at his shirttail, flapping just inches in front of her grasping fingers.

"I'll git you Raphe if it's the last thing I ever do, then I'm going to snatch you bald-headed, do you hear me?"

"Momma, Momma, make her stop!" Raphael laughed breathlessly as he grabbed her skirt to help him make the loop around, then shot back across the yard to reenter the house with Gabriella hot on his heels.

She heard their rapid footfalls on the wooden cabin floor, and then the kitchen door slammed open as the boy burst forth anew into the morning sunshine.

"You kids, break anything, I'll snatch you both bald!" the woman called after them, then picked up one of the man's shirts and shook it out before pinning it to the line.

The day was clear and warm, and it felt good to get outside and hear the birds in the trees fighting over nest-building sites as spring blossomed in every direction. The sun was big overhead, and the sky peeking between the tall green pines was the same shade of blue as a robin's egg. Clean sheets billowed in the breeze, and the odor of fresh laundry filled the air. It was good to see the kids shaking off the winter doldrums after being confined to the house for so long.

The woman thought the children were still playing as she bent down to pick up one of Raphael's nightshirts from the basket and heard the terrified scream come floating over the cabin.

"Momma!!" it was Raphael, then long seconds of silence.

"Wolves! Momma, wolves, has got Raphe! Oh, Momma!" came Gabriella's heart-rending screams.

The woman said, "Oh my dear God, not my babies!" and started running toward the back door of the house.

When she came through the open kitchen door and onto the planks of the porch, she could see her daughter halfway to the barn; she looked so tiny standing there with her hands covering her mouth, mesmerized by the horrible spectacle just feet in front of her. Raphael was being jerked and dragged between the two massive beasts that had attacked Mary Magdalene the day before. Their blood-red eyes glowed with the same intense hatred that had been there in the brute that she had killed.

She could now see why she had heard no more from her son because one of the big curs had a firm grip on his throat, and the other tugged at his bleeding legs. The boy's shiny black eyes found hers, and as his body was brutally snatched from the ground, they silently cried out for her help. Juliet brushed past her and bound into the fray, snapping and snarling at the attacker at the boy's head, but to no avail.

Maria was paralyzed, there was a scream in her throat, but it was trapped there by the horror. Her son was dying, and she would rush to him if only she could get her petrified body to move. If William were here, he would save him; he would make his feet carry him to his son's side. He would put his hands in the dog's jaws and pull his boy free. He would yank the life out of the beast and put it back into his son. He would carry Raphael and lay him in her arms.

Was this William's fault for taking Miguel away from her to teach him his absurd trade? No, that wasn't it; it was her fault for being too weak. She couldn't save her father, she couldn't save her mother or her sister or brother, and now she couldn't save her son.

She remembered what her father had said with his dying breath, "God loves you, mi bebita."

"No," she had thought, "God surely hates me!"

All that she wanted then as now was to reach out and stop the world from turning, to roll back time and undo every bad thing that was happening, but the world would not stop, and time would not be turned back, and it was not within her power to keep her loved ones safe.

She had been a girl of sixteen then and all alone when she held the hands of each of her family, pleading with them, in turn, not to leave her alone. Slowly, silence crept from room to room and then into the streets. She assumed that all in the village had died, but most had simply fled. The home that had kept her safe and warm all her life was now as cold as a tomb, a place of death accusing her for remaining alive. Finally, her time came. She somehow found her bed, the only one not occupied by a waxen, shrunken figure that looked vaguely like someone she had loved. She gratefully closed her eyes and waited for the relief that only death could bring.

Then, she slowly became aware of the shadow of a stranger, of a man. He sat by her bed, held her hand, and wiped her brow. He said soothing things in a language she did not know but somehow understood. He chased away the cold and silence and replaced them with warmth and hope. She suspected him of being an angel, come to guide her home, but an angel doesn't feed you soup, change your sheets, or sing haunting tunes to encourage you to live. Until she came fully awake, he never left her side.

He buried her family and burned all signs of the disease, and when she had recovered enough, he helped her to their graves and stood with her while she prayed. It never occurred to her to question his motives or to refuse his help. He packed her clothes and the things she pointed out, put them all in a wagon, sat her on the seat, and tied his horse to the back. He climbed up next to her and snapped the reins, and the mules carried them far away to his place in the mountains.

It was almost a year before the man made her his wife and a couple more before Miguel was born. During that time, they built a cabin and cleared the land. Maria was young and strong, but William was forced to shoulder much of the responsibility for the child, for she found herself reluctant to completely commit her love to the boy, or his father, for a fear that she could not describe. She only knew that she would never be strong enough to survive the loss of another loved one. Eventually, as the boy grew and became strong, the mother in her could no longer be denied, and then the twins arrived. If William was the source of the family's strength, then she became the source of its love.

She turned to God as insurance against all things evil and believed that if she were devout enough, pious enough, He would protect this new family that she had found. But now, the protective walls she had so carefully built came tumbling down. Was she being punished again for having a perfect life? Had joy somehow become a sin? Had she not suffered enough?

She opened her eyes, but she could not see. She took a breath, but there was no air. With her last bit of strength, she reached out for her son, and to her surprise, she found him. She pulled him to her and held on as the dogs tried to rip him from her. She would fight them to the death.

"Momma, turn me loose!" cried the boy as he flipped and flopped, trying to turn in the bed to face her.

Gabriella shouted out an unintelligible warning in her sleep, and she became a part of her mother's dream, but it had been Raphael's cry that had startled the girl awake. In moments Gabriella was on top of her mother, weeping without knowing why.

Maria finally shook loose from the horrible dream and sat breathless, great sobs wracking her chest, still feeling the same unbearable anguish she had in her nightmare. She released her son, and he spun toward her and reached for her face with both hands.

"Momma are you hurt?" he said, shaking her, demanding an answer.

"Yes, yes, I mean no, I'm not hurt," She sat up and found a child snuggled beneath each arm. Soon she caught her breath and calmed the children, and they both went back to sleep, clinging tightly to her. The thought that kept running through her mind was, "God, please take me before my family!"

When the early morning light crept in through the window, she kissed the boy and girl a last time, slipped from the bed without waking them, went to the kitchen, and automatically began making a fire in the stove. She sat in the dim light of morning, feeling the pain of loss as if the terrible thing had actually happened. She made a silent vow to God that no family member would ever die alone again.

Before long, Gabriella came padding into the kitchen carrying the doll her father had brought back from Mexico the last time he was there.

"Momma, I think I had bad dreams last night," the girl said as she sat down and rested her head on the doll she had placed on the table in front of her, looking sideways up at her mother.

"What did you dream about, baby?" asked Maria, looking for a link to her horrific nightmare.

"It was about them wolves that came yesterday; I think they was chasing Raphe and me."

"Well, it was just a bad dream, baby, so try not to think about it."

Maria got up, made dishwater, and began washing the things they had left the night before. Gabby watched her for a while, then closed her sleepy blue eyes and napped until Raphael walked in and dragged a chair from beneath the table.

"What's for breakfast anyways?" the boy asked, with his chin resting sleepily on his crossed arms on the table. "I didn't sleep at all last night thinkin about them dogs."

"Them was wolves, dummy," Gabriella stated, without even bothering to look up at the boy.

"Shows what you know about wolves," Raphael retorted. They were both too tired to fuss, so the argument died.

Maria's hands stopped washing as she gazed out the window, "We will see how Mary is this morning, and if she is all right, I might try to milk her." She had just remembered the poor creature who had suffered the attack of the dogs the day before.

After breakfast, they all got their coats, Raphael got his egg bucket, Gabriella carried the milk bucket, and they all held hands going to the barn.

This time Maria looked around to ensure that Juliet wasn't there, having dreamed her up during the night. She was relieved to see that she indeed wasn't.

Mary Magdalene was calmly munching hay when they opened the manger door to let her in. If it wasn't for the flap of loose skin on her tail, you could hardly tell that anything had happened. After gathering the eggs, Raphael went to inspect the ashes of the fire with a stick and came back to report that the dog was gone, bones and all.

Maria milked the cow but then dumped it on the ground outside the barn for safety's sake.

That day no one mentioned the dogs again, but the children didn't play outside anyway. It was laundry day, but Maria baked bread instead, preferring not to repeat anything that had happened in the terrible dream.

She couldn't help but wonder how Miguel and her husband were doing. She seldom worried about William as he was the unshakable rock she had built her entire life on, but she felt that her son was vulnerable, especially after last night's dream. Dreams for her fell into the same category as unburied bodies and omens. One couldn't prove they meant anything, but you couldn't prove they didn't.

A sense of dread had settled upon her, and only the sight of all her family together at home would shake it.

CHAPTER 7

In 1920 Alejandro Rodriguez Pena found himself on the wrong side of history when Madero, Zapata, and Villa successfully led the overthrow of the dictatorship in Mexico. Over 900,000 people lost their lives in the bloody conflict that ended the rule of the aristocracy and land gentry.

Alejandro lost everything when his father was bound and executed in his Mexico City estate courtyard. He went from wealthy and privileged to poor and alone, finally realizing that he was nothing more than a well-fed, well-spoken, well-educated orphan, entirely without the skills to support his family on his own. He would spend the next fifteen years hiding in plain sight as Alejandro Hernandez.

In 1935, with a low-level bookkeeping job in the town of Saltillo, his luck ran out. One day, a patron walked into his office and recognized him as his father's son. He made accusations as a one-time employee and victim of a family known for taking cruel advantage of those at the bottom of the caste system. Alejandro voiced his denials, but the political system was still dominated by one-time revolutionary generals seeking to root out the remnants of the aristocrats they had fought so hard to defeat.

Alejandro took what little money he had and loaded his wife, Camila, son, Mateo, and daughter, Natalie, into the only vehicle he could easily steal, a peasant's wagon and donkey, and headed north in the middle of the night. He hoped to cross the border into California before the Federal Police discovered where they had gone. They were headed to Mexicali just south of San Diego but were forced to cross prematurely into Arizona to avoid capture.

They just had time to send a telegram to Camila's sister in San Francisco, laying out their situation and planned route. After six weeks and no further word, the sister filed a missing person's report with the U.S. government. This brought into motion the events that caused William Strider and company to search for the lost family in the Mojave Desert.

"My husband," said Camila, "are there no towns or villages in this country where you have brought us to die? I begged you to send the children and me ahead by train, but Don Rodriguez would not travel alone. Now we are dying of thirst, and you sit in the dust like a lost dog crying for your bad luck. God will judge you for the murder of your family."

"Quiet woman, have you no respect for the master of your house?"

"The master of a broken-down cart, you mean!"

"Silence! I must think, to devise a plan to get us out of this wilderness. Perhaps we would not be in this situation if you were a help instead of a millstone."

"Do you mean the situation where you dragged us from our beds in the middle of the night to ride like ignorant peons into the desert?"

Alejandro said no more, reaching once again the point in the argument with his wife when he realized the futility of sparring with one armed with the truth and more capable in a fight than he.

The children sat in the shade of the wagon, unimpressed by the noise their parents made, continuing a running dialogue that they had heard their entire lives. At first, they had enjoyed the adventure, stopping at day's end at the home of a goat herder or the modest adobe hut of a farmer, all bound by hundreds of years of tradition to open their doors to any traveler in need of food or bed.

Everything in Mexico reflected the war years, throwing most of the country into abject poverty. For weeks after Mexico City fell, the country was one huge fiesta financed by the looting of the great Houses in the cities, and the huge Ranchos recently divided up among the ranking officers of the rebellion. Slowly, most of the country returned to their neglected and ruined farms to wait for the prosperity that had been promised.

Had these people known that Alejandro represented everything they and their campaneros had fought against and died to defeat, the reception might have been different. They were often welcomed by someone who had lost an arm, leg, or eye while fighting to overthrow the dictator. Despite these malformities, Alejandro accepted their hospitality, although with an air of disdain.

Only now were Mateo and Natalie beginning to appreciate the seriousness of their situation. Water was running out, and they had hardly eaten in days. The vastness of the desert was on display in every direction, and the hazy images of mountains looked a thousand miles away. There had been a brief rain shower the night before, but the small party of travelers was ill-equipped to collect more than a few drops of it. An argument between their parents had erupted as the storm clouds passed, each accusing the other of incompetence and stupidity.

Travel was slow, but the time of year meant that the opportunity for more rain was at least a possibility. The family forged ahead a few miles each day, but the lack of water for the donkey was taking its toll, and it was only a matter of time before they would be forced to walk with only the supplies they could carry. The rifle they had brought held only one bullet at a time, and Alejandro was no marksman, so an occasional skinny rabbit was the extent of their food.

When the donkey could pull the cart no more, a bullet to the brain was its reward for its toil. Although they didn't know it then, the camp they made that night could have become their home for the remainder of their lives. The meat lasted them a week, but it was impossible to keep the flies and other insects away, and the maggots consumed more than the doomed family.

Alejandro tried several times to convince Camila to stay with the children while he returned the way they had come for help, but she called it an attempt to abandon them and vowed to follow and slit his throat while he slept. Ultimately, he saw that his only choice was to stay with his family, no matter the consequences.

CHAPTER 8

Miguel noticed that once they entered the desert, all talk stopped, and everyone took on a demeanor befitting the seriousness of the task. Til now, this had just been a camping trip and a visit to a grandpa he never knew existed. The talk of dead people and the images it suggested caused him to ponder what lay at the end of this trail. His father and mother seldom spoke of the details of any of the man's assignments, so they were never a real part of day-to-day life for the Strider children. Pappa left and returned in a week or a month with fresh supplies, and if he had been successful, maybe a new goat or pig or some bobble for their mother. Occasionally, if they were lucky, a new toy, doll, or steel trap came out of a pannier, and a celebration would break out among the children. It was enough to have their father home again but presents made it seem like Christmas.

When they stopped for the night, William stayed mounted. He looked at his father and pointed south, perpendicular to their path, then leaned forward in his stirrups and started in that direction. Juliet was on the move as soon as he pointed, and they were quickly out of sight in the gathering darkness.

Miguel looked to his grandfather for an explanation, the same way he looked to his father when the question was so apparent that words weren't necessary.

"It's a Indian thing," the old man explained, looking in the direction his only remaining son had gone. "It started back when we were fight'n with the whites. Indians ain't sneaky cowards like them, soldier boys. They would come up on you in the dark if they could. So, we took to riding a big circle around the camp come sundown, lets you slip up behind somebody followin you and cut the track of 'em if they are layin' for you up ahead. Your daddy will be back before the moon's up."

The thing that stuck in Miguel's head was 'fighting with the whites.' Isolated on the homestead the way he had been his whole life and with the few people he had met, he would have more likely categorized them as either clean or dirty rather than light or dark. Fighting conjured up images of battles on horseback, war cries, and the roar of cannons, so he was pretty sure what his dreams would consist of that night.

They stripped the horse and mules, hobbled them for the night, and arranged the camp. No tent was needed, for the silent canopy of stars seen in every direction promised no rain. Looking up into the endless firmament made the boy feel small and humble; the vastness suggested that one who looked long enough might see forever; where you stood was today, ahead lay tomorrow, and behind yesterday. He could almost feel the day's oppressive heat being sucked into the void of space as a chill rose from the ground.

Miguel made a fire, and the old man pulled out his clay comal, picked off a few more dog hairs, then started mixing tortillas in a gourd bowl.

"Will you answer me somethin?" Miguel asked.

"I will if I can," said the Indian.

"Poppa said not to mention to Momma about us coming to see you," the boy began.

"Thought you was going to ask me somethin," replied his grandfather.

"Yessir, why would he tell me not to say anything to Momma?"

"Did you ask him?"

"Yessir, but he said what he usually says, nothin'."

The old Indian shook his head knowingly, "Well, maybe you better wait til your poppa's ready to say."

Miguel didn't know his grandpa very well, but he knew what it sounded like when his father was through talking about a thing, and this sounded just like that.

"Can I ask somethin else?" continued the boy.

"Fire away," said the old Indian.

"Do I have any more kin that I don't know anything about except you?" he asked slightly accusingly.

"Well, sir, your poppa has a mother, two brothers, and a sister, all buried in Mexico. They died while he was off to war. Far as I know, I got a brother still livin over in the canyon country; that's where we all come from, you know; I guess he'd be your kin."

Miguel considered his grandfather's answer and tried to gauge how far he might go to fill in the gaps in his family's history. He finally decided on what he felt was a safe tack to take in his quest for details.

"Where did you all live when my poppa was a boy?"

The old man stopped kneading the flour and lard and looked into the distance. He knew this clever boy was trying to lead him somewhere he didn't want to go. The past was a place that he avoided visiting, mainly because his memories always left him stranded in the same dark place. He was afraid every time he went there that he might be unable to escape. But on this occasion, he determined that his grandson deserved to know.

"I remember," he said, "the first time I took your poppa with me up to the rim; he didn't know the world was made of anything but sand rock bluffs and a strip of blue sky. Our village was on the sandy bottom of a canyon that took you almost two hours to ride out of. I set him in front of me on my horse, and we rode the trail up. When we came out on the level, he started to cry for want of them rock walls around him. The same thing happened to me when I was a boy. That was in the Great Canyon country in Arizona. I told him that everything he could see, mountain, plain, and sky belonged to him, for that's what my poppa told me, and back then, it was so. Your daddy was the firstborn to your grandma and me, and then his two brothers and sister came. We had cattle and a little bark hut up on the rim where we spent the summers, and we went there to hunt in the winter. We traded cattle and pelts with the white men, and most of us took up their language, that and Mexican. We traded red clay (red ochre) with the other tribes, Navajo and Hopi, dug from secret caves in our canyon, and lived a good life.

Then the soldier coats come, and they told us we couldn't go more'n a few miles away from our canyon. Then they come back and started takin away our children; the government said we wasn't teachin em' right how to be Americans. Some of us fought em', but it weren't no use.

When your poppa was about grown, they come and took him and some others off to fight in a white man's war in a place they called over the seas. While he was gone, the soldier coats came again and said that now we can't go out of our canyon. Said the Great White Father in Washington would take care of us like we was his children. We wondered if he starved his other children too, because we never had enough to eat. Finally, me and your grandma loaded up the kids and everything we owned and slipped on down to Mexico to live. We got his sister to write a letter to your poppa, tellin him where we was going to, so he would know how to find us when he come home.

When your daddy did come back from the war, he comes lookin for us, but by then, everybody was dead of the fever cept'n me. Spanish flu, they called it. Your grandma went first cause she was out helping them that was sick. We didn't know how bad it was till everybody started dyin. In a week, they was all gone. I buried em' there in Mexico and come back to the canyon, but he never come back that way again. In a couple of years, I got a letter your pappa had wrote, sayin he had a wife, and where he was livin at, and would we like to come and live closer to them. It was just me, so I went lookin, and I found him on his mountain. I built my home in that place you come to, and it was close enough that we could see each other from time to time. I help him with his trackin, and he brings me the things I need. We get on all right, I guess."

Miguel sat cross-legged in the sand, watching the images that his grandpa painted for him with his words. They flowed like flipping through the pages of one of his mother's books. In the end, the mystery remained.

"From now on, I will come to see you too, Grandpa," the boy offered, and the conversation ended.

When William completed his circuit around the camp, he reported seeing a fresh set of horse tracks that paralleled their path into the desert but off by a couple of miles. He had followed them for some time, but when they turned north toward the mountains, he quit them to continue his route.

Nothing was said about the conversation between the boy and his grandfather, and a look passed between the two filed the subject away for another time.

Miguel lay awake late into the night, picturing his grandfather riding a camel down on a troop of soldiers, all standing gape-mouthed at the sight.

**

"I told you it wasn't a good idea messin around with these Indians, didn't I?" said Skinner.

"Shut up; who rides around in the dark in the desert anyways?" said Bodine.

"You mean besides us? Will Strider does, and if that dog of his hadn't jumped a coyote, he would have rode right up our backsides I guess, and made camp!"

"Well, he wasn't smart enough to follow us on upland," said the big man.

"No, but you can bet he won't forget about us, neither."

"It won't matter; by mornin, we'll be ahead of 'em."

CHAPTER 9

Each morning and night, Maria and the children walked apprehensively past the chicken coop to the back of the barn to watch Mary Magdalene through the fence. They had released her from the confinement of the corral to graze in the meadow, and so far, she was showing no signs of the illness that they suspected the wild dogs of bringing.

"Momma, is Mary going to be ok?" Gabriella asked hopefully.

"It's too soon to tell, baby," Maria answered, gazing over the split rail fence at the cow.

"How will we know if she's sick?" the boy wondered.

"Your daddy told me about a cow he had when he was a boy that got bit by a mad skunk; they called it moon madness back then. He said she was ok for about a week, then suddenly, she quit giving milk and started slobbering, and you couldn't get close to her. They put her down and burned her like we did that dog."

"How'd they know a skunk bit her?" Raphe wanted to know.

"Well, they seen it bite her dummy!" mocked Gabriella.

"Your father said that they didn't see the skunk bite her, but he did see it chasing her around the field, and he went out and clubbed it to death. He said it's pretty easy to tell an animal with moon madness because it staggers around and foams at the mouth like nothing you've ever seen. We'll keep milking Mary as long as she acts all right, but we won't drink the milk."

"If I seen a mad skunk," Raphael boasted with an excited glint in his wide eyes, "I'd club it to death!"

"If either of you ever sees an animal acting like that, you run away from it as fast as you can. Do you hear me?"

"Yes em'," Raphe slowly answered, but his eyes retained their shine as if imagining the clubbing scene.

"Yes, ma'am," Gabriella said meekly. "I wish Daddy and Willy would come home."

Life got back to normal. They didn't see the wild dogs again, and Mary Magdalene stayed healthy. Still, Maria's sleep was fitful, and she moved the children back to their beds so she could get up in the night without waking them. She knew better than to guess when William and Miguel would return because it only made time move more slowly.

Some days were spring-like, and others were colder. Still, when the sun shone brightly through the trees, the two little ones got back to well-established routines, with Gabriella playing doll house in the barn loft and Raphael leading raids on outlaws holed up in the smokehouse or defending the corn crib against a wide array of adversaries.

Maria had enough to keep her occupied with the two children that she was compelled to put her eyes on every little bit to assure herself that they were still breathing and not bleeding and that no monsters had crept into the yard to attack them. Not to mention three meals to prepare, dishes to clean, and clothes to launder. The cow had to be milked, and there were chickens to tend. She spent a fair amount of time praying for her son and husband to return quickly and safely.

On the morning of the fifth day following the wild dog attack, they were all in the barn, and Maria had just finished milking Mary when Raphael's head appeared through the hay well in the loft floor.

In an excited, subdued voice, the boy said, "Momma, there's people at the house."

Maria sat the milk bucket down and picked up the shotgun that now accompanied her anytime she was outside.

"Gabby, get up in the loft with your brother, and neither of you come down until I call you." She pointed to the ladder and waited until her daughter disappeared through the ceiling before opening the barn door.

Sitting in the lane before the yard gate sat an Army escort wagon, pulled by a team of two mules and driven by an Army cavalry soldier. Beside him sat a Mexican woman who looked a little older than Maria herself, wrapped in a shawl that could have been one of her own. There was another soldier mounted on a big bay horse sporting a McClellan military saddle; he wore knee-high leather boots that hinted of regular buffing, though the dust of the trail obscured some of their shine. He sat erect as if nailed to the horse with an iron rod driven through his spine. When he spotted Maria coming from the barn, he dismounted and saluted stiffly, waiting for her to acknowledge him.

Raphael had the haymow door open by now, and he and Gabriella stood staring down at the visitors. The first thing the boy noticed, even before the people, were the two large crossed sabers printed in black on the white wagon cover. He turned to head back toward the ladder, but Gabriella grabbed his shirt collar and jerked so hard that the boy's teeth snapped shut with a click, and he had to scramble to keep from falling backward.

"Don't even think about it!" the girl growled.

His pride was bruised, but he said nothing as he rejoined his sister at the opening, realizing that his impulse to get a closer look at the wagon and soldiers went against everything his father had ever told him about obeying his mother in his absence.

Maria felt awkward holding the gun at the ready and lowered it to a benign attitude as she walked up to the saluting soldier. She nodded her acknowledgment, and the man dropped his hand smartly to his side and said, "Ma'am."

"It's a surprise to see you here, Lieutenant; what can I help you with?"

With a sweep of his arm, the soldier directed her attention up to the wagon seat where the woman sat with an uncertain smile.

"May I present Mrs. Ortiz to you, Ma'am?"

Maria stepped nearer the wagon and said, "Would you like to get down, Mrs. Ortiz?"

The seated soldier hopped from the wagon and reached up to help the woman down, and when she was on the ground, he stepped back to allow the two women to meet.

"Are you the wife of Mr. William Strider?" the woman asked politely.

"Why yes, I am," answered Maria, a little taken aback.

"I believe your husband has been tasked with finding my sister and her family, who seem to be lost in your desert."

Maria took a moment to digest the information before speaking. This woman could easily have been her departed sister, and she felt an immediate kinship with her. She knew that most of the people her husband was sent to find were not expected to be found alive, so she took a moment to look into the woman's face, hoping for a clue on how to respond. Behind the woman's smile, a stress-hardened brow and searching eyes betrayed the sleepless nights and long journey that had brought her to this place.

"He is away with my oldest son 'en una tarea (on an assignment)' for the government, that is true."

"Gracias a Dios te encontramos (Thank God, we found you)," the woman said as one holding their breath, hoping for an affirmative reply, as this was not the first homestead that she had been taken to in her search for the man that she prayed would bring her family safely to her.

"Ma'am," the lieutenant interrupted, speaking to Maria. "We have been on the trail for three weeks, a week longer than our commander allowed us to bring Mrs. Ortiz to you. We had hoped to spend this last week here anticipating your husband's return, but I see that we were overly optimistic, and well, one way or another, the corporal and I have to get back to the post."

Maria saw mild panic in the eyes of her countrywoman. She was obviously exhausted from her journey and probably her fight with the military bureaucracy to have gotten this far, only to be turned around and sent back home.

"Surely, Lieutenant, you wouldn't deny Mrs. Ortiz a good night's sleep and a home-cooked meal before you drag her back through these mountains. I suspect that you and your corporal could both stand that as well. I know it is days by wagon to the nearest Army outpost, so one more night can't hurt. Rest your animals, sleep in a good soft bed, and get an early start in the morning."

The lieutenant hesitated, weighing the pros and cons of the decision.

He, too, was exhausted from trying to persuade this determined Mexican lady to turn back at every crook in the trail, and he was stymied by the prospect of arguing now with two women.

While the two ladies waited for an argument to ensue, a small strained male voice floated up from the barn.

"Momma, can we come out now?"

The group turned in unison to the sight of a young boy being restrained by his smaller sister with her arms wrapped around the boy keeping him from launching himself from the hay loft door.

The lieutenant sighed, "I guess we can stay one night."

Maria motioned to the two children to come on out.

CHAPTER 10

After Alejandro chose to stay with his family, even in the face of probable death, he turned his efforts to creating a shelter that would keep them alive for as long as possible with the hope that God would eventually intervene to save them.

As he worked, the young Mexican man of privilege thought of a statement he had made as his father was being executed, "someone should do something!" Peculiar, he thought that this should come to mind at this moment. He also recalled the face of a young peasant woman, dressed in rags but with a fierce look of nobility in her eyes as she had charged a cannon emplacement outside the walls of his father's home with nothing more than an antique muzzle-loading pistol. Until now, he had never understood what could have possessed her to perform such a doomed act. But perhaps she too had thought that someone should do something, and so she had, and so too would he. Alejandro Rodriguez Pena would do a husband and father's duty for his family, even if it were the first and last time in his life.

They had stopped their wagon at the bottom of a deep arroyo carved by flash floods from the mountains to the north and west, caused by Pacific storms colliding with the Sierra Nevada and spilling over their peaks. Volumes of water were squeezed from the clouds by the rapid ascent in altitude and subsequent descent down through the canyons and valleys toward the basin. The powder dry sand provided no evidence that water had ever flowed there, and the inexperience of the travelers let them see only the shade of the mornings and evenings created by the abrupt eastward and westward banks.

Relative to the heat of the sand above, the base of the wash, when in the shade, was a good twenty degrees cooler. Quilts and blankets suspended on straps made from the leather harnesses, drawn across the wagon and staked to the ground near the tops of the banks, provided shade during the hottest part of the day until the arc of the sun dropped low enough for the land to block its rays in the evening. Following the depression, hot breezes wafted beneath the shelter to evaporate their sweat and make the heat at least bearable.

"My husband, what are we to do?" Camila asked hopelessly as she looked up from scraping the husk of a small cactus fruit. "The moisture that we get from these will not sustain us."

"I know," replied Alejandro softly so as not to wake the two sleeping children. "I have few cartridges left for the gun, and when they are gone, we will have nothing to eat."

Each looked deeply into the other's eyes and found that the hostility they usually met there was gone.

"Out in the sun," said the man, "we would not last a day, and the mountains are a week's walk away. Without God's help, we shall all perish beneath this wagon." He placed a hand on his wife's cheek and continued, "I swear I would cut out my own heart if that would save the rest of you."

"Say no more about it, my husband; if it is God's will that we should die here, then so be it."

In the early morning light and the evening's dusk, the Mexican man roamed the nearby desert in search of game and the small cactus fruits that were their only source of moisture. His wife and children spent the predawn hours huddled in the makeshift lean-to waiting for the passage of night in anticipation of the day's heat. Each day they all became noticeably weaker and survived only with the thinnest thread of hope promoted by the man, for he knew nothing else to do for them.

On his forays into the wasteland, Alejandro's thoughts were haunted by the wrenching images of his family being slowly tortured to death in this unrelenting heat, and he was to blame. It was becoming increasingly apparent that it was his duty alone to spare them this ordeal. He spoke with Camila privately and asked her what she would have him do when all hope was lost; she had answered him only by looking back at their children and making the sign of the cross on her breast before turning desperate eyes back to him. He made up his mind then to save four bullets for the end.

CHAPTER 11

The old Indian was up with the sun, cooking tortillas on the campfire when Miguel rolled from his blanket and pulled on his boots in the chilled air of the morning. William sat astride his saddle near the fire, hands cupping a tin of hot coffee, talking with his father in subdued tones. Both men looked up as the boy walked over, dropped his saddle, sat cross-legged between it and the fire, and wrapped his blanket around his shoulders against the cold.

"I thought it was supposed to be hot in the desert," complained the boy, scooching closer to the flames.

"You better enjoy this cool," said the man. "Because when that sun gets up, you will find out what hot means," nodding toward the eastern horizon.

"I've seen the sun so hot out here," the old Indian mused as he lifted the edge of the tortilla he was cooking, "it burnt the warts off the back of your grandma's neck."

"For real, Grandpa?" gushed the boy.

The old Indian just smiled at the gullible young face of his grandson.

After a light breakfast, they packed up their camp and rode single file in the direction they had traveled the day before. As the sun cleared the horizon, it dropped a blanket of warmth, heat, then oppressive heat across the land. Miguel started to remove his blanket coat but was warned off it by his grandfather, who told him to loosen the straps and drop the collar but not to remove the coat entirely. Otherwise, the desert sun would have unimpeded access to his defenseless back and shoulders.

Miguel thought it was contrary to basic logic but kept the coat on anyway.

It was a typical day in the Mojave, with stark blue skies faded only by the omnipresent sun's glare. Looking back at the mountains, the boy could see the permanent halo of misty clouds clinging to the heights. The exception today was the presence of an occasional silent flicker of light from an unfortunate storm front that had strayed too close to the coast and tripped over the peaks from which there was no return.

From time to time, the old Indian would guide his mule fifty yards to either side of the trail and then gradually angle back to resume his position at the lead of the small troop. The first time this happened, the boy stopped his horse and twisted around to see his father, who motioned him on and said, "He's cutting for sign," and on they went.

Early in the evening, with the sun descending behind the mountains and the shadows growing, Miguel looked up to find that he had run upon the mule his grandfather was leading and had to jerk the reins to avoid a collision. The old man had stopped and was standing in his stirrups, staring out across the scrub. Following his gaze, the boy located Juliet standing on a small knoll, looking back toward the mountains with her nose high in the air, trying to locate the origin of the odor that had gotten her attention.

"What does she smell, Grandpa?" asked the boy.

"Dust where there ain't no wind," the Indian replied, sniffing the air.

"Get to high ground!" his father yelled, pointing off the trail toward a slight hump in the terrain as he put his heels to the horse's flanks and guided her in the same direction he was pointing.

Sensing danger, Miguel's horse bolted after William's, causing the boy to grab to keep from losing his seat. When they were safely on the rise, all eyes turned toward the mountains, where it looked like several invisible locomotives were racing in their direction, kicking up plumes of dust in their wake.

"Flash flood," William explained to his son. "A big one!"

"But it ain't even raining," the boy said, aware that he was stating the obvious.

"It's raining somewhere in the mountains," his father said, following the path of the water with his eyes as it careened down ancient routes across the arid land.

"Will we be ok here?" asked the boy.

"We will be fine," his grandfather said calmly, "but I wouldn't want to be in the way of one of them things."

As the dust grew nearer, a slight breeze rose, and the smell of moisture filled the air.

"Wy, I seen a flood so big one time…" the old Indian began.

"Don't, Grandpa!" Miguel stopped him, exercising a newfound sense for detecting his grandfather's malarky.

The old man grinned his toothy grin and waited for the water to arrive.

Like a serpent racing down a well-worn path, the water rushed by them. Logs, limbs, and all sorts of other debris tumbled along ahead of the beast as it whooshed past at an unbelievable speed.

"Jesus," said William as they were hit by the air rushing up out of the arroyo. "Hang on to the mules!"

It was as if a dam had burst somewhere high in the mountains unleashing a great torrent of water to careen down the slopes and speed out across the desert, a flood whose tail constantly threatened to overtake its head, which was taking the time to collect timber and brush as it coursed through the canyons and arroyos that this band of searchers had traversed only hours before. Miguel and his father and grandfather were miles into the flat wasteland, yet tons of dirty water and debris rushed by them, spilling from the banks of the depression created by other such events throughout the ages. The noise made by the tumbling logs and rushing water was enough to panic the horses and mules, and it was all they could do to hold them.

"How long will this last?" yelled Miguel above the fray, unsure how long he could pretend that he wasn't as scared as the animals he was trying to control.

The deadly engine of destruction continued to be heard echoing across the plains as it traveled mile after mile for what seemed like hours but, in truth, had taken only a few minutes to both come and go.

Finally, it was as if the silence of the Mojave slipped back in to fill the space that the juggernaut had ripped through the dusty air of the desert. The air smelled freshly scrubbed as it does after a rain, a gift from the cool breeze that had followed the rushing waters out of the mountain passes.

"They go as fast as they come," William commented. The three sat watching the water as it receded toward the southeast.

"It might just be a good idea to follow that water to the south," the old Indian stated. "We know them folks ain't behind us, and on the outside chance they are still moving, we couldn't ask for a clearer sign than someone crossing this ditch coming up from Mexico."

"I was thinking the same thing," said William. "Even if they ain't moving, if we get close to the Mexico border and haven't struck sign, then we can loop back east until we hit the Colorado river and follow it north, and we will just about have to cross their trail."

"What if they crossed the Colorado further south?" asked Miguel.

"Well, we know they crossed from Mexico into Arizona from the telegram they sent to their folks, and they would have to go north before turning west again. That puts them somewhere above where we would start back."

Within an hour, the pools of water left by the flood were disappearing into the thirsty sand, and in two hours, you could only tell that something had happened by the stain of brown mud that marked the water's path.

The old Indian on his tall mule, with the blue tick hound leading the way, resumed the march toward the south.

CHAPTER 12

Raphael barely touched the ladder as he flew out of the hay loft on his way to the house; his anxious sister stayed at the haymow door, looking down at the soldiers and the Mexican woman with a sense of apprehension. In Gabriella's short life, few people had come to the Strider home, and each time she had stood breathless, hidden behind her mother's skirt, waiting for them to leave. Of course, for weeks after, all she could talk about were the strangers and how she wondered where they were and what they were doing now. Her fascination with the outside world did not extend to wanting to see it, for she had inherited her mother's phobias concerning strangers and strange places.

"Mrs. Ortiz, would you like to come into the house and rest? I know you must be tired from your journey," Maria said kindly.

"Please, call me Margarita," said the Mexican woman.

Suddenly Raphael slid to a noisy halt in front of the lieutenant and stood saluting up at the tall man in uniform.

"This is my son, Raphael," Maria explained to them all, "and the one hiding in the hay loft is my daughter, Gabriella."

The soldier snapped a smart salute, then offered his hand to the excited boy and said, "Lieutenant Samuel Geoff at your service, sir."

Raphael accepted the handshake and smiled back broadly, "Just call me Raphe."

"Well, Raphe, maybe you could show Corporal Donovan and me where to park the wagon and pasture the animals?"

"Yessir," said the boy. "Just follow me," and he started toward the barn.

"Don't put them in the pasture with Mary," Maria warned, then turned to lead the Mexican woman into the house without further explanation.

By now, Gabriella was down from the loft, hurrying not to be left behind by her mother.

"Ma'am," said the lieutenant, touching the brim of his hat as the young girl passed them coming up from the barn. Gabby couldn't stop a shy smile from escaping as she slowed enough for a quick curtsy and then dashed on to the house. Just before she entered the door, she stole a glance back at the tall soldier leading his horse behind her brother.

The corporal climbed back onto the wagon seat and snapped and pulled the reins hard right to get the mules started, and the wagon rattled toward the barn lot.

"Where's your sword?" asked the boy as he slipped the lock on the pasture gate and pushed it open.

"I only wear that when I'm going to a fight," said the officer, looking up as he started to unbuckle the cinch strap to remove his saddle before turning the big bay into the lot.

It wasn't long before they had the mules out of their traces and in with the lieutenant's red horse. The saddle and the harnesses were stowed inside the tack room of the barn, and the wagon was left out of the way near the chicken pen.

"Do you want to see where we burned the mad dog?" Raphael asked the two soldiers, afraid they would go inside with the women.

"Mad dog?" asked the corporal. "You mean it had the hydrophobia?"

"Yessir, we got a cow locked up that got bit too."

The soldiers looked at each other with concern, and the lieutenant said, "Yes, son, maybe you better show us."

The dark-haired boy started down the split rail fence at a trot and stopped where his mother had collapsed after shooting the beast that had threatened her.

Raphael described the battle in fine detail as the two men stood looking at the black circle burned into the ground where the bonfire had been.

"You and your momma were very brave to stand your ground when that dog attacked," said the lieutenant. "Now, let's go see that cow."

"Yessir, right around here," and he led them past the chicken coop to the back lot where Mary Magdalene stood grazing.

"She looks ok, but how long since she was bit?" asked the corporal.

"It's been almost a week, and we've been milkin her every day, but Momma says we can't drink the milk."

"You'll know soon enough if she's rabid or not," the lieutenant mused.

"What's a rabid?" the small boy asked, looking up at the officer.

"That's what they call the hydrophobia now, rabies. They say a French fellow found a cure, but I have yet to hear about anyone surviving it in this country."

"If I ever see a rabies skunk, I'd club it to death!" said the boy excitedly.

"If you ever see a rabid skunk, you run like your tail is on fire, do you hear?" said the lieutenant.

"Yessir," said Raphael dejectedly.

In the house, the ladies went to the kitchen, and Maria put a pot of coffee on the cook stove, and they both sat at the table with Gabriella standing behind her mother's chair.

"Mrs. Strider, at the Army Station, they said that your husband is the most accomplished tracker in these mountains," the Mexican woman said earnestly, implying a question.

"Please, call me Maria, and yes, I believe he has an excellent reputation with the Army."

"I haven't heard from my sister and her husband and two children for almost six weeks," the Mexican woman said, "and I fear for their lives in the desert for that long."

"How old are the children?" Maria asked with genuine concern.

"Mateo is fourteen, and Natalie is thirteen."

"Don't worry," Maria assured her with finality. "I have no doubt my husband will find them; we can only pray it will be in time."

"My poppa and brother won't come back without them!" Gabby said reassuringly over her mother's shoulder. "I can't wait to meet them."

Margarita responded with a grateful smile.

The kitchen door burst open, and Raphael walked proudly in, followed by the two soldiers.

"We checked on Mary Magdalene, and she's ok Momma," said the boy.

"Thank you," Maria said. "I want you to meet Mrs. Ortiz; her family is who your father and brother are looking for."

"Are they dead then?" asked the boy.

"No, they are not dead!" Gabriella said, leaving her mother's side and walking to stand immediately in the boy's face and grabbing the front of his shirt.

"Gabby, don't you hit him!" Maria said with haste. "You two go outside and play until I call you for supper!"

"It's ok," said Margarita. "It is a question I have been asking myself for weeks."

The two soldiers stood uncomfortably by until the children were out on the porch, then they ducked their heads and followed them out. They watched as the boy walked toward the barn with his shoulders humped and head down, doing his best to guard against possible physical harm as his sister dogged him every step of the way, almost chewing on his ear. As she unleashed her fury, the boy was confused, for he thought he had asked a simple enough question.

"You must be the stupidest human being in the entire world to say that poor woman's family is dead right in front of her," the girl yelled in his ear, making him wince even harder at the threat of her balled-up fists swinging up and down with every stride. "If it wasn't for Momma, I would find a club and beat you like a mad skunk."

Suddenly, Raphael stopped short, and Gabriella stumbled a few steps before coming to a halt and turning to face the boy.

The two soldiers looked on, not knowing what was coming next.

"What do you think our poppa does anyhow?" he asked his sister.

"He finds people for the government!" she answered defensively.

"They send him to find dead people, Gabby, and if they sent him to find Mrs. Ortiz's family, then that means they don't think they are alive."

"Well, maybe your daddy finds dead people," the girl uttered, "but mine saves them! "

Embarrassed, having finally realized how hurtful his words to the Mexican woman had been, he struck out one last time at his uppity sister. "What will you say to that lady when Poppa and Miguel bring back her family's bodies then?"

Tears came to the girl's eyes, tears that the anger had allowed her to hold back. She was forced for the first time to seriously consider where her father went and what he was doing while away from home. To think what it meant to people like Mrs. Ortiz when her father delivered the remains of people they loved. How hard it must be for her father, whom she knew to be kind and caring, to face those people and see their pain. To have to do it over and over again to provide for her and Raphe and Momma. Worst of all was imagining what she would feel like to be in those people's shoes. This realization was heartbreaking to the innocent child.

Raphael walked on, feeling ashamed of having made his sister cry. Within a few paces, he stopped and turned to face her.

"I hope it's your daddy that finds Mrs. Ortiz's family, Sis," he said kindly, then turned and walked on.

The scene was touching, and the two soldiers searched the sky as if looking for rain clouds to avoid facing each other, then slowly wandered off in different directions.

CHAPTER 13

Alejandro sat looking at the product of his early morning foray into the desert, a half-starved rabbit, a small burrowing owl, and a dozen small eggs from a quail's nest. He separated the eggs into three groups of four for his wife and two children and prepared a lie about having eaten his portion already. He grabbed the rabbit by the skin of its back, stripped away the hide in one quick motion, then cut the feet off and slit its belly from stem to stern with his knife, and removed the intestines saving the heart, lungs, and liver. With the owl, he took the time to pluck the feathers to retain the skin which contained most of the fat, then placed them both into a pot that sat by the fire and pushed it down into the bed of hot coals.

Camila woke at the sound of the cast iron lid being placed on the pot and pushed herself into a sitting position, leaning her back against the wood of the large wagon wheel.

"Did you find no water?" she asked, already knowing the answer.

"No water but these," he said, carefully handing her the portion of eggs he had separated for her. "Chew the shells well so they don't scratch your throat."

"Is it allowed, to eat the shells?" she asked doubtfully.

"Yes, when I hunted pheasants with my father, we often came upon their nests, and the men with us ate the eggs whole. They are like a drink of water."

"Are there more for the children?"

"Yes, mine I ate from the nest when I found them, and these are for the children," he said, pointing at two small depressions in the sand.

"Mateo, Natalie, wake up and come to the fire," said the woman.

The kids stirred but neither got up and only pulled their covers tighter against the morning chill.

"Let them sleep," said Alejandro as he lifted the pot lid to check the condition of the meat. A small amount of steam rose with the top, and he quickly replaced it.

Maria hesitated but finally placed one of the eggs in her mouth and bit down. She was pleasantly surprised at the burst of moisture and how easy the fragile shell was to chew. Moments later, she popped the remaining three eggs in and savored the much-needed liquid they contained. She quickly rose, gathered up the children's eggs, walked to where they were sleeping, made each rollover, and forced them to accept one of the tiny morsels and told them to bite.

They were both as reluctant as she had been, but upon feeling the moisture on their dry tongue, they sat up for more.

"It's heavenly," said Natalie, reaching for another and another until they were gone.

Mateo dropped all three remaining eggs in his mouth and chewed them with relish.

Their father removed the cast iron pot from the fire, and they all gathered for the rare feast. They sat on blankets in a circle around the food that Alejandro fished out of the pot with a large wooden spoon that had made the trip from Mexico with them. A plate was used to hold the cooked remains of the rabbit and bird, and they took turns picking morsels off the bones until nothing was left but two disassembled skeletons cleaned of every speck of meat and drop of moisture.

As they all sat contemplating the pitiful remains of the meal, the man began the apology he had constructed privately in his mind over the last several days.

"My beloved family," he began, meeting their wan and forlorn faces with as much strength as he could muster. "Our situation is dire, and I fear that I have doomed us all to perish in this God-forsaken wilderness with my lack of preparation and skill. In my haste to flee from my accusers, I thought of only my safety at your expense. I was as frightened to be alone again as I was when my father was taken from me, so I dragged you with me on this desperate journey, and for these things, I humbly apologize."

Camila made as to comfort him, but he stopped her before she could rise with an upraised hand.

"No," he said softly. "We have a decision to make as a family. As I see it, we have two choices: we can stay here or try to walk to the mountains. If there is truly a God, we will survive in one way or another."

The woman said, "Do not tempt God, my husband. We will survive if it is his will, but if you make it a test, you condemn us all."

"Then let us vote," said the man. "Those for staying, raise your hand."

They all looked to see a hand go up, but none did.

"Then, with God's blessing, we will begin our journey at sundown. With food in our stomachs, we will rest until then."

That evening, as the sun neared the mountain tops to the west, they gathered the things they would carry with them. Each had a blanket for the cold nights and shade for the daytime. They took pans for cooking and containers for water in case it rained. Alejandro carried his gun with the few remaining bullets and a knife that his father had given him. Camila took her Bible, and the children took other odds and ends. Natalie looked through her belongings and selected a small, tattered doll that had been a present from her aunt, with whom they hoped to live in California. She slipped it beneath the serape that her mother had made for her.

The small troop of Mexicans walked single file up and out of the depression that had been their home for more than two weeks. They paused to look back at the shelter and prayed they would not regret their decision. As they gathered their bearings for the nearest mountains, a noise like they had never heard echoed across the desert. In moments the sound was upon them, and their small wagon flew up out of the arroyo with a crash, then tumbled back in and raced away, pushed by a wall of water that rushed against the steep banks and flew into the air, soaking them with warm muddy water. In only moments the flood settled down and became a stream from which they quickly filled everything they were carrying that would hold water.

"From this day forward," said the man. "I will never again doubt the grace of God."

As tempting as it was to drink the murky water to slake their terrible thirst Camila made them wait until she could pour cups full through a cotton cloth to filter out the worst of the sand and debris.

Later, when Alejandro contemplated the events of this day, he saw two possibilities, the violence of the flood suggested an attempt to end their misery by delivering a swift death. Still, their miraculous escape felt like they had been given a second chance and an opportunity for life. He preferred to believe the latter.

CHAPTER 14

William noticed that Miguel was keeping his horse near his own as they followed the general path the old man and dog laid down.

"Son, you look like your chokin on a frog or somethin; what's on your mind?"

"I don't know Poppa; I guess I just wanted to tell you that it's nice havin Grandpa along."

William sensed a more profound feeling than his son's statement indicated but wasn't inclined to explore the subject further.

"I feel the same way son; now let's spread out in case your grandpa misses something."

Miguel was disappointed that he hadn't the courage to ask his actual question about his mother and grandfather but resolved to bring it up later.

The small party of searchers continued for the rest of that day and the next and the next until finally, in the early afternoon of their fourth day following the flood, Juliet's bell-like voice split the silence with one short choppy note followed by an excited whimper that meant that she had struck a trail and it was a fresh one.

Miguel and his father brought their animals to a halt and turned to the old man standing in the stirrups of his peculiar saddle, looking for all the world like a sultan surveying the desert for signs of his lost caravan.

When they rode up beside the old man, he pointed down into the sand at a set of tracks made by several persons walking single file, having come up out of the freshly scoured water course, heading in the direction of the nearest foothills.

"I make it four people afoot, headed in that direction," said the Indian. "They crossed sometime before the flood."

"It could be them, gauging the small prints bringing up the rear; they said there was a young boy and girl," said William.

"Look," Miguel said, pointing at a pile of mud-stained trash that looked to have once been part of a wagon spread over the ground beside the wash.

"If that was theirs," William mused, "somebody must be lookin out for em'."

They rode three abreast at a good pace, with Juliet leading them away from the ditch. The signs were only a few days old, which meant that there was a chance that a body retrieval had just turned into a rescue mission. Hope slowly turned to apprehension as, mile after mile, evidence of desperation appeared on the trail. At intervals, they came upon sites where the people must have rested through the heat of the day, and each was marked by piles of discarded items like water containers, cooking utensils, camping gear, and articles of clothing. Along the way were personal items that would be the last things to go as life-sustaining objects became the only thing valuable enough to carry.

The intimate nature of some of the personal items they saw unexpectedly disturbed Miguel as he began to imagine the people who had dropped them. A woman's hand-made wrap similar to the one his mother wore, a boy's kerchief like one his brother had used as a robber's mask only a few weeks ago, a girl's small doll dressed as a ballerina complete with a tiny diamond necklace. The last caused him to pull up, lean down, scoop it from the sand, and tuck it into his coat.

At sunrise, the searchers were still pushing ahead as fast as they could without losing the winding trail of dying people fighting to stay on their feet. Miguel was the one who spotted the single-shot rifle that had been tossed into the brush alongside the trail; upon inspection, they found a spent bullet in the chamber. It was the last thing they found before coming to the tragic end of their search.

They saw the buzzards, first one, two, then a dozen riding the rising air heated by the sun's reflection off the desert floor. Before they reached the apex of the living black tornado, at least a hundred scavengers were in the flight pattern, lazily descending on an unsavory banquet to which they knew there was no hurry, served up by death, cooked in the blazing sun, and catered by decay.

The path led them toward a depression carved by hot winds flowing over smooth stones that seemed so out of place that they looked like they had been dropped from the sky. In truth, they had been excavated from the hardpan and then honed smooth by wind-driven sand over the eons. They stopped at the edge of the arroyo, and William pulled his rifle from the saddle scabbard and fired into the air to set the few birds to flight that were milling around on the ground. Instead of scattering, the birds rejoined the silent, circling watch party in the sky, refusing to abandon the bounty they considered rightfully theirs.

William pushed his mare over the edge, and the rest followed. The fine sand, disturbed by the horse's hooves, followed them down, causing only a muffled whisper as they descended. The sun was low enough in the west that the sandy banks cast black shadows across the floor of the false waterway.

The old man warned, "Watch out for ghosts," Miguel could tell he wasn't joking this time. It triggered in the boy an unfamiliar feeling of dread that would have been more natural to his mother.

As they came near the bodies huddled together against the bank, Miguel said, "Look, they are just sleeping," but no one agreed with his assessment. As they got nearer, they could hear the hum of flies disturbed by their presence taking to the air.

The young Indian boy found himself willing the people to be alive, for the alternative proved impossible for him to contemplate. First to the ground, needing to prove his observation to be accurate, ignoring the swarm of flies that rose into a cloud above the bodies, Miguel knelt and touched the shoulder of the man, snuggled to the back of a woman, and her to the back of a boy.

William and the old man leaped down from their saddles but too late to stop the boy's actions.

"Hey, mister," Miguel said, barely above a whisper.

As unsubstantial as a ragdoll, the man rolled toward him onto his back, exposing a large black stain of dried blood and matted hair belonging to the woman he had embraced. The motion of the man's body caused the hair plastered to his shirt to pull the woman's head around as if she were peeking over her shoulder through jagged empty eye sockets to discover who the intruder was. It was evident that the milling vultures had begun with the choicest morsels.

The woman's gaping stare petrified the young Indian boy, whose horror only increased as the flies drew his gaze into the depths of the hollow cavities. His attention was only diverted when the Mexican man groaned, and upon looking down, Miguel saw the man's eyes spring open.

William and his father watched as the young boy slowly sank into the sand.

As the veil of blackness faded, Miguel heard his grandfather say, "He will be fine when he wakes up; he's just fainted, is all."

"I know," said William. "This wasn't the way I had this trip planned. Would you see to him while I get some water into this poor fellow over here?"

The old Indian placed a cool hand on his grandson's brow and distractedly began to hum as his mother had done when caring for any of her ailing children many years ago.

William took a canteen from his saddle, walked to the prostrate Mexican man, and helped him drink, avoiding the face of the man's wife as much as possible. He then took the sharp hunting knife from his belt and cut the strands of hair stuck to the man's chest, releasing the woman's head to return her attention to her dead child.

As the man stared skyward, he asked weakly through blistered lips, "¿Encontraste a mi Hija (Did you find my daughter)?"

William had no response until he leaned over the woman to look at the single child lying dead in her arms. It was a boy about Miguel's age, but there was no sign of a girl.

"No, no encontramos ninguna chica. (No, we found no girl)."

***

The smaller mountain man rolled over onto his back, tired from watching the desert below.

"Bodine, if they was comin this a way, they would've been here by now!"

Jack Bodine threw down the stick he had been using to scratch in the sand as he killed time while they waited for the party of Indians to appear somewhere in the desert below the hillock they were perched on. He stood up, dusted off his leather pants, and looked down at his partner.

"Ok, they either got washed away by the flood or changed direction. They could have turned back, but I don't think they're the turnin back kind."

"No, they sure ain't that," replied Skinner as he stood and looked up at his partner. "Maybe we oughta go back and try to pick up their trail."

"Maybe instead of wandering around in the desert taking a chance on being spotted, we just go someplace we know they will come back to," said Bodine.

"You mean we lay for them on the return trip back up the mountains?" said Skinner.

"That's what I mean; from here, there is only one good place to leave the desert, and it's the same way we came in. There is good high ground to watch from and even better to shoot from," said the big man.

"Now your talkin!" agreed Skinner.

CHAPTER 15

Mrs. Ortiz, Margarita, as she insisted when she was addressed formally, was as at home in the kitchen as was her host, and accounted for at least half the meal they prepared. The soldiers went again and again into the dishes of potatoes, gravy, fried chicken, and homemade bread on which they slathered the fresh butter; thank you, Raphael.

The soldiers provided an experience the young Strider lad had no notion was missing from his life. His world to now had consisted of a father and mother he loved, an older brother whom he idolized, and a twin sister whose mission in life, he was sure, was to ruin his. Most of his days were spent alone, inventing games involving one small boy and a myriad of fantastical creatures, inspired by stories his mother read him from the Bible and tales from books that she had carried with her from her home in Mexico. But these soldiers were flesh and blood men, walking, talking embodiments of all the heroes he had conjured to help him fight off hordes of Philistines and Romans and bandits and thieves. But more than that, he considered them to be friends. They patiently listened to his fantasies, for men and boys all share common childhoods, most of it lived in imagination, very little in reality. Their arrival had quelled the mysterious ache he felt when his father was away, and his brother was off on more grown-up adventures that didn't include him. Every moment with them filled him with joy, even though he knew their answers to his many questions were primarily out of polite tolerance.

Gabriella viewed the two men's presence with apprehension and was mainly quiet throughout the meal. She remembered Raphael's words at the end of their argument last night. It was the first time that she could recall her brother saying anything that sounded remotely like there was a grain of thought attached. Had she misjudged the boy all this time? Was there some small cavity in his thick head that contained a tiny wad of brains? She turned to look at him with an eye intent upon rediscovering that spark of caring and intelligence she had witnessed before. Instead, she saw a boy with fried chicken grease and bread crumbs covering his mouth, a blob of gravy in his hair and one on the front of his shirt, and the grin of a moron permanently plastered on his face. The picture was complete when a small red tongue flicked in and out of the gap left by his missing front teeth. A shiver of disgust ran up her spine, and her sky-blue eyes rose toward the heavens.

After the meal was settled, the soldiers went to the porch to smoke, and Raphael followed, peppering them with questions. The two Mexican women and Gabriella cleared the table and washed and dried the dishes, for they were all members of the same sisterhood who, throughout history, have cooked and cleaned and served men. Men, to whom it has never occurred to question a system in which they perceive themselves as one rung higher on the ladder. From a woman's perspective, it is an illusion that she is content to perpetuate to keep her male counterparts under her control. This control was soon to be demonstrated to the naive young lieutenant.

Margarita was shown to Miguel's bed, but only after the women had talked until the wee hours, each happy for the unaccustomed companionship. After refusing the offer of the children's beds, the soldiers had made soft nests in the hay of the barn loft, where the boy made a late-night clandestine visit that lasted until the red glow of morning.

Maria woke with a small girl tucked warmly beneath her arm, not remembering when she had appeared and not minding the intrusion.

Breakfast was a happy affair with the two soldiers rested and glad to be heading back home, anxious to resume their lives of discipline and routine. The children were still excited by the seldom-experienced distraction of guests in the cabin. Only Maria and Margarita were subdued, pensive about the news that they were about to break to the two soldiers.

Lieutenant Geoff rose from the table to address Maria, "Ma'am, the corporal and me would like to thank you for your hospitality and to tell you that we will remember your family fondly to our superiors when we arrive back at our post."

The corporal rose and dipped his head in a sign of respect and said, "Best grub I've et since my Momma's," and he pushed his chair toward the table in preparation to leave.

"Corporal," the lieutenant said, "If you will prepare the wagon, I will help Mrs. Ortiz gather for the journey home."

"Samuel," Margarita said, addressing the young officer. "I shan't be joining you on your return trip. Mrs. Strider has kindly invited me to stay as her guest until her husband concludes his search and arrives with my family or with news of their demise."

"But, Ma'am," the lieutenant implored. "My instructions were to accompany you here to ascertain the status of your family, then ensure your safe return to the post."

"I don't yet know the status of my family, and I refuse to return until I do."

"But our orders Ma'am," the lieutenant protested.

"I am sorry for your conflicting orders, young man, but I didn't issue them or agree to them before we left your station. I am quite happy to release you from any further obligation in this matter, but here I am, and here I will stay."

At a loss, the lieutenant asked, "Are you willing to write a letter to my commanding officer to that effect?" He was not at all sure how the situation had slipped so quickly and entirely from his control.

"Most certainly," replied Margarita with satisfaction. "I thank you for your forbearance to this point and your much-appreciated help, and I hope for your understanding in this matter."

"Certainly, Ma'am. Corporal, hitch your mules and prepare to leave."

The corporal stood uncertainly for a moment, looked from his lieutenant to the two ladies, then said, "Yessir," and marched stiffly out the door.

"Ladies, Raphe, I take my leave," said Lieutenant Geoff, and he rose to his full height and saluted.

Raphael slid his chair back, stood to attention, and returned the soldier's salute, who smiled, then turned and walked solemnly out the kitchen door.

Tears of disappointment filled the boy's shiny dark eyes as he watched the only friend outside his family that he had ever known walk out of his life forever. The look he offered to his mother was so full of pain that it startled her, for she had never before witnessed such a display of emotion from her young son. A look of sad confusion was all that she could muster in return. In desperation, the boy turned to his sister; what she saw in his watery eyes was true heartbreak, and she took it as evidence of the presence of the thing she had sought to find in him the evening before. She placed a hand on his shoulder, which he promptly pushed away and turned to follow the lieutenant out the door.

Sierra Sunrise

CHAPTER 16

Alejandro was having difficulty focusing, but the words the Indian had spoken finally found their way through to his dull consciousness. His reaction was barely discernable through the mask of puffy, dry flesh and tortured cracked lips, but one look into his vacant red eyes provided a glimpse into the depths of a truly lost human soul.

William offered more water from his canteen, but instead of accepting the life-giving moisture, the Mexican rolled back toward his dead wife, who embraced her dead son.

"God grant you mercy," William uttered as he spotted a smooth, bloody stone at the Mexican man's feet.

The old Indian had helped Miguel to sit up in time to hear the short conversation his father had with the Mexican man, and the boy asked weakly, "Poppa, where do you think his daughter is?"

"I'm guessing that we passed her somewhere on the trail," the man replied without optimism.

The boy tried to rise with the intent of looking for the lost girl, but his grandfather pushed him quickly back to the earth.

"Dog and me will find her," he said with finality and rose to walk back to his mule and shinnied up onto the contraption that served as a saddle.

"Dog!" he said without looking for her and pulled the reins to turn the animal back in the direction from which they had arrived. Juliet appeared as from thin air, beat the mule to the top of the bank, and disappeared into the desert. The big hound was happy to leave this place behind where humans lay dead. She had helped find dozens of lost souls in this wilderness, but being in their presence had been troubling to her, and she always found a place far enough away that she didn't have to be bombarded by the sickening odors while her master did what he had to do.

The man looked back at the Mexicans, and Miguel did the same.

"What happened to the woman and boy?" Miguel posed.

"What do you think?" asked the man, concerned about how his young son would interpret this situation. He had learned in the Great War not to pass judgment on the appearance of a thing, especially one that would surely be judged by God. The Bible passage, 'Judge not that ye be not judged,' was one that he had lived by after the things he had willingly done during the war.

The boy had no answer but continued to look at the three people lying against the bank.

Juliet, unaccustomed to tracking a quarry in reverse, ran ahead and waited to be sure the old man was still following.

They went almost five miles back to where Miguel had spotted the rifle in the brush. The tracks of the four Mexicans converged into a group where cartridges were trampled into the sand. Someone on their knees had raked through the dust. A picture played in the Indian tracker's mind as he read the signs. This had happened in the dark, or the search for the shells would have been successful. Some confrontation had taken place, resulting in the discarded gun. A single set of footprints led north into the desert, and those of two adults continued on their original course; it was apparent the man had carried the boy. As he picked up the scattered bullets, he surmised that the missing girl had made the lone tracks into the desert. He couldn't help but wonder at the spent round they had found in the rifle.

The old man said, "Dog!" and pointed in the direction the child had gone. Juliet disappeared once again into the scrub.

Within moments the dog's cry of discovery floated back to him as he dodged his way through a forest of small Joshua trees and saguaro cactus. When the Indian caught up with her, Juliet was sitting, staring down at a young Mexican girl lying with her face in the dust. Long ebony hair covered her head, which protruded from a faded serape that looked to have once been gay with color, now dingy with weeks of constant wear in the desert.

As he knelt carefully beside the child, he brushed her hair aside, placed one hand beneath her neck and head and the other on her arm, and gently rolled her toward him into his lap. He could see no apparent wounds as he brushed the dust and sand from her face, but the inside of her mouth and nose were caked with dried mud from inhaling the powdered desert after she had fallen. In the failing light, he could see where she had tangled her feet in half-buried vines when she reached this point in the chaparral. Her unconscious state had been more likely caused by exhaustion and dehydration than the effect of a poorly aimed bullet. Blistered skin and swollen lips were testaments to the hardships endured.

The girl coughed weakly but didn't open her eyes until the tracker poured water from his leather canteen onto her sunburnt skin, rinsed her mouth and nose, then rubbed away the grime with his soft, weathered hand.

Her eyes opened, and her body tensed as she tried to reconcile her situation in the early evening shadows cast by the creosote bushes. If her condition had been less severe, she might have tried to escape the cradling arms of this strange-looking old man whose unreadable liquid eyes spoke neither friend nor foe. Her response was total surrender to a fate unknown. She closed her eyes and slipped gratefully back into unconsciousness.

**

Miguel walked unsteadily to one of the smooth alien stones and sat, seemingly no longer aware of the three bodies that had caused his brief fainting spell. The fading sun was teetering on the mountaintops to the west, perhaps reluctant to leave before this small tragedy in the desert had played itself out.

William pulled a short-handled Army shovel from its place on his pack mule and began digging a hole at the base of one of the enormous stones. It would be a permanent marker for the woman and child if some relative ever wanted to retrieve the bodies. More than a resting place, the grave would be protection against desert creatures who had no more respect for the human soul than that of a lizard or rabbit. The woman and boy would have to remain in the desert. Usually, he would carry them back with him, but the survivor was his priority for now. He prayed that if a virtue could be assigned to the dead, it was patience, for it would be a horror to imagine that they have a capacity for marking the passage of time.

Miguel took a swallow from the canteen and numbly watched his father dig. His mind did not even question what the hole would be used for until his gaze fell upon the bodies resting silently in the shadow of the sandy bank. As if made curious again by the discovery, he stood and walked slowly to the Mexicans and stared down upon them.

"Miguel!" the man called, "Come away!" But the boy was already puzzling the pieces together. Exposed skin blistered almost black, lips swollen and cracked, the man still alive but embracing the dead, the bloody stone lying near the bodies, the woman and boy having shared the same fate.

William watched apprehensively while the boy processed the evidence.

"I think he must have loved them very much," the boy said.

The words drifted through the dry air to his amazed father, who stood holding the shovel and looking on.

"Yes," said the man with a measure of relief, "I suspect that he did."

Juliet appeared on the bank above and looked down at the boy and then at William standing waist-deep in the hole he was digging. Moments later, the old Indian eased his tall mule down the sandy slope into the arroyo, balancing the limp young Mexican girl seated on the saddle in front of him. Miguel hurried to retrieve a blanket from one of the mules and then met his grandfather to help ease the girl to the ground.

As the old man dripped water on the girl's blackened lips, she seemed to drift between oblivion and life and finally, reluctantly, chose life. She opened her eyes to the eager face of the young Indian boy who knelt beside her. He suddenly remembered the toy in his pocket and lifted it shyly toward her, an offering of kinship from one child to another. Recognition glimmered faintly in the girl's eyes, and she made a weak attempt to raise her hand but failed and let it drop back to her breast. The boy gently reached out, opened her fingers, then wrapped them around the small doll and closed them on it. The girl grasped it while watching the boy's gentle eyes; then, she closed her own again.

**

Bodine pulled his horse up on the rise where the old Indian had stopped before he and his party had entered the desert.

"That bluff up yonder will do for me and my sharps, and you can find a comfortable nesting place in them cedars over there. All we have to do is kill Strider before he gets a chance to use that damn rifle; the rest'll be easy pickings."

Skinner looked around nervously and said, "All I can say is, we better not miss because Will Strider is one man who won't waste bullets. How bout I get up on that bluff, and you hide in them trees?"

"You've seen me use this buffalo gun; you got nothing to worry about. When you hear this cannon go off, start shootin anything alive with that repeater of yours."

"All right," said Skinner apprehensively, "just look for that big spotted mare of his, but don't forget, you just got one shot before all hell breaks loose."

"All I need is one shot!" boasted the big man.

CHAPTER 17

Margarita asked her hostess for pen and paper to write the letter she had promised the lieutenant. Maria went to her chest in the bedroom, where she selected an unused sheet of precious rag paper and a small bottle of India ink that had been her father's, taken from her home in Mexico long ago. She took a sharp knife, put a new point on a feather pen, and placed it all on the kitchen table, then led Gabriella onto the porch to watch the men preparing the wagon and mules for the journey.

After the Mexican woman composed the note, she signed and folded it, then walked outside to join the woman and girl as they waited for the soldiers.

They saw the corporal climb to the wagon's seat and pick up the thick leather reins. He braced his heels against the toe board, then slapped the mules lightly on the rump and shouted, "Gee Carl! Gee Toby!" to get the mules to pull the wagon around to the right toward the gate to the lane.

The lieutenant was walking toward the cabin, leading his big bay horse, with Raphael hurrying alongside him, taking two steps to the man's one, talking nonstop, hoping to delay the moment of departure as long as possible.

The two women stood on the wooden porch waiting for the officer, and when he arrived, Margarita stepped down and handed the paper to him.

"Thank you, Lieutenant, for all you have done for me."

"Welcome, ma'am; I wish you luck with your sister and her family." The lieutenant was surprised at the sadness that he felt at this parting. He fitted his left foot firmly in the stirrup and swung up into the saddle; he fumbled an awkward moment with his right boot to find its place in the other stirrup, then motioned with his chin for the corporal to move out.

They all watched until they lost sight of the wagon as the lane followed the mountain's contour. The women all went back inside the cabin, but Raphael ran through the woods to a bluff that overlooked the path as it descended from the plateau into the valley below. He caught an occasional flicker of white from the wagon's canvas top through the tall pines as his new friends left him alone and lonelier than he had ever been in his short life. As a rule, he only shed tears due to out-of-control anger, but on this occasion, he allowed a few pity tears to help dampen the pain.

After the soldiers were gone, the day trudged along, as days tend to do when the routine, broken by the coming of visitors, is repaired by their leaving, and quiet slips from its hiding place to fill the house once again. The women made small talk about things of no consequence, and Gabby remained close but quiet. Her silence was more due to the absence of her brother, whom she assumed was off sulking in the woods, than the stranger's presence in the house. Margarita was desperate to make herself useful as thanks for the kindness she was being shown, and if her hands were not busy, then even short stretches of silence became awkward.

When the last glimpse of white was just a memory, Raphael dried his eyes on his shirt sleeves and stood to throw a stone dejectedly in the direction of the departing soldiers. He began a meandering walk back through the pines to the lot fence, intending to follow it toward the barn.

The boy was enjoying the soulful quiet of the woods, bathed in the chilly morning sunshine, until the angry chatter of a fox squirrel caused him to stop his aimless ramble. He stepped onto the bottom rung of the rail fence to peer over at the commotion. He was surprised to see Mary Magdalene squared off and stiff-legged, facing the small tree rodent, not ten feet from where he stood.

"What are you two fighting about?" asked the boy, amused at the awkward pairing of participants in this unusual barnyard standoff.

Instead of scurrying up the tree, the defiant squirrel barked at this new intruder. He had already exhausted his daily allotment of patience on the former dullard that refused to leave his buried food cache and now was faced with another.

The cow turned her head to look in the direction of Raphael's voice, and the motion caused her to stagger sideways with unsure steps. When she recovered her balance, she leveled her gaze in the boy's direction. He didn't recognize the family's pet cow in the wet glassy eyes that stared back at him. A froth of mucus and saliva dripped from her nose and mouth, and she swayed from side to side as if trying to focus her vision on this new opponent.

"Rabies!" the boy whispered to himself at the realization.

Suddenly, having been provided a stationary foe, unlike the flitting rodent, the cow made a lurching, unorganized charge. Unable to distinguish the source of the sound from the rails of the fence, she ran headlong into the barrier near where Raphael was perched. The impact knocked two horizontal members loose and threw the boy to the ground. It took the cow to her knees, but she staggered back up and managed to mount another charge. With her full weight behind her, the fence toppled over this time, landing on the terrified lad. Blood from the damage of the two full-on impacts to the cow's face and froth from her nose and mouth sprayed the boy trapped beneath the fallen fence. Mary stumbled through the tangle of split rails and continued through the woods, deviating only when a tree stood its ground and forced her to give way.

Raphael knew he was hurt but was more terrified by the mucus and blood clinging to his clothes. He knew that the spittle transmits the disease from an infected animal, but usually, he thought, through a bite. He was unsure of the effect of its contact with bare skin. It was like standing by as a stick of dynamite went off, the blast might not kill you, but the proximity was enough to terrify you.

The boy watched the cow stagger off through the woods in the direction of the bluff where he had sat just moments ago. When he was sure she wasn't coming back, he began extricating himself from the rails of the fallen fence. Carefully, one timber at a time, he rolled the triangle-shaped logs away from his body, then sat up in the wreckage to assess the damage. He knew there would be scrapes and bruises on his legs which had taken most of the weight of the logs because he could already feel the numbness coming on. Cautiously, he stood, testing his legs for severe injuries, and finding no broken bones he began to limp across the lot toward the gate at the back of the barn. He tried not to look down at his ruined clothes for fear of the disease he knew was clinging there. He poured all his concentration and effort into the single task of reaching the cabin and help. He tried but failed to push aside his feelings about the prospect of dying the most horrible death he could imagine. He didn't know all the details of the disease, but the look in his parent's eyes when they spoke of it was more than enough to frighten an eight-year-old boy.

"Momma?" the boy began calling weakly as soon as he made his way through the gate and started limping toward the house. "Momma!"

Now that he was nearing his goal, panic began taking control. Tears were streaming, and he could no longer keep the crying out of his voice.

"Momma, where are you?" he sobbed pitifully as he neared the porch and watched the kitchen door, desperate for someone to emerge. Strangely he felt apprehensive, as if he were about to be discovered having done something terrible that he was ashamed of. He felt sorry for the hurt that he was about to cause his mother. He felt sorry for himself that he was likely to die.

When Maria first heard the boy's voice, she was standing at the stove, tending a skillet of ham to be the meat for their noon meal. The sound was like a whimper at first, and she looked around to see if her guest, or maybe Gabby, had uttered something, but she saw only curiosity in their faces as they had heard the same faint cry. She slid the skillet to a cool part of the stove, carried the fork with her to the kitchen door, and looked out through one of the wavy panes of glass toward the barn. She saw her son cowering just beyond the porch steps and knew something was wrong. She dropped the fork to the floor, quickly opened the door, and stepped out onto the treads. What she saw confused her; the boy was standing with his shoulders humped, holding his arms away from his body as if he had fallen in the mud and was waiting to be scolded for ruining his clothes. His face was twisted with silent sobs, and tears dripped from his chin. His hopeless shiny black eyes once more begged for her help, echoes of the terrible dream that had to be pushed from her mind.

"Raphe honey?" she queried, searching for a clue as to what was wrong with the boy.

"Rabies, Momma," was his sorrowful confession.

Gabriella and Margarita crowded through the open doorway to stand beside Maria.

Sierra Sunrise

"Did you see those big dogs again, honey?" asked Maria fearfully.

"Them was wolves anyways," spouted the small girl, thinking that her brother was making up a story to get attention.

Suddenly Raphael was angry, and now he had a focus for it. His sister hated him, and for the first time knew he hated her.

"It was Mary!" he said with venom.

Maria walked toward the boy with the intention of a closer inspection, but when she got near, he backed away. He was afraid to expose his mother to the terrible disease he might be carrying.

"Raphael?" she asked as the boy recoiled. Being closer now, she could see small tears in his pant legs and traces of blood and dirt on his shirt.

"What's this about Mary?" she asked before she remembered the cow's condition. "Did she hurt you? Is that her blood on your clothes?" her voice rising with alarm. The consequence of a yes answer was unthinkable.

The boy's downcast face told the whole story.

The two women and young girl were stunned into silence, for everyone knows that hydrophobia is a death sentence to all who contract it, and the worst is that death doesn't come fast enough. There is the agonizing wait for the first symptoms to appear, then a period of sickness and fever, then the strangling when the victim can no longer swallow, which accounts for the slathering. Then the last stage, as the victim slowly goes mad with rage.

Maria's mind raced; what could she do for her small son? There was no doctor; there was no medicine. Should she put him into the wagon and try to chase down the soldiers? But why? she finally concluded, for there was no place to go and no help to be had, and then it hit her, Raphael was going to die! She found that she could no longer move or even breathe.

Margarita suddenly stepped down from the porch, grabbed the stunned mother by the arm, and turned her urgently toward her. Looking over her shoulder, she called, "Gabby, draw a bucket of well water and bring me a bar of your mother's lye soap." Then looking Maria intently in the eyes, speaking slowly so that her words would penetrate the panic that she found there, she said, "You go get your bathtub and bring it to the porch. Then fill it with clean water while I strip Raphe and get him ready to wash. Now everyone, go quickly!" and she pushed the stunned and inanimate woman toward the house.

The Mexican woman knew that what she was doing now was merely a ruse, a distraction for the boy, his mother, and his sister. A lie to keep them all from facing the utter hopelessness of the situation. She hovered over the boy and tried to give him a reassuring smile but only managed to produce a grotesque, twisted leer in which Raphael read his fate. They stood stiffly waiting for the soap and water to arrive, and when they did, she dispatched the girl back toward the well and sat the bucket of water between her and the boy. She worked the soap into the water until it was gray and cloudy from the wood ash from which it had been made.

"Raphael, honey, first I'm going to soap my hands, and then I will remove your clothes." The boy's response was a look of hopelessness and a simple nod of obedience.

Margarita slipped the suspenders from his shoulders, unlaced the boots, and carefully pulled them from his feet; then, her hands went back into the lye water and rubbed the soap bar again until suds reappeared. As she carefully unbuttoned the young boy's long sleeve cotton shirt, she heard the tin bathtub rattle against the rough planks of the porch and the hurried steps of Maria going to the well. She concentrated on slipping the garment from the boy's body, trying not to expose herself or the boy to the debris clinging to the outside of the shirt. She saw scratches on his hands and neck, which troubled her, but she didn't slow down in her deliberate task.

The boy stood shivering and unclothed, and he tried to cover himself with his hands, but Margarita stopped him, led him onto the porch, and helped him stand in the cold bathwater. Maria came out of the kitchen door with a large kettle of steaming water she had prepared earlier to warm the dishwater, but now she poured it into the tub, careful not to burn the boy.

Gabby carried wash rags and towels out onto the porch that her mother had pushed into her hands and held them there for the Mexican woman. She avoided looking at her brother out of respect for his nakedness, even though they had taken countless baths together in their young lives. This seemed different somehow because the boy was so exposed and vulnerable.

Beginning with his head, with soapy rags, the visiting stranger methodically cleaned the boy, sometimes making him groan with the roughness of her scrubbing of the scrapes and scratches. Maria used a drinking dipper and a fresh bucket of cold well water to rinse the soap and soil off as the Mexican woman worked her way down his body. She had forbidden anyone to touch the boy or the water except herself. When his feet were cleaned, the tub water was cold again. Raphael's lips and fingers were blue, and his shivering had become uncontrollable.

When Margarita finally wrapped him in towels and lifted him into her arms to carry him inside, the small boy was almost unconscious with cold and exhaustion. She tucked him snuggly into his bed, towels and all, and although it was early afternoon, his sister lay watchfully from her bed. With each fitful twitch and moan from her brother, another image from the ordeal was brought fresh to her young mind.

In the kitchen, a pot of black coffee was made, and the two Mexican women sat at the table, now sisters, bone tired, feeling as if they had been put through a washing wringer. Shaky hands added sugar and cream to cups, and their wide eyes looked, but all they saw were shadows of the small boy, shivering in the cold tub of water.

"I didn't know what to do," said Maria helplessly, touching her new sister's hand. "Thank God you were here. But how did you know?"

Margarita grasped the woman's hand in both of hers and explained by recounting events from long ago.

"My husband was a physician in Mexico during the war," she began, "and I was his nurse. We were lucky to have escaped to California when it became apparent that the monarchy would fall. I still remember the horrors and countless terrible wounds we treated. Ultimately, all we could do was cut and cut, trying to leave enough viable flesh that might support life. But most vivid are the images of two young brothers who came to us, bitten by a rabid dog; one had tried to pull the animal off the other. We read everything we could find about the disease, and still, there was nothing to do but watch them suffer daily, waiting for them to die. For we had no medicine to stop the disease."

After a few moments of silence, Maria looked into the nurse's eye's and instead of seeing herself reflected there, she saw them turned inward, looking upon a thing from the past.

"Near the end," the woman said with a pensive melancholy, "when their fits became uncontrollable, my husband brought men to help bind them to their beds. He locked the doors, and only he held the keys. I came with him each day to help tend them, but then came a day when he entered there alone. It isn't easy to describe the sounds coming from that room, none that could be attributed to human beings for certain. It was like wild animals being burned alive, and in between the screams, their voices, like the demons who wielded the torches, mocking their pain. Then came the silence, which became the most terrible sound of all. When my husband emerged, he was dejected and defeated."

Maria was stunned into silence as these ghosts, conjured from the woman's past, filled the room.

Suddenly Margarita came to herself and said, "Oh Maria, please forgive me, for I should have told you none of those horrible things!"

Then her speech became clinical and monotone, and she recounted the symptoms of each stage of the disease as if reading from a book. She was obliged to tell the boy's mother how to recognize the progression of the disease as if she would not be present, and she sincerely hoped that she would not.

Finally, she confided that what she had done for Raphael would not prevent the disease if it had entered any of the many apparent cuts and scrapes on his young body.

"If it entered his feet," she said, "then it might be weeks, but if it were nearer his head, then perhaps days. For it is an illness that destroys the mind."

Gabriella heard the two women's voices and crept from her bed to listen at the door. As the Mexican woman told her story, the small girl realized that Raphael might not survive his horrible ordeal. And that the ordeal for them all could only be just beginning. Overwhelmed with guilt, and with despair creeping into her heart, she recalled the meanness and jealousy that marked her relationship with her brother. Beware the wrath of God; she had heard her mother say. Could this be a punishment for her? As if the small girl had sprung a leak, whatever sustains us flowed from her tiny body, and she collapsed like a heap of rags onto the wooden floor.

CHAPTER 18

The two mountain men set up camp deeper into the woods and began their vigil, waiting for the Strider party to appear across the vast flat stretch of desert approaching this well-known mountain entrance. There were other places to start the assent but none so accessible or well-traveled, at least not within a day's ride of this one.

Bodine spent most of the daylight scanning the wasteland with an Army spyglass he had won gambling with a drunken soldier, who had stolen it from a careless officer, both posted at the Three Forks Station. Bodine and Skinner spent an inordinate amount of time at the Station enjoying the recreational opportunities that tend to blossom around permanent Army installations, especially the saloons. Being there also gave them a jump on the other trackers eager for the assignments doled out by the military for jobs they didn't want to bother with.

Will Strider had a unique arrangement with the governments of the U.S. and Mexico, being able to speak the languages and having family ties to both countries. His ability with the Enfield rifle and unmatched record of completing assignments put him at the top of most tracker lists. He supported himself and his family through the snowy winter months by hunting and trapping predators like wolves and mountain lions, which preyed upon the domestic herds of cattle and horses of the ranchers who populated the lowlands between the mountains.

Skinner was relegated to tending the camp and cooking the food over an almost smokeless fire at daybreak and dusk to lessen the chance of discovery by the targets of their assassination plot.

Bodine would climb down from his bluff overlooking the Mojave after he felt that the Indians would have gone to ground for the night. He rose before dawn to eat, then resumed his lookout post high above the sandy plain.

**

After the Mexican man's wife and son were safely in the ground beneath the sizeable smooth moonstone, the group moved away from the depression. They fled from the flies who refused to abandon the macabre sight of death and those ranging far and wide in search of the missing bodies. Another reason to move on was the hapless buzzards who could not fly at night but refused to leave the site of such bounty and glided to earth in the dusky dark.

Few words were exchanged as the camp was set up, and a fire was made for warmth and cooking. The old Indian began preparing a meal for them all, and William and Miguel made the two surviving Mexicans as comfortable as possible.

Miguel stayed near the young girl, ready to rush in if she showed signs of waking, but there were none. If it weren't for his father, he would have happily sat by her side all night, but a look from him kept the boy away.

Later, William managed to coax the young girl awake enough to eat a few bites of food and take more water, but then he let her sink back into sleep for the night.

The Mexican man accepted a little water but refused all food, hoping death would somehow find him in his misery. He realized he was slowly losing the battle between survival and his conscience and cursed his weakness.

William and Miguel spent the next day tending to the man and girl. It was determined that it would be several days before she could ride alone, so the old Indian made a foray into the desert looking for material to make a travois. They decided that it was necessary to begin their journey out of the desert as soon as possible, for water was becoming a factor with the two-extra people to provide for.

When the old man returned to camp, he went to the fire to prepare another meal while William and Miguel began constructing the sled to transport their young guest.

They began by crossing two long poles over the mule's back and tying the ends together; then, they set them between the front and rear saw buck trees on a pack saddle. The back tree would bear the dragging weight, while the front would keep it from sliding forward. They let the other end of the poles sit on the ground behind the mule. Then they placed several shorter bars across the two main beams to make a platform upon which a person could ride. The short poles were secured with leather strips, and the canvas panniers were collapsed to form a pad. When the travois was completed, they lifted it from the mule's back and laid it on the ground, ready for use.

In the early twilight of the evening, they ate their meal and then prepared for departure, deciding that night travel would be more comfortable than the heat of the day for the two Mexicans.

They were all surprised when Alejandro called William in Spanish and asked to speak with him. The Indian walked to the Mexican's blanket and waited while the man rose and stood unsteadily.

"How are you feeling?" asked William in Spanish.

"I am conflicted," said Alejandro, "for I had committed my soul to

God's keeping before you came. And now, as you can see, I am faced with an entirely different set of circumstances. My wife and son are dead, and I feel certain that my daughter will condemn me as a murderer at the first opportunity. If you would but loan me the method, I would gladly end my life before she recovers enough to know of our situation."

William looked closely at the man but found it difficult to muster enough sympathy to try to comfort him. If a man decides to end his wife and son's lives, then surely the justification for doing so does not diminish simply because fate robs him of a convenient way to avoid judgment, at least human judgment.

"My advice," William responded, "is to wait until you can have that conversation with your daughter, for she might surprise you. Trust God's plan and face it like a man. Right now, all I need to know is, can you ride?"

The surprised Mexican man took this as a refusal of his request and affirmed that "yes, he could ride."

"Miguel," the man said, "rig up a saddle on Rachel."

They put all the remaining food and cooking gear into the old Indian's pack panniers and folded blankets to make a riding saddle for Rachel. Then they rigged up makeshift stirrups out of rope so that the Mexican man had something to support his legs. They made a cot on the travois, tied the girl securely to it, and then started toward the mountains.

William led Rachel, whom the Mexican man rode, just in case he took a notion to ride off into the desert to finish dying. He wasn't as concerned about the man as he was at losing the mule.

The Indian and Juliet led the way under a clear moonlit sky with stars so brilliant that they hurt one's eyes. Riding through the creosote bushes, horses and pack mules looked to be floating as their legs could not be seen through the foliage. The Mexican girl and her sled were invisible, gliding beneath the shadows of the three-quarter moon.

"Poppa, when do you think we will get to the mountains?" Miguel asked over his shoulder and past the mule that pulled the girl's sled.

"My guess is sometime in the morning, the day after tomorrow, as long as we don't have to stop too often," William replied, glancing back to make sure the mule he led still had her passenger.

They stopped about midnight to give the girl water and ensure she was enduring the ride on the travois. Miguel stood next to his father and watched the young girl's face as she sipped the water from the canteen. After she drank, William asked her how she felt, and she spoke for the first time since they found her alone in the desert.

"Much better," she rasped, barely above a whisper. She lifted the small doll she had clung to in her sleep and held it up to Miguel to show that she still had it. The boy rewarded her with a big embarrassed grin but said nothing.

William offered water to the girl's father, who remained astride the mule, for it was awkward to dismount from the pack saddle with the makeshift stirrups.

They resumed their steady march to the mountains and didn't stop again until toward daylight. They helped the Mexican man down so he could stretch and relieve himself, then continued until the sun rose high enough to become uncomfortable for the girl.

Miguel helped the old Indian build a cooking fire in the shade of a stand of Joshua trees, and they moved the girl to a blanket spread out in the relative coolness of the shadows. After eating their fill of the late breakfast, the men found their places in the trees and napped, waiting for sundown to continue the journey.

Miguel placed his blanket in sight of the girl and propped himself up against a tree so that he would see if she woke. Finally, the afternoon's heat caused him to drift into an uneasy sleep where he dreamed about the woman and boy lying against the sandy bank. Only in his dream, he saw himself lying in the man's place, and the woman spoke Spanish to her son. She told him to close his eyes if he wanted a surprise and held the smooth stone raised in her hand. He woke, reaching in vain to stop the descent of the rock.

His heart was pounding, his mouth dry from his rapid breathing, and he was afraid that he had cried out in his sleep. But looking around, it didn't seem that he had drawn any attention, so he guessed that his dream had been silent. Suddenly he remembered the girl and was surprised to see her sitting up and looking around as if she was lost. She must have caught sight of his movement because she looked directly at him. They sat peering at each other for some moments, then the boy rose and walked slowly to where she sat, hoping not to spook her. As he neared, he sensed some recognition in her eyes but also confusion, as if she couldn't quite place him in her memory.

"My name is Miguel," he said in his best Spanish.

"Where am I," she croaked, putting her hand to her throat as if speaking caused her pain.

"Can you tell me your name?" he asked softly to show her that she didn't have to speak loudly.

"Natalie," she whispered, "Where am I?"

"Me and my poppa and grandpa are taking you to get help," he replied, as he doubted that the middle of the desert would satisfy her for an answer.

"Then where is my family?" she asked with some alarm, and Miguel panicked, realizing that he should have anticipated the question.

William heard the voices and quickly grabbed a canteen and hurried around the bushes that separated the men from the two children. He correctly feared that the boy had strayed beyond his depth in his conversation with the girl. As he arrived, he knelt down and almost forced the water on the child.

Startled, she accepted the drink and then allowed herself to be pushed down onto her blanket. Without letting her speak, William began to tell her about the seriousness of her condition and cautioned her about overexerting herself. When she tried to ask another question, he shushed her and said there would be plenty of time to talk after they reached the mountains and cooler climes.

There was a bustle in the camp as William announced they would leave early, and preparations were made to get underway. Miguel sat down next to the girl he now knew as Natalie and watched as she drifted in and out of sleep.

The old Indian carried two tortillas filled with meat to the children and handed them to Miguel, who gobbled his down as quickly as he could, then slowly fed the other to the girl.

William encouraged the Mexican man to avoid letting the girl see him, and by the time they had rigged the travois on the mule and secured the girl to it, she was back deep in sleep.

The company of Indians and Mexicans moved easily across the dark desert as they had joined one of the many trails that led to the approach to the mountains, so the way was chosen for them. The silent giants loomed ever higher as they followed the path of the yellow moon toward the irregular peaks that formed the western horizon.

They were only a few miles from the beckoning foothills as the sun's red rays washed over them from the east, chasing away the shadows. When Miguel recognized the rise in the distance where he and his father and grandfather had stopped on their way into the desert, he twisted in his saddle, eager to tell the girl that their destination was near, but saw that her head was lolling from side to side with the motion of the sled in her sleep.

CHAPTER 19

Maria went to the bedroom to check on her son before going to bed but found her daughter lying on the floor in the doorway with her legs drawn up, hugging her knees. In the darkness, her mother didn't notice her unblinking eyes, so she lifted her without trying to wake her, placed her on her bed, and covered her with her quilt. Raphael was breathing the deep, steady rhythm of an exhausted sleeper, so she didn't bother to wake him.

The following day the two women rose early and met in the kitchen, where Margarita assembled a pot of coffee and Maria lit the stove to prepare breakfast. The children were not up yet, so when the coffee was made, they poured themselves cups and sat at the table. They had talked late into the night, so they had little to say this morning. On different schedules, the women glanced down the hallway every few minutes anticipating one or both of the children to appear, but neither did.

Finally, Maria could wait no longer and had to walk down to peek into the children's bedroom. When she got there and looked in, she saw that they both lay almost precisely as they were the night before.

Back in the kitchen, she asked Margarita to stay with the kids while she took care of the barn chores. She took Raphael's egg and milk buckets and started for the door. The Mexican woman called her and asked if she really thought she would milk that cow, given the boy's previous experience with her. Maria smiled, left the milk bucket by the door, and headed to the chicken house.

After feeding the chickens and gathering the eggs, she looked into the pasture for the cow but saw only the gap in the back fence left by Mary's charge at her son. Curious, she sat the eggs down at the lot gate and walked across the meadow to look for the pet cow. All she saw were tracks through the needles and leaves where she had stumbled away after demolishing the section of the fence. The path was plain, so the woman followed the trail through the trees, often stopping to look around and listen in case the cow lingered nearby. She heard only the incessant chatter of a squirrel high up in the pines. The trail led toward the bluff where Raphael had sat, watching as the soldiers drove the wagon away.

Upon reaching the edge, Maria carefully leaned over and looked down to see the cow at the bottom of the cliff, burst open from the fall to the rocks. Her body was resting against the base of a big pine tree. She also saw several small woodland creatures fighting for dibs on the carcass.

Quickly she returned to the egg bucket and hurried to the cabin. She told the nurse what had happened to the cow and her fear that the disease would explode throughout the countryside from the animals she had seen feeding on it.

Together the women reasoned that it was too late for them to do anything to prevent the spread, and all they could do was be cautious outside the cabin and never let anyone go out alone.

"Besides," Margarita said, "the disease can only survive in a dead body for about twenty-four hours, and it only lasts for seconds outside the body. It isn't always necessary, but it usually takes a bite to transfer living bacteria from one victim to another."

As they spoke, Raphael stumbled into the kitchen and sat down without saying anything, an unusual entrance for the boy. His nose was runny and his eyes puffy, but otherwise, he seemed fine.

"Raphe, how do you feel this morning," asked his mother, frowning with concern.

The boy coughed and wiped his nose, then replied, "I'm sore all over," then gently touched his ribcage and looked at his scuffed knuckles as if trying to figure out what had happened.

Margarita turned her chair toward the boy so that she could feel his forehead for fever, but feeling no warmth, she told Maria so. "I'm not surprised that he has a cold though."

"What would you like for breakfast this morning, son?" his mother asked.

"Could we have flapjacks?" the boy wondered.

"Anything you want, baby," she answered, happy that he seemed to have a good appetite. She went to the stove to prepare the meal, not wanting to bring up the boy's ordeal with Mary Magdalene.

"Momma, I couldn't wake Gabby up," said the boy, "and I shook her good too."

Maria stopped what she was doing and hurried down the hallway without taking time to respond to the boy. Margarita followed her to the bedroom and stood while she lowered the covers and rolled the girl onto her back while cooing her name.

"Gabby?" she said when she saw the girl's glassy staring eyes. She lifted the girl into a sitting position, looked closely into her face, and shook her gently.

It was a few moments before Gabriella's eyes focused on her mother, and when she did, she began to cry.

"What's the matter, baby?" Maria asked as she hugged her daughter to her.

"Raphe is going to die," the girl said through tears, "and it's all my fault."

"No, darling, Raphael is fine, and he is sitting at the kitchen table waiting for his flapjacks," she said soothingly to the girl.

"He is?" the girl asked through the tears.

"Of course he is dear," as she picked her up. "Come on, and I will show you." And she carried her into the kitchen where her brother sat at the table, scratching his elbow and grinning.

CHAPTER 20

William urged his horse on, wanting to overtake his son and father, who were riding ahead. He could see them going up the knuckle of ground where the three of them had sat surveying the vast expanse of desert on their way out of the mountains. That seemed ages ago now, a time of innocence for his young son.

Most of the man's previous assignments had consisted of playing a guessing game, predicting the mind of the target of his search, and eventually discovering the details of yet another lonely tragedy that had unfolded in the wasteland. At the end of each, there was the satisfaction of another puzzle solved and the challenge of bringing the body back to whatever entity had commissioned the search. There was little or no emotion involved, for he was simply doing a job that he was good at and one that provided well for his family.

The difference this time was the unavoidable drama of dealing with living people. Something that the parameters of his job customarily allowed him to avoid. And in this case, the presence of his son was forcing a new perspective on the nature of his trade. He was beginning to understand his wife's opposition to bringing their son into his chosen profession, especially after the events of this last trip.

On the other hand, as ugly as his discovery of man's fragility had been, his young son had also experienced the deep satisfaction of saving a life. God had chosen to spare these two, whether for mercy or destiny remained to be seen.

As they neared the mountains in the breaking dawn, he realized that his preoccupation with these matters was distracting him from doing his job correctly. Now, to make up for his lapse, he was hurrying to alert his father to watch for the tracks of the men whose path he had crossed their first night in the desert. As he approached his father and son, the deafening report of a buffalo rifle harangued down from the stony bluff above, causing his horse to rear.

Miguel was stunned by the explosion but what drew his attention was the ear-splitting scream from his father's horse, Sugar, behind him. He looked back in time to see the big mare's front legs fold beneath her and to watch as she crumpled to the ground. The bullet had pierced the Appaloosa's throat, her spine, and then his father's leg. It broke the large bone in the man's thigh and sent the horse and rider tumbling backward down the slope. The horse's lifeless tumble took Rachel's legs out from under her, and the mule and Mexican joined the tangle as they all slid and rolled to the bottom of the steep sandy bank.

Dotty pulled to the right, away from her fallen mother, and stumbled back down the sandy knoll, fighting to stay on her feet. The mule that Miguel was leading, still attached to the stretcher the girl rode, had no choice but to follow the horse to the bottom. Other shots rang out from a smaller caliber gun, but the boy was too busy to notice where those rounds were directed.

As soon as the old Indian heard the blast from the big rifle, he dug his heels into his mule's sides and drove toward a stand of cedars. Halfway to the trees, the mule he rode brayed in pain and tumbled into the dust of the ridge. A hole the size of a man's fist appeared through the animal's hindquarters as Bodine redirected his fire after Will Strider had disappeared. The mule continued its odd, terrifying screeching as it thrashed its useless legs in an attempt to escape from the danger.

The old man hit the ground and rolled, then came up on his feet running, still holding on to the lead rope of his second mule. He completed the distance to the trees with plumes of sand rising around him as Skinner pumped rounds from his repeating rifle at him as fast as he could work the lever.

The brow of the knoll provided cover for the Striders and Mexicans and gave Miguel a chance to dismount and rush to where his father lay. He had seen flashes of his poppa, rolling and tumbling, his injured leg gyrating grotesquely with every revolution. Somehow the man had remained conscious, and with his son's help, they put the leg back into its proper orientation to where he sat in the sand. William immediately began working the waist strap from his coat and commanded his son to give him his belt. They wrapped the wound with the thick strip of cloth and placed Miguel's wide leather belt over the bandage; then, the man asked his son to tighten it until the blood stopped gushing.

It was the hardest thing that Miguel had ever attempted to do; with tears of fear and concern flowing down his cheeks, he pulled the wide leather belt through the buckle, braced his feet on either side of his father's wound, and leaned back with all his might. His first attempt cut the flow of blood in half, and he looked to his father, who said, "Harder!" The boy, choked with emotion and effort, leaned back again and got another notch on the belt. The man finally patted him on the arm to stop.

With the flow partially staunched, William lay back in the sand. He reached for his son and brought their faces close together. He knew he was close to fainting because his vision had already begun to narrow, so time was short to get some strategy into place to save their lives.

"Did you see what happened to your grandfather!" he asked the boy, none too politely.

"He was making for the trees on the right," Miguel replied, frightened at his father's abruptness.

William looked up while calculating the odds of the old man making it to cover from what he could remember of the terrain. Pretty slim, he decided.

"Ok, you will need to get my rifle," he said, looking back into his son's eyes.

Miguel started to rise, but his father held him fast.

"Do you remember how I showed you to fire my rifle, how to use the sights?" he asked the boy.

He knew he was about to ask his young son to do something practically impossible, but he didn't know what else to do. This was war, and he knew that you do impossible things in battle.

"Yessir," said the frightened boy.

"I figure a hundred yards to the bluff and sixty feet to the top," William said before the pain from his leg could no longer be held at bay, and his head dropped back against the sand.

"Poppa?" the boy implored.

"Bring me the rifle, and I will set the sights, but you will have to take the shot," the man said haltingly, forcing the pain away by sheer will.

This time he released his grip on his son's coat, and the boy flew to where the man's horse lay in a jumble of crushed bushes, broken bodies, and busted gear.

Alejandro had tried to jump free as his mule went down, but the makeshift rope stirrups bound him to the pack saddle. He was lucky to land on top of the heap at the bottom of the slide, where he was able to extract himself from the pile. He now lay in the sand, not knowing what had happened or where he was. Rachel, the mule the Mexican rode, hadn't fared so well, as somewhere on the trip down the slope, the mule's neck was snapped, and she now lay a dead companion to the big Appaloosa mare.

Natalie had fared better because neither Miguel's horse nor the mule had lost their footing completely and waded successfully through the sand during their descent. She had been tied to the travois and remained aboard when the boy ran by to retrieve his father's rifle. A hurried glance told him that she had fared well enough.

Another shot rang out, fired from the buffalo rife, but no bullet appeared to strike near the boy.

The custom leather scabbard was all that had saved the long gun from being broken into pieces. It had clung loyally to the saddle throughout the ride, alternately above and beneath the big horse's body as it tumbled. Upon settling in the soft sand, the rifle lay trapped between the horse and the ground, and only the butt end remained visible. Miguel located it quickly and began digging the sand away until he could unlash the leather flap guarding the stock. He was able to slip the gun from its stiff leather sheath without too much difficulty.

Miguel had always admired his father's rife from afar because the man cared for it like a new baby. The birch stock always gleamed through the fresh linseed oil from a rag folded in a pouch built into the scabbard. The man used it to clean the gun each time before placing it back into the saddle holster. The young boy took a half moment to admire its beauty and test its weight, then thumbed the precision Galilean sights that his father had several times tried to explain the workings of to him. There was a round flat half lens mounted on the muzzle end of the barrel about an inch in diameter that, as his father said, produced a two-and-a-half times magnification of the target. A small dot at the center of that lens was the aiming point to be lined up through a peep sight mounted on the rifle's rear. There was an elevation knob that allowed you to set the estimated distance to the target and a windage knob that moved the rear sight left or right to compensate for the estimated drift of the bullet. The boy understood the mechanics of the sights, but the skill was in calculating the distance and wind speed. The man had started going over projectile weight, powder grains, and muzzle velocity but quickly left him far behind. He knew how to line the sights up and pull the trigger; that was about the extent of his confidence.

When the boy returned to his father's side, the man's eyes were clenched against the pain as he willed his mind to keep functioning until he had performed his part in the plan to save them.

"Poppa," the boy said, breathless from the run, handing him the weapon.

The man lifted both hands to receive the rifle without raising his head or opening his eyes until he held the gun. He felt for the folded rear sight and lifted it into place as he had done thousands of times. At last, he opened his eyes and focused on the minute graduations etched into the hardened steel, then quickly dialed the position that matched the image he had concentrated on keeping clear in his mind, for he knew that delirium was rapidly approaching.

"You will have to find a place to shoot from, and when you see the target in your sights, squeeze the trigger. If they fire first, you will have plenty of time while they reload to take your shot. When you do, don't wait to see if you've hit anything; get another round in the chamber and fire again."

When the man closed his eyes again and eased the gun to his chest, Miguel knew that he had finished his job and was now drifting into a world without pain. The boy took the rifle from the still firm grip of his father and began scanning the ridge for a spot to shoot from.

Slightly to the left of the trail that led up the rise was a stand of young Joshua trees, and Miguel made for these as fast as he could crawl, careful not to let the gun touch the sand. He hadn't heard any more firing in the last few minutes and hoped whoever was on the bluff had remained there. He knew that there was more than one person above from at least two distinctive-sounding guns and doubted if he would be able to hit one of them, much less both. The boy stole a glimpse back at his now silent father as he reached the firing position he had chosen, and his breath caught in his throat; his poppa's body was limp. The hard lines of determination that had been present on his face as he had fought to remain in control of the pain were gone, replaced by what the boy interpreted as the expressionless continence of death. Tears welled, and loneliness that he had never before felt knotted in his chest, but his father's determination flowed through his veins. He frantically wiped the tears, and his thoughts returned to the task. He would do this to avenge his father or die in the trying.

When he raised into a firing position to look at the bluff, a bullet from the huge gun above struck the trunk of the small tree beside his head and shattered it to shreds. Remembering his father's words, he neither ducked nor flinched but steadied the long rifle and peered through the optical sights. A man's head came into focus through the cloud of powder smoke left from the last shot fired from above. As the sights aligned with the target, he squeezed the trigger. The recoil pushed him backward, but his right hand was already on the bolt, ejecting the spent shell and shoving another into the chamber. He settled again and looked for the man, but he had disappeared behind the rock shelf.

Fear took hold; had he missed, had he done something wrong, had he wasted his father's efforts? Then slowly, a single stone fell from the bluff and bounced off a bolder into the sand of the desert, and then a shape like a massive bear in slow motion tipped over the ledge and somersaulted into the dust of the ridge.

The boy saw movement from the trees on the other side of the plateau; it was another man. He swung the rifle around and tried to focus the sights, but the target was moving too close. He raised his eyes above the gun and thought to shoot by chance, but when he saw the man again, he recognized the big toothy grin of his grandfather. He was walking toward him as if taking a stroll in the sunshine. Undoubtedly one of the other attackers would see, but seconds passed with no shots ringing out, and the old Indian continued to come. That's when Miguel noticed that his grandfather was wearing a strange wide-brimmed hat that he'd never seen before, and in his hand was a repeating rifle that he also failed to recognize.

When he was nearer, the old Indian said, "Good shot, William Miguel Strider! Where's your poppa?"

CHAPTER 21

Back at the homestead, the two women and two children were still enjoying the big breakfast of flapjacks, sugar syrup, and fried ham that was just a bit chewy, having sat overnight in the skillet on the stove. Everyone was in a good mood, as yesterday's ordeal quickly became a fading memory.

Raphael was the center of attention and cracked silly jokes that everyone laughed at for no good reason; even Gabby participated in the generous laughter. Maria couldn't help but notice that the small girl was particularly attentive to her brother and sat smiling at him, even when someone else was talking.

Finally, the women rose and began clearing the table while the boy and girl giggled at their sticky fingers. Raphe held his fork out and released his fingers from it, which stayed glued to his palm until he shook it loose. This started a new round of laughter from him and his sister.

"Raphael, you will need another bath if you don't get away from this table soon," Margarita joked, picking up the coffee cups for the wash water.

Suddenly, the boy stopped laughing and looked up at the Mexican woman, bursting into tears as an image of the hard scrubbing he had endured at her hands only a few hours ago flashed through his mind.

"Oh, honey, no," she moaned, realizing her careless mistake.

Maria looked over and saw tears streaming down Gabriella's cheeks as the small girl stood and walked to her brother and wrapped her arms around his neck, trying to absorb some of the boy's hurt as penitence for her past behavior. It reminded the woman that this terrible ordeal wasn't nearly over.

"You kids, come wash your hands in the dishwater, then go get some clothes on!" their mother said, wanting to break the mood for Margarita's sake. The two children recovered somewhat and stood, still huffing, but obeyed their mother's orders.

They all spent the rest of the day going about their business as normally as possible, and the incident at breakfast was mainly forgotten as the kids had come out of the bedroom dressed. Gabriella was chasing her brother, pretending to be trying to poke him in his sore ribs. The laughter was welcome and caused the two women to smile, and the tension evaporated.

The children had to amuse themselves indoors as the grown-ups discussed the situation with the unfortunate cow. All three females had to take a turn scolding Raphael for trying to recruit them each to go with him to the bottom of the bluff to inspect the carnage.

Later in the day, Margarita commented on the frown she noticed on Maria's face anytime her thoughts seemed to wander from whatever chore the two women were engaged in.

"It's hard to explain," said the mother, "and my husband would say that it is just a waste of good worry, but I get these feelings sometimes when any of the family is out of my sight for too long."

She was referring to her husband and oldest son, as the two little ones were sprawled on the kitchen floor where Raphael was trying to explain imagined army tactics to his sister. He had enlisted the aid of some small potatoes that had sprouted eyes over the winter, large enough to make them stand on their own, transforming them into cavalry horses.

"You see," Maria continued, "this is the first time my son has accompanied my husband on one of his assignments, and at first, I was afraid for him, but now I don't know. I keep seeing William's face, which hasn't happened to me in all the years that he has been doing this job, and I feel like something terrible may have happened to him.

"I understand your concern," said the Mexican woman, "I have had the same feelings about my sister since we arrived here. All we can do is pray for them and trust that God will bring them home to us."

Maria felt a little better after talking about it, but she was still preparing herself for the bad news.

The following day after breakfast, Maria reached the shotgun down from its pegs, Raphael got his egg bucket, and all four of them left the cabin to feed and water the hens that hadn't been out of the roost for two days. Gabby held the Mexican nurse's hand, Raphe walked by his mother's side, and they all made the trip to the chicken pen, anticipating a rush of moon-mad varmints intent on harming them.

It wasn't until they had opened the roost that the coyote stumbled through the open lot gate, having just found its way through the broken pasture fence. When it saw the people, it stopped, looked at them through the chicken wire, and snarled. It was unusual to see a coyote in broad daylight and unheard of to have one stand and growl at you.

Everyone froze in fear and then jumped and squealed as the roar of the shotgun ripped the moment of silence apart as Maria fired on the infected animal. The coyote was blown head over heels backward through the open gate, where it lay stone dead behind a wall of rolling white smoke. Everyone looked at the woman who had pulled the triggers with new respect as she calmly broke the gun down across her forearm, pulled the spent shells from their chambers, and felt in her apron pocket for two new ones.

"Man alive!" the young boy exclaimed, then bent to pick up the bucket that had somehow flown from his hand.

"Momma?" Gabriella whimpered, standing with her knees bent and legs together. The others looked at the small girl and saw that she had wet herself.

"Don't worry, honey," Margarita smiled, "I may have wet myself a little bit too!"

No one felt safe again until they were all in the cabin with the door closed behind them. Maria placed the loaded shotgun back on its pegs above the door, took the spare shells from her pocket, and stood them on the wall's ledge where they were kept handy.

Margarita went with Gabriella to the bedroom for fresh clothes, and Raphael stood admiring the big gun hanging above the kitchen door with scenes of who knows what playing in his head.

"Momma?" the boy asked his mother.

"Yes, son?"

"When do you think Poppa and Willie will come home?"

"Soon, baby," she replied, "I hope very soon!"

CHAPTER 22

Miguel was so relieved to see his grandfather alive and well that he rushed out of the brush from where he had fired and ran to the old man. He found that the emotions he had been fighting so hard to hold in check were now running down his cheeks, forcing him to wipe them away from his eyes before he could see the friendly old face. He might have hugged the father of his father had he not been too grown up to do such things, but instead, he tried to put on his grown-up face.

The old man placed a gentle hand on the back of the boy's neck and gave a squeeze that transmitted all the relief and love that a giant bear hug would have accomplished had either of them been so inclined.

The Indian man looked down at the rifle his grandson now held and asked, "Where's your daddy at, son?"

Miguel glanced toward the brow of the ridge and said, "He's shot, Grandpa," and his face became that of a thirteen-year-old boy again and fresh tears brimmed his young eyes.

"Show me," said his concerned and suddenly frightened grandfather.

The boy led the way down the bank to where his poppa still lay unconscious in the stain left as the sand had so greedily absorbed his blood as it was gushing from the wound.

The old Indian looked his son over and lay his hand on his chest to confirm that he was still breathing, then pointed to the bandage on his leg and looked at Miguel.

"It's broke," said the boy.

"Looks like a lot of blood come out."

"A lot!" confirmed the boy.

"Could be a good thing, cleans the wound sometimes. We need to get it braced before he wakes up, or we'll have fits holding him still. Where's that fancy rifle scabbard your daddy keeps his gun in? It might be just the thing."

Miguel jumped up and ran down the bank toward his father's dead horse, recruiting the Mexican man to help him on the way over. Alejandro was kneeling beside the girl and confirmed to the boy that she was well in answer to his unspoken question. Together they dug the now empty leather holster from the sand.

By the time the boy returned with the scabbard, his grandfather had gathered water, soap, rags, and a box of sulfur powder from one of the pack panniers, along with a blanket. He had removed the man's boots and split the pant leg from cuff to crotch, skipping over the bandage and then around at the top. He was about to unwrap the cloth belt from the wound but stopped to prepare the splint first.

Estimating which section of the stiff leather tube would best fit the leg, he started sawing with the razor-sharp hunting knife he carried on his belt. He made the splint long enough to immobilize the leg from the calf to the crotch. This would ensure that the shattered bone would remain stable through the healing process. The last thing was to split the seam up the long side of the leather where it had been sewn together. This would allow the circumference to be adjusted as the straps holding it on were tightened or loosened and would enable it to be removed entirely if the dressing needed changing.

"Now I will lift his leg, and you two slip that blanket underneath to keep it out of the dirt," said the Indian. After the blanket was spread, he settled the leg back down and prepared to tackle the more serious part of the operation.

"When I take this bandage off, it's like to bleed like the dickens again, so be ready to hand me what I ask for fast."

"Yessir," said the boy, thankful that his grandfather was present and seemed so confident and capable.

When the cloth was removed, the wound did start bleeding again, but it didn't spurt blood as it would have had the artery been severed. The pressure from the tight belt had done its job.

"You do the water, and I'll do the soap," said the Indian to the boy. The old man held the bar of lye soap and a rag together above his son's leg as Miguel poured from the canteen. He worked up a lather in the rag, then carefully cleaned the injured limb from top to bottom, signaling again and again for more water. When the cleaning was complete, he carefully dried the leg, then began his inspection of the entry and the exit wounds made by the bullet that had thankfully spent most of its energy plowing through the horse's neck and spine.

He probed into the discolored wounds with his finger, feeling for bone fragments, making the man moan with pain even in his unconscious state, but he found only the smooth ends of the broken bone, fractured by the glancing force of the lead projectile.

Satisfied that they had cleaned the wound as well as they could, he dusted the now freely bleeding wounds with sulfur and wrapped the injury tightly with a clean cloth.

"Lay across your poppa's chest," he told the boy. "And don't let him move when I set the bone back into place."

Miguel lay his body diagonally across his father's chest, placed one arm over the unconscious man's shoulder behind his back, and the other around the opposite side. He worked his hands through the sand beneath him to hold them securely together. A strange sensation filled the boy as he lay his head on his poppa's chest and listened to the subdued beating of his heart; he realized that this was the first time in his life that he had shared such an intimate and unhurried embrace with his stoic and sometimes distant father. A pang of sadness overcame him to think that it had taken thirteen years and a gunshot to bring them this close together, and he somehow knew that the older he got, the further the world would push them apart.

The old man lifted his son's leg up between his arm and body, noticing the unnatural looseness of the limb as he leaned back. He felt a slight give as the muscles stretched, allowing him to set the bone and remove the obvious misalignment of the thigh. With his left hand on the break, he guided the big bone back into its place and slowly eased off the pressure. When satisfied with the feel, he released all pressure and let the muscles pull the bone back together while still supporting the weight of the leg.

"Ok, Miguel, you can let go now, work the splint around the leg and put your straps on both sides of the break and pull them tight." When this was accomplished, he eased the leg they had encased in the stiff leather splint to the blanket.

They placed more leather straps up and down the cast, and the Indian adjusted each one below the break to a tension that he hoped would hold the leg immobile without stopping the circulation. He checked the foot's alignment to ensure they weren't going to leave it at an awkward angle to the leg and had the Mexican hold it while he tightened the straps above the wound.

Sierra Sunrise

Finally, he looked his grandson in the face and blew out a breath that it felt like he had been holding the entire time they were working on his son, and let slip a nervous smile that reassured the boy.

The rest of the morning was spent unraveling the mess at the bottom of the rise, salvaging the equipment that wasn't ruined in the wreck. Natalie was scooted to one side of the travois to make room for the Indian man, and Miguel walked the mule and sled up to level ground at the top of the ridge.

Alejandro was no worse off for his tumble with the mule and bustled about assisting the others in any way he could.

When everything was accounted for, the boy took his father's rifle from the travois where he had stowed it for the ride up the hill and pulled the linseed cloth from his coat pocket where he had jammed it when they were cannibalizing the scabbard. With reverence, he carefully wiped down the gun just as he had seen his father do a hundred times before, then wrapped it in a blanket and tied it securely to his horse Dotty's saddle.

The old Indian came walking down from higher up the bank leading two horses and a donkey that the mountain men had picketed out of sight in the trees near their camp. He told Miguel that it looked like they had surprised the two Bandidos by their early arrival from the desert, as their breakfast had been abandoned over the fire and had burned to a crisp.

"Might account for why your poppa's still livin," speculated the old man. "If you will give me a hand, we will dig a grave for those two yahoos that shot your daddy."

CHAPTER 23

Life got back to normal at the homestead, and Margarita soon found her place in the rhythm of the Strider family's day-to-day life. For the women, it was breakfast, lunch, supper, and fighting with the little ones to get them to bed. For the children, it was eat, play, and repeat, except for bedtime, then it was begging, whimpering, and finally, sleep.

There were late-night discussions about the twins, William, Miguel, and endless speculations about the prospects for the Mexican woman's family in the desert. Other times Maria spoke of her life in Mexico before coming to these mountains and the mystery of how she happened to be married to an Indian man. They had talked about places they had both visited in their youth and where they could have crossed paths. It usually ended with Margarita speculating about what her husband might be doing and thinking.

More infected animals were killed and burned, a joy for Raphael and a horror for Gabby. Every day began with someone feeling the boy's brow for fever and rolling him over and over, checking his cuts and scrapes and bruises for infections, with Gabriella looking on, anticipating the worst.

As the days marched by, they all became more comfortable with their situation and spent more time with what was happening at home than speculating about the people they had waited for but who never came.

There was a casual nervousness, and everyone, including the children, had been guilty of staring off into space at times of idle distraction. It is usual for nothing significant to happen when you are isolated in the wilderness; you become accustomed to it and expect that nothing will change. Of course, everyone knows, or suspects, that these unguarded times are when the worst things happen.

The storm hit the cabin with gale-force winds, and black clouds that looked like they could have been produced from the smokestacks of some huge steel smelter poured over the peaks from the Pacific, pushed by a massive tropical storm that had tried but failed to come ashore over southern California. The cold south-flowing California Current, which acts as a hurricane repellant, was able to turn the main body of the storm. Still, it couldn't keep the moisture-laden clouds from splashing up and over the Sierras and down into the Mojave Basin. Rain by the wagons fell from the sky and ran down the face of their protective mountain and caused cataracts of water falling hundreds of feet to inundate their usually peaceful plateau. Cold dampness seeped into every crack and caused even their bones to ache as it invaded the cabin. The moisture, driven by the relentless wind, found its way through even the thick logs the home was built from.

The cabin and barn were in no danger, being built on the highest ground of the plateau, but the mirror pool that was the reservoir that fed the meadows was turned into a torrent of fleeing rainwater. Who could have imagined that there could be a flood halfway up the tallest mountains in the United States? It rained day and night, and normal thought or conversation was impossible for those trapped indoors. Before it was over, the children were crying from fear, and the women would have been, too, if it weren't for the children's sake.

Sometime during the early morning hours of the second day, Gabriella stumbled into her mother's bedroom. The rain was barely a patter on the roof, and the sounds of dripping and flowing water had replaced the violent sounds of the tempest.

"Momma, something is the matter with Raphe," said the girl softly, not wanting to disturb the relative calm after the storm.

When there was no response, she said again a bit louder. "Momma?" then waited.

"Momma, Raphe is making funny noises!"

Maria woke and sat up in bed.

"What, honey?" the mother replied.

"I can't make Raphe stop making those noises!" the small girl said again.

The woman's feet touched the floor, and she led the young girl back down the hallway to her bedroom.

Raphael was making grunting and groaning noises, and they could tell he was having difficulty breathing by his raspy air intake.

"Raphe, baby?" his mother implored. "Raphe, can you wake up?" She rolled him onto his back so she could feel his forehead.

By now, Margarita was up and standing in the bedroom doorway.

"He's burning up!" Maria said aloud and looked fearfully up at the Mexican nurse, who could only look on in horror at the revelation.

The more they tried to wake the boy up, the worse his breathing became until the nurse finally put him on his side and drew his knees up, which helped to relieve some of his distress. She tucked the boy's covers around him and waved his mother to follow.

Back in the kitchen, the Mexican woman got the dishpan from beneath the cabinet, dipped water into it from the drinking water bucket, picked up the lye soap, and implored Maria to wash her hands.

The woman looked down at her hands and then at the water and would have covered her face, but Margarita grabbed her wrists with force and shook her until she looked up.

"You can't afford to give yourself this disease, or you will be worthless to us," she said, looking sideways down at Gabriella, indicating what she was talking about.

Numbly the woman walked to the dishpan and began washing her hands.

"Do you think he has it?" she asked, unable to say the word.

"I can't imagine it is anything else, dear," the nurse admitted. "Gabby, you wash next, and don't go back into the bedroom alone."

The small girl stood, and her icy blue eyes stared at nothing.

CHAPTER 24

Will Strider lay quietly on the travois beside the resting girl, his broken leg, sheathed in the stiff leather splint that his son and father had constructed, sat comfortably on a soft pad of wool blankets they had placed beneath it.

The Mexican man stood away to one side; he was staring uncertainly at his young daughter, asleep and innocent on the sled. His face was a picture of indecision and dread, reflections of the task he knew he couldn't avoid much longer.

Miguel looked from the sleeping girl to his father but noticed his grandfather carrying his oddly made saddle. He had just removed it from his dead mule that he had ridden to the ground when it was shot. The boy read neither sadness nor sorrow in the old man's face, but he had long since stopped trying to discover his grandfather's inner thoughts simply by looking upon his countenance, another of those Indian things he guessed that his mother often spoke of. Only the fact that he paused for one last look hinted at an emotional response to the loss of the animal.

The boy walked over to stand beside the Indian, and after a silent moment of respect for the dead mule, he asked, "Grandpa, what do you think we should do now?"

"Well," the Indian said, shifting the saddle's weight and turning toward the boy. "Your daddy needs to be home as soon as we can get him there, but if we carry him up these mountain trails, we might shake them bones and ruin his leg. All I can figure is to go a long way around and catch a wagon trail and follow it up to your place, take a couple of extra days, but it can't be helped."

"Do you think it would be better if we had a wagon then?" the boy offered, wondering where they might get one if the answer was yes.

"No, those long poles on that drag sled have more spring than a wagon wheel, so they orta ride softer. We need to get that girl up on a horse, so we can narrow the sled to go through the trees. Let's move everything to where those two yahoos was camped; I seen grass up there, so the animals can eat and rest while we see if we can rearrange your daddy's ride."

They had lost two mules and a horse to the two mountain men's ambush but had gained two horses and a donkey. They led the animals through the trees to the clearing that Bodine and Skinner had chosen for their campsite and unloaded their entire kit to be redistributed before they resumed the journey. They unsaddled and hobbled the animals, then sorted and combined their gear with that left by the assassins.

Miguel went to speak with the girl whom the move had awakened, and he found her trying to rise. She had pushed herself up on her elbows, but her restraints held her.

"Do you think you might be able to get up now?" the boy asked and started slipping the knots on the safety ropes.

"Yes," she replied in English, for he hadn't used Spanish to ask the question.

"Can you speak American?" the boy asked with surprise.

"Yes, I can," she answered, with a heavy accent that reminded him of his mother's.

He helped her sit on the side of the sled with her bare feet touching the sandy ground.

"What happened to him?" the girl asked, looking at William lying unconscious behind her.

"That's my poppa," Miguel said. "His leg is broken," hoping to avoid a longer explanation.

The boy had tried to prepare for the conversation he knew he was about to have. He had spoken with his father at their last rest stop in the desert and asked his advice on how he should respond if the girl should corner him again about her family.

"All I can tell you is," his father had said, "keep still and let the girl do the asking. When you answer, be sure you are truthful. Don't offer any opinions or do any guessing. That's advice I was given once, and it has served me pretty well."

Miguel looked down into the dark pools of the young girl's eyes, past the sun-reddened skin and cracked lips and tangled hair, and found that undefinable something that sooner or later disrupts every young boy's life. It's the something that starts a boy on his journey from boyhood to manhood. It is impossible to say whether these feelings awoke coincidental with the boy's first real test on his way to becoming a man or if they happened due to it. Fortunately, chance and Nature are responsible for boys becoming men. Otherwise, a mother's love would keep a boy a child far beyond all practicality. This unfamiliar feeling caused him to blush and shift his gaze away from the young girl's face.

"I dreamed I saw my poppa," the girl said. "He was holding my hand."

Miguel understood the implied question, took a deep breath, and chose his words carefully.

"Your father is here with us," and then, despite his father's suggestion, he continued, "but your mother and brother were not alive when we found them."

"My mother and brother? Where are they now?"

"We buried them in the desert, at the base of a great stone that is a marker for their grave."

Somehow the girl's reaction hadn't aligned with the boy's expectations.

"My father, then, have you spoken with him?" she asked cautiously.

"I have not, but he told my poppa you were missing; that's how we found you."

Miguel was relieved, for he feared that the following questions would require reasons and explanations that the girl's father would be far more able to supply.

Without asking if she wanted him to, he said, "You just sit here, and I will get him for you."

The boy quickly started in the direction he had last seen the girl's father, but before taking five steps, he heard Spanish being spoken back at the travois. Looking back, he saw the girl's father kneeling in the dust before her, clasping her hands in his. Miguel guessed that the man had been near enough to hear their conversation and had stepped from concealment as he had left.

He was curious about what was being said but not enough to get caught up in what could become an uncomfortable situation. He looked around for his grandfather, and when he located him, he walked quickly there. They were too far away to follow the conversation but near enough to intervene if things got out of hand.

The old man and boy waited at a polite distance, but finally, all worries were put aside when they saw the two stand and hold each other in a tearful embrace. Once again, Miguel was troubled by the girl's reaction.

The rest of that day was spent deconstructing and remaking the travois after Miguel and his grandfather pulled the injured man into the sand on his blanket. They widened the front of the sled by securing a cross piece to the sawbuck trees, allowing the long poles to lay parallel to each other just wide enough that they didn't rub the mules' sides. With the slats all trimmed to the same length and tied to the long poles, the sled became narrow and rigid but retained the flexibility to soften the ride over uneven ground. They calculated that if the mule could get through a place, the sled could follow. After testing the device by pulling it through the trees, they unsaddled the mule to let her graze.

By dark, they had resurrected the mountain men's campfire, and the old Indian got out his clay comal to cook tortillas. By scavenging through the supplies confiscated from the would-be killers, he made them a banquet of odds and ends by using the canned goods he found. They couldn't carry all they had acquired, so they splurged and ate their fill. Even Juliet shared in the bounty.

William woke eventually, and although he was in considerable pain, he hadn't developed any fever and could eat a little. His leg had swelled enough that his foot became numb, so the old man adjusted the bindings on the splint to restore circulation. When they had done what they could for the leg, Miguel and his grandfather moved the man nearer the campfire, using his blanket again as a sled.

The two Mexicans seemed to have resolved whatever questions they had for each other and remained near each other throughout the evening. When they made pallets, they placed them together for the night.

After everyone else had fallen asleep, Miguel moved his saddle and blanket nearer to his father and watched as the fire burned down. The boy was too troubled to sleep and sat staring into the glow of the wind-stirred ashes.

"Son," William said weakly.

With a start, Miguel looked up to see his father looking over at him.

"Yessir?" said the boy, surprised and pleased that the man was awake and speaking.

"I guess you must have made that shot then?" the man said with evident pride.

"Yessir, but I don't rightly remember how it all happened just yet," the boy said, a little bewildered.

"Don't worry; it will come back to you in a few days, then you can tell me all about it. How do you feel about having to shoot a man?"

"I suppose it might be wrong of me, but Poppa, I was glad he was dead."

"Son, when you're protecting your own, there's nothing you can do that's wrong. Is that why you're not sleeping?"

"No, sir, that's because of another thing."

"Want to talk about it?"

"If you are up to it."

"I am; what's on your mind?"

"Well, sir, it's about that girl Natalie and her daddy. They talked today, and I don't know if he didn't tell her the truth or if she just didn't care."

"What makes you say that?"

"I don't see how she could be so happy if he was honest about her mother and brother," said the boy.

"Did you hear what they said?" asked the man.

"No, sir."

"I did," the man said gravely. "I'm not sure why I woke up, but I did; maybe it was just the Spanish they were speaking. The girl's father was trying to explain to her what had happened after she walked off into the desert. But she stopped him; she said she knew they were dead from what you told her. He told her that he wanted her to know they didn't suffer; she seemed satisfied not to know more. I felt she had a pretty good idea of what went on, but she didn't want to hear the details."

After a moment of thought, the boy mused, "I wonder why she left them to go off by herself?"

"You may find out one day; I think the reason may explain what happened after," the man replied tiredly.

The plan for the next day was to go south toward a different mountain approach, one on a wagon route that would take them to the Three Forks Station Army camp, and from there over lesser traveled wagon lanes and eventually to the Strider homestead. What wasn't in their plan was the storm brewing off the pacific coast headed for the western seaboard.

CHAPTER 25

Few words were spoken in the cabin the rest of that day as if stating their worst fears aloud might somehow bring them to pass. And since fear for the small boy had crowded out every other thought, that left little for them to hang a conversation on. Every few minutes, one of the two women would impatiently rise and walk to the boy's bedroom door and stand and watch him struggle to breathe, then return teary-eyed to sit and stare. Gabriella was finding it impossible to release her grip on the hem of her mother's dress, so her tiny feet shuffled down the hall and back each time Maria went.

Raphael remained asleep, and beyond his rasping breath that was driving them all mad, the only thing worse was when the sounds he made ceased for long moments, causing them all to catch their breaths and hold them until the terrible noise began again.

The only treatment the Mexican nurse could recommend was to place blankets, wet with cool water, over the boy to keep down his raging fever. She and her doctor husband had proved all other remedies useless when trying to treat the two men in her story.

Silent looks exchanged between the two women while trading out the wet blankets were filled with shadows of unspeakable alternatives to allowing the boy to suffer through the ravages of the disease that had been witnessed by one and imagined by the other. Both knew that a time would soon come when silence would no longer suffice, and words would have to be said and actions taken, else madness would consume the rest as surely as the disease was destroying the young boy's mind.

No one slept that first night until Gabriella succumbed to exhaustion in her mother's lap sometime in the morning hours. The sounds from the bedroom were relentless until they weren't, during the brief interludes of silence that echoed more ominously than the sounds of his labored breathing.

The storm and rain were over, but blue skies and sunny weather went unseen by the inhabitants of the cabin where death stalked a small boy who was stubbornly refusing to go gently.

The days were endless and nights eternities, but somehow, they all endured them. On the third morning after the storm, Maria and her young daughter left the cabin to tend the chickens and gather the eggs. Stepping into the sunshine was like being wrapped in a warm blanket after the dark chill of the house. Their spirits were lifted simply by escaping the gloom that cloaked the cabin.

"Momma, is Raphe going to die?" the young girl asked flatly, all emotion having been spent.

"I don't know, honey," her mother answered, not wanting to perjure herself more than just this small lie.

"Do you think he will go to heaven?"

"Well, of course, he will, dear; what makes you ask?" the woman replied, conceding his death.

"I'm afraid God won't let rabies into heaven," the small girl said tearfully.

"Hush now, and don't think such things," scolded her mother, and they walked on.

After they had gathered the eggs and released the hens from the prison of the roost, they walked to the barn for feed and the well for water. Maria returned to the house with Gabriella still attached to the tail of her skirt.

Back inside, the Mexican woman was removing a pan of biscuits from the oven, and she had cooked eggs and ham for their breakfast. They all sat down and ate, but the meal was consumed mechanically, more out of habit than hunger.

About midday, Raphael's fever broke, so the women stripped his bed, took the damp mattress out into the warm sunshine to dry and air out, and temporarily moved the boy into Gabriella's bed. He woke briefly during the move and had a coughing fit that produced clots of greenish phlegm, and he seemed confused about where he was and had difficulty getting enough air. After he was settled in the girl's bed, he fell back to sleep, but it was a troubled sleep marked by incoherent rants plucked from fragments of memories. Just before sunset, they brought the boy's mattress back inside and moved him to his bed. Sometime after midnight, the boy's exhausted sister finally fell asleep again, and her mother pried her dress hem from the rigid claw of her hand and tucked the girl into the big bed in her room.

One or the other of the women constantly stayed with the boy, and when his breathing became so distressed that they were frightened of a strangle, they sat holding his head and shoulders on their lap until it passed. Each time this happened on the nurse's watch, she couldn't resist thinking that it would be a kindness to all concerned if she helped nature bring the child's life to its inevitable end. In the early hours, just before dawn, as Raphael slept quietly and Gabby napped in her mother's bed, Margarita came into the front room of the house where Maria sat before the hearth.

"We need to talk," said the Mexican nurse.

Maria looked up at her forlornly as if she were the condemned being finally called to execution.

"All right, my dear," she replied hopelessly.

"I want you to know," said Margarita, "that I will support whatever decision you make. But as a nurse, should your son's suffering become so great that you feel it would be a mercy to end it, you should know that I am aware of methods neither cruel nor painful to help ease him on his way."

Maria carefully considered the woman's words, then replied, "That is as kind a way as I can imagine for you to make that offer, my friend. If I were fearless, I would say yes, do it now. But I am afraid of what God will think of me for asking it and of you for doing it. If I were capable, I would gladly trade my place in heaven to save my son one hour of the agony that is sure to come, but I would go mad I am sure, and botch the deed. So, in the end, if it comes to it, I may be tempted to risk both our souls for the sake of my son."

"If you ask it, I swear I will fulfill my promise," replied the nurse.

"Then let this be the last word we pass on the subject," Maria replied. "We are both in agreement that we are prepared to risk our immortal souls to save my child the agony experienced by those two men you spoke of. I will pray for God's forgiveness for you, but not so for myself. I trust you to know the time, but until then, let us hope for a miracle."

It was unfortunate that neither of the women had thought to check the location of Gabriella before having the morbid conversation about her brother. The child seemed to have an intuition when she or her twin was the subject of grownup discussion, and this was no exception.

CHAPTER 26

The following day Miguel lay listening for his grandfather to stir before he rose to begin preparing for their journey. The sun had not yet appeared in the east, and the skies were a mystery of blackness. The stars he had watched long after his father had drifted back to sleep were gone, and he knew there should be a moon, but that was also absent.

Soon he heard the old Indian rise in the darkness and walk toward the smoldering campfire to resurrect it for the light. The boy was instantly up and into the trees searching, primarily by feel and intuition, for his horse, Dotty, whom he had been tracking by the sound of her snuffling as she grazed. The Indian knelt, blew on the spent embers, and dropped some grass onto the red coals, which burst into flames. The flickering light from the newborn fire found the boy leading his horse and mule into the open where their gear sat.

"Big storm comin," he heard the Indian say gravely, looking up into the endless darkness and sniffing the heavy air.

The boy followed his gaze but knew that whatever signs were being read lay beyond sight. Juliet came to him and let slip a peculiar whine before taking a seat in the dust and gazing up toward the mountains.

"We better skip breakfast and see if we can find some cover," said the old man. "I know where there's a gold miners shack that orta keep us dry till this storm passes. Get them folks up, and I will saddle their horses for them."

Miguel walked to where the Mexican man and his daughter had made their beds and nudged the man's foot to wake him.

"Mr. Alejandro," the boy called to the sleeping man, then nudged his foot again.

The man stirred and then sat up with uncertainty in his eyes. When he recognized the boy in the dim firelight, he relaxed and put a hand on his daughter's shoulder to wake her.

"Please, just Alejandro," the Mexican man requested. "My name is Alejandro Rodriguez Pena, but to our rescuers, it is simply Alejandro."

"Miguel," the boy responded to the belated introduction, "Miguel will do just fine for me." He had only heard the man's first name but had added the Mr. out of respect for an elder.

The girl sat up in the dim light and looked at the boy standing awkwardly by.

"Could I help you up, Miss Natalie?" he offered. The young Mexican girl took his extended hand to rise and seemed in no hurry to let it go. She stood smiling warmly up into the slightly taller boy's face, and he suddenly felt like his feet were on backward and quickly dropped her hand.

"We are leaving," he said abruptly, "my grandpa says that there's some pretty nasty weather on its way, so if you could help us gather the camp to go, we would appreciate it."

As they all worked to prepare to leave, a cool breeze slid down on them from the foothills above, a harbinger of the storm to come.

Minute by minute, the temperature dropped as the cold air, pushed by unseen forces on high, moved glacier-like toward the desert. Tongues of lightning teased the cloud bottoms and outlined the peaks far above, but their source was distant, and the following sound was little more than a rumble. It was as if an armada of phantom ships were approaching from the sea, warming up their big guns, preparing for the battle. The Strider cabin would feel the attack first, but the exposed travelers were in the most danger.

Miguel and his grandfather placed the reconstructed travois flat on the ground just beyond the injured man's head and used his blanket to drag him up and over the slats. They then secured him with the tethers they had used on the girl. With the Mexican man's help, they raised the front of the long narrow sled and tied it to Leah's sawbuck saddle.

Miguel saddled Dotty, and the old Indian, leading the pack donkey loaded with two large canvas bags containing their supplies, walked to his remaining mule, waiting to be saddled. When the feather bed saddle was secured, they were ready to go.

William was awake and aware and had requested that his rifle be placed on the sled next to him in case they encountered unexpected friends of the two dead bushwhackers. He had them put his saddle behind him to support his head and shoulders so that he could watch the trail behind them as they traveled. His son was happy to have the gun back in his father's capable hands, relieving him of an unwelcome responsibility.

With the old Indian leading the way, a donkey in tow, Mexicans following, and Miguel leading Leah dragging the sled, they struck out. They backtracked down to the relative level of the desert floor and turned south, abandoning the more direct trail that would have taken them on a winding path toward the Strider cabin. This way would lead them to the wagon trail they were seeking.

Sierra Sunrise

After about an hour on the move, the sun in the east crept above the horizon and spread out to meet the advancing storm. It supplied light to guide their way but soon climbed above the clouds, and all became dusky dark again. The wind came in swirling banks, carrying leaves and dust as it found the freedom of the flat sandy desert. They stayed as close as they could to the trees for relief from the sporadic wind, but the going continued to deteriorate as rain joined the tempest.

The miner's shack had been some five miles from the site of their last camp, and by the time they reached it, the storm winds had reached gale force. The rain came down in sheets, and how the old Indian could find his way astonished the rest of the party. They sat their horses like turtles with heads drawn inside their coats. When they stopped at the cabin, they saw tall pines forming a protective shelter over it. Otherwise, the rickety structure would have never survived the onslaught. A shed was attached to the side of the building, large enough to shelter the livestock, and they rode beneath it before dismounting.

William, who was trapped on the sled, face to the sky, had been forced to cover his head with his blanket to keep from drowning in the relentless rain, and he had slipped the rifle beneath his covers down alongside his body to protect it from the weather.

It took all four of them to manage the man on his wet blankets into the old cabin, but once inside, they found it mostly dry, and in no time, they had a fire going in the stick and mud fireplace. Since everything they wore or carried was soaked through, they decided to hang the wet blankets around the fire to dry first, as there was no doubt that they would at least spend the night here.

Miguel and his grandfather tended to the animals and brought the leather tack inside to drip in the corners of the one-room dwelling. With each passing hour, the storm raged harder and louder, and the occupants prayed a humble prayer that the roof stay on at least till morning. They all sat with their faces toward the hearth, cheeks and foreheads rosy reflections in the dark. They listened to the old logs surrounding them creak and groan under the pressure of the wind, and occasionally, the rain came down so hard and battered the low roof so violently that new spiles of water were formed in the ceiling, and seats had to be moved to avoid them.

This defined the travelers' experience through the night, and someone wondered out loud what would have become of them without the cover of this humble shelter. They were trapped inside by the storm for a night and a day and another night before they dared to venture out to watch the remaining clouds dissolve with the coming sun.

Miguel hoped his mother, brother, and sister had fared as well as they, and now he had a new apprehension about arriving home after leaving them alone for so long.

CHAPTER 27

The nurse, who had sat up all night with Maria, followed her into the children's bedroom and sat on the young girl's vacant bed while the mother rested the boy's head in her lap.

Raphael's glassy eyes were open, but he seemed unaware of the women's presence. He muttered and jerked spasmodically as if random and incoherent thoughts flashed through his damaged mind, calling his body into involuntary action.

"Gabby?" he whimpered, searching the room with urgent eyes, "Gabby, come back here!"

Maria looked worriedly to the Nurse, who stood and took up Raphe's hand. Leaning forward, she stared into the boy's eyes.

"It's the disease," muttered the Mexican woman, deep in thought. "First, the fever and choking, and next, hallucinations. Soon he will no longer be the son you know. It's the madness that will cause pain for him and us. We must prepare ourselves for what is to come."

Maria sat holding her small son, listening to the awful sentence of pain and death for which she was responsible.

"I should have destroyed the cow immediately," she muttered. "How easy it would have been to prevent this whole thing from happening. I have no right being a mother; I was supposed to die with my family in Mexico; Now I have traded his death for mine." Desperate, hopeless tears flooded down her cheeks.

Margarita recognized in her new friend, an inconsolable mother, rendering words useless. Best to leave her to her grief; besides, a plan was agreed upon to cut this misery short, a strategy she now felt compelled to carry out. She let go of the boy's hand, turned quickly, and walked from the room.

Sometime later, Maria joined her in the kitchen, but neither spoke, and they each had reasons for avoiding eye contact. The nurse didn't want to reveal the resolution she had just made and the boy's mother because she was afraid her eyes might betray an involuntary request for the thing they had spoken of last evening. She finally wandered distracted to the door and stepped out into the warm sunshine. Standing there in her misery, she heard a call from the kitchen.

"Maria, where is Gabriella?"

"She is still in my bed," the girl's mother answered.

"No, she isn't," came the immediate reply.

Quickly back inside and down the hallway, the woman looked into her bedroom and then on to the children's room, where Raphael lay alone. She had put the sleeping girl into her bed late last night but hadn't even thought of her this morning.

The two women had a thorough look inside the house, each searching rooms already searched, in a desperate need to find the child. After exhausting all reasonable hope that the girl was inside, they both emerged into the bright sunshine, still hoping to resolve the question quickly, but slowly pulses rose, and breaths came faster.

"Gabriella!" they both called as Maria went around the house and the nurse to the barn. In minutes they met back at the chicken coop, and in full panic, turned to yell in every direction for the child.

"If she has gone into the woods," said Maria, "those infected animals there could tear her to pieces. I will get the gun and search the pastures; you should stay in the house with Raphe in case she returns."

"Yes," the nurse agreed. They both hurried back to the cabin and were shocked to see that in their haste, they had left the door wide open, breaking a hard and fast rule they had made the day they killed the coyote.

The girl's mother headed toward the mirror pool behind the house with the shotgun in hand. She walked beneath the towering escarpment overlooking the plateau where the children often played.

Margarita knew that an unbearable situation had become impossibly worse. She had been aware for some time that the imminent death of the small boy was destroying her friend but feared the loss of both children would drive her entirely out of her mind. With a nurse's cold logic, she knew she should be out with Maria looking for the girl, for she felt that the distraction of Raphael had become unaffordable.

It was almost an hour before the woman returned from searching the plateau with no sign of the girl.

"We should both be out looking for Gabby!" the nurse told the now frantic mother as she entered the kitchen.

Maria considered the proposition but quickly dismissed it, feeling like she was being asked to choose one child above the other.

"As long as Raphe is alive, we can't abandon him," she answered. "I will go below the bluffs," she continued, not daring to say what she thought she might find there.

"As you wish," said the Mexican nurse, and she watched the mother hurry toward the lane, then solemnly to herself, "We must each do what we must do."

Maria walked as quickly as she could out of the gate to the lane gripping the shotgun fiercely at the ready. She followed along the wagon track, down and around the homestead plateau, looking for a sign that her daughter had come this way. She stopped to call her name and to listen, only to hurry on. What must her state of mind be that caused her to run away? Perhaps, she'd gone looking for her father and brother? Could she have witnessed last night's exchange between her and the nurse? It was impossible to say, and she realized that her mind was playing distracting games with her, trying to keep her from imagining the sight of her young daughter's frail body, torn and bleeding.

The road was steep and rocky, being no more than a game trail when William had discovered it, an accident of nature just like the shelf of land itself. It provided accessibility, without which the homestead could not have been possible. She thought of the many trees they had removed to widen the trail used to build the cabin and barn, preserving the giant pines and oaks that stood watch over those same buildings above. Maria thought of the wagon loads of supplies and building materials that she and her husband had hauled up this path, all of these things more idle mind tricks.

The trail reached the bottom, where the sloping ground joined back up with the mountain and then reversed course to skirt back around the belly of the slide. This section of the road could be seen from the bluffs above. Maria knew that soon she would pass by the carcass of the pet cow responsible for this dilemma. She stopped calling out and stepped cautiously, anticipating the scene that might include her young daughter lying among the strewn boulders.

As the carnage came into view, she saw several small creatures slink into the trees. Knowing that the carcass was no longer a source of the disease, she stepped off the wagon road to look among the enormous stones wedged between the tall pines. The small body of her Gabriella could be in any one of a hundred nooks created by the fallen rocks.

High up in the limbs of an ancient dead oak, vultures sat preening and arguing, waiting for another turn at what remained of the body of poor Mary Magdalene.

When her search revealed only fragments of the now disassembled milk cow scattered by the competing scavengers, she breathed a sigh of relief and turned to return to the top.

The Mexican nurse waited until she saw Maria go out of sight before going to her bedroom to retrieve the tool she needed for her task. It was a four-inch-long stiff metal hat pin, one of several that she used when wearing the straw sun hat she had brought on her arduous journey from San Francisco. She selected the one with the most delicate point, took it into the kitchen, and ladled water into the wash basin. Next, she ceremoniously cleaned her hands and the tool, dried all on a linen towel, then wrapped the pin in the cloth and walked softly to the boy's bedroom.

Raphael was still unresponsive and gave no resistance as the nurse rolled him over to his stomach, exposing the back of his head and neck, which were the focus of her intent. Minor spasms stiffened his body as the new position caused his breathing to become more distressed.

"Momma?" the boy mewed weakly in response to the handling.

The simple word pierced the Mexican woman's heart unexpectedly, as this utterance had never before been directed toward her. She had always wanted children and tried to have them, but it was not meant to be. Now, at this moment, she couldn't resist indulging in the maternal fantasy.

"Yes, baby?" she stammered, eyes brimming.

She waited, but no response was forthcoming. Not wanting the moment to end, she supplied the sought-after answer.

"I love you, Mommy," she choked through the tears.

"I love you too, darling," she answered herself.

The nurse, ignoring the tears, unrolled the towel exposing the instrument of death, then held it in her right hand. With the fingers of her left hand, she located the small indention at the base of the boy's skull. She placed the pin's point at an angle, just above her finger, then paused.

"Mommy's taking you home, sweetie," she sobbed. "Don't fear, for it will all be over in a moment."

As she steeled herself to thrust inward and upward with the killing tool, a blood-chilling squall like that of a doomed raccoon caught on the ground by the hounds echoed off the walls of the small bedroom, and something from beneath the boy's bed wrapped itself around the woman's ankle and seized on it with tooth and nail.

Margarita screamed the desperate scream of one condemned to death, then, with effort, she jerked her leg free and flew out of the bedroom, down the hallway, through the kitchen, and outside onto the porch, where she collided with Maria.

The desperation in the nurse's cry had hit the mother in the chest like a hammer as she approached the steps, and she froze until she was staggered back by the woman's rush to flee her attacker in the boy's bedroom.

The breathless nurse clung desperately to Maria, saving them both from falling to the ground.

"Thank God you're here! There is an animal beneath Raphael's bed, and it bit my leg!" the woman gasped at her startled host, then looked down at her scratched and bleeding leg.

The boy's mother led the way back into the house, still carrying the gun at the ready. They cautiously stalked through the kitchen, down the hallway, and into the children's bedroom, hoping to kill the beast before it harmed the boy.

The big gun led the way into the room, and the women knelt to peer under the beds, only to see Gabriella's blank face staring defiantly back at them like an animal in a cage.

CHAPTER 28

It was a stiff and tired group who woke after two days and two nights huddled in the leaky, musty confines of the prospector's cabin. On the good side, they were all still alive and relatively dry, thanks to whoever had constructed the rickety dwelling wedged between the ancient pines. A modest breakfast was assembled by the young Mexican girl and the old renegade Indian man enjoying the rarely experienced companionship of so many people.

Miguel shouldered open every available portal in the cabin walls to welcome the morning breeze and cleansing sunshine that raised everyone's spirits.

Juliet was thankful to be outdoors, away from the stifling odor of humans, which had multiplied in the confined space of the small cabin. She busied herself by scouting the country around their location.

William had endured the most discomfort since the stiff leather cast had to be carefully removed and dried by the fire. The necessity of removing the brace also presented an opportunity to clean and re-dress the jagged wound that had bruised purple and black from kneecap to hip. The first thing the old Indian did was to put his nose close and sniff up and down the leg looking for putrefaction. Finding none, he cleaned the entire leg and applied new sulfur powder and bandage while the onlookers grimaced and groaned for the boy's stoic father. Next, a soft blanket was carefully wrapped around the injured leg before reapplying the brace, something that afforded just a bit more comfort to the man and gave the others a feeling of relief to no longer be forced to see the damaged limb. The old man said it would take the large bone many weeks to heal enough to bear any weight, even with crutches. Although William slept a considerable amount of the time, he had listened carefully to the tales their two Mexican guests told, prompted by questions from his son and father.

Alejandro spoke of the war and the extinction of his childhood family. Even Natalie learned things that she had never been told before about her long-dead relatives. He recounted the events that led to their departure from Mexico and the trials they endured along the way. There was no mention of, and no questions about, the details of the last few days before their rescue as he told of his wife's sister and her husband in San Francisco, who had offered them sanctuary if they ever chose to leave Mexico. William speculated that it must have been they who initiated the search that resulted in the rescue. Several times the Mexican man expressed gratitude for his and his daughter's lives.

Miguel was astonished to hear a man speak so openly about such a wide range of topics, including his thoughts and feelings about family, home, and country. It made him look at his father, who was reluctant even to comment on the weather, much less reveal a personal detail about his family or give up a revealing opinion. Somehow the man speaking so freely made it seem that he was offering these things up for approval or disapproval. Two things he knew that his father would never ask for, nor accept from anyone, with perhaps the exception of Mrs. Strider.

Natalie recounted tales of her life in Mexico and described her mother and brother, who now lay dead in the desert. She gave her impressions of life in the United States, formed from years of stories of the relative richness and prosperity enjoyed by all who lived there. Miguel was most interested in her third-hand but flowery descriptions of great U.S. cities like New York and San Francisco and depictions of the vast plains and the towering mountains like their own Sierra and the Rocky's, of railroads and steamships and the unending oceans that covered the world. All of these things were familiar from his mother's teachings, but even she admitted never having seen any of these wonders firsthand. Of course, the Mexican girl was describing these things from impressions formed by listening to the often-repeated, fantastic tales told by people who desperately needed to believe that this mythical country existed somewhere in an often too-cruel world.

Miguel was awestruck to listen to his grandfather's account of his father having been plucked from his people's canyon to cross the vast sea on a ship with engines larger than a locomotive to fight in a war that involved the entire world. It was troubling to hear how the old man's family was forced from their home in the canyon only to die tragically in Mexico.

It was disheartening for the wide-eyed young girl to hear how her hosts lived in such isolation and without their share of the wealth that all Americans were assumed to be privileged to. More disturbing still was the history of abuse and lack of consideration by the U.S. government for the indigenous people of North America, recounted by the old man and affirmed by his son.

William advised their new Mexican friends and his son by saying, "The biggest places, with the most people, can be the most difficult to survive in, so don't discount too easily the comfort of the hearth and home that you know."

As the mood became more somber, the Mexican man turned to the old Indian and asked him if he had any advice for two people entering this country where white men rule. The graying, year-worn old man sat somberly looking into the coals of the diminishing fire, then, without emotion, spoke of his people's history.

"My grandfather told me the old stories his grandfather told him; about the great ancient nations of our people, whose numbers were more than the stars in the sky. He told about the first foreigners who came to this country, how they arrived in ships so large that the people thought they were floating islands, and how they brought magic weapons that shot fire, of animals on which men could ride. More came and brought iron tools that they used to cut down the trees for making lodges of wood, and still more with iron that cut the earth and rolled the grass under. About how his people looked upon them with wonder, like greedy children craving these new things, and how jealousy made them fight one against another to be the friends of these invaders. How finally the Great Spirit could abide the foolishness and shame no longer and sent terrible sickness and death to punish them, how they fell dead as do the leaves in winter. By the time our people knew the evil these foreigners had brought among us, they had become too many and we too few. Even as we fought them, we became strangers in our own land. Now, we are like the visitors who have stayed too long, a problem that the government must solve, and their solution is to turn us into white men or kill us in the trying. These are the things that I know, and you will soon see that you have not come to a welcoming country, for you too will have to live in the shadows and on unwanted ground, for in this wide land, there is no longer room for people like us."

This speech was delivered not as a plea for sympathy or an accusation but simply as a statement of facts, acknowledging his own people's failures and complicity in destroying their nations.

"The strong will last while the weak fade away," he said in closing. "All of our treaties were made after defeats at the hands of the invaders, hoping that pity would soften their hearts toward us, for we had wasted the time of our power over them in lusting after their shiny metal toys."

The solemn group spent their last night in the cabin listening to the wind that could have been the lamenting of the Great Spirit of the sky, whose journey had been interrupted by the old man's story.

The following morning, after breakfast, everyone collected their gear and left the confines of the cabin to resume their journey. The horses, mules, and donkey, which had been released from the shed, were happy to be free to graze and move about freely and were now reluctant to give up the green grass and freedom to resume the trek up the mountains.

The mud was still deep, and rivulets of water rushed down from the higher ground to remind them of how fortunate they had been to find the sanctuary of the small cabin. By late morning, the sky was clean and blue again, and as the sun melted the lingering fog, they turned upland. The runoff from the rain turned the wagon ruts into tiny streams and made going difficult for the sled. It glided smoothly on level wet ground, but the ditches were deep and torturous to the wounded man.

Natalie rode her horse side by side with Dotty and kept up a one-sided conversation with the young Indian boy. On the rare occasions when she paused to listen, he was more often than not too startled to speak. She entertained him with daydreams about where she might go and things she might do now that she was in this country. After a few hours of this, Miguel felt a new appreciation of his father's aversion to speech, both in himself and in others. Although he liked the girl, her idle prattle made him long for the extended stretches of silence that had accompanied his time traveling with his father and grandfather. For his part in the conversation, he was sure that the less he said, the higher this young girl's opinion of him would be, especially since he didn't understand half of the things she said.

As they rose from the depths of the desert basin, the air grew fresher, and the canyons and creeks, flush with new water coursing unrestrained, reminded the boy of their destination and his home and the family waiting for them there. Despite the drone of the girl's voice, he called up a picture of his young brother's face, who would need to hear every little detail of their journey, and his tiny sister, who would feign disinterest but sit wide-eyed as she eavesdropped on the telling. He had been guilty of giving them both a hard time, but the truth was that they were his best friends, and he was theirs, as up to now, none of them had gotten to know anyone outside the family.

They occasionally stopped to let William rest from his bouncy sled ride, which required a particular vigilance and tension on his part to protect his injured leg from the inevitable jolts and jostling caused by the uneven trail. He endured the ordeal without complaint, but it was evident by his strained expression and beads of perspiration on his face that he was in constant pain.

It would take them another day to reach the Army outpost and then at least two more before they would be home. They hadn't spoken about it, but they all assumed that the Mexicans would make arrangements at Three Forks Station for their continued trip to San Francisco.

For Miguel, the prospect of being home and the successful conclusion of his first true adventure would be more of a relief than he could have ever imagined. It felt like months had passed since he and his father had ridden into the woods, leaving his mother on the cabin's steps. Meeting his grandfather had given him a feeling of connection to a world outside the small orbit of bluffs, trees, and mountain streams that had satisfied his young boy's expectations—but knowing of a great canyon someplace where his father had grown to be a man, among a tribe of people who had existed for hundreds of years, instilled in him the need to explore and want to know his roots and ties to the past. The words Indian, Mexican, and white up to now had had abstract meanings, like up and down and sideways, but he realized that at this point, they had developed definite meanings. He was determined to one day understand the mystery behind the things that his grandfather had spoken of in the prospector's cabin.

After they made camp that night deep in the foothills of the Sierras, and as the old man and young girl prepared their food, the boy went to sit next to his father and waited for an invitation to speak. The man recognized the signs of a question coming on, and he settled himself to the task with a look of attention.

"Poppa, do you hate the white people?" the boy asked cautiously.

William searched his young son's face for clues as to where this conversation might be going. All he found was a look of confusion in the innocent eyes of a child with no experience in this big cold world outside the protective warmth of his family. He felt a dread come over him for the boy's sake, not because he was an Indian in a white world but because he was a boy in a man's world. He knew how difficult it was to enter the company of men, and he also knew that it would be a mistake to try to spare him the wounds that were sure to come.

"When I left my family in the canyon," William said, "I was young and afraid, but I learned that all whites are not bad, and all Indians are not good. I have been harmed by both and helped by both, but mostly I have found that people mind their own business and don't care one way or another about you. Your grandfather has had more than one man's share of hurt done to him, and he is angry at what our people have become. But he blames our people as much as he blames whites for that. So, to answer your question, no, I don't hate the whites. I wouldn't give anyone that much control over me."

Miguel walked away, well satisfied with his father's answer and less concerned by his grandfather's story of their history.

CHAPTER 29

"Gabriella, honey, what are you doing under there?" questioned Maria as she pushed the gun aside to reach beneath the boy's bed to retrieve the small girl.

Her daughter allowed herself to be extracted from the dark cave that she had chosen as her post for protecting her helpless twin brother. When she was fully out, she wrapped her arms around her mother's neck and legs around her waist and rested her tiny chin on her shoulder. Her cold blue eyes sought the face of the Mexican nurse and transfixed the would-be assassin with an icy stare that struck the woman like a stone knife. Margarita found herself unable to hold the child's gaze for more than a moment because of a feeling she had experienced as a girl when reaching into a hen's nest for eggs. She had wrapped her fingers around the cold bony body of a snake; fear had gripped her heart in the same way that the small girl's stare now was. She turned away but could still feel the snake crawling up her spine and coiling about her throat. She only found relief when she was entirely out of the room.

Gabby didn't speak the rest of that day but seemed to sense that the immediate danger for her brother was over. It was as if her actions that day had happened in a trance, for by the next morning, she was acting her old self again.

The Mexican nurse kept a wary eye on the young girl, though, as if at any moment she expected the snake to reappear, and each time she touched the child, she had to suppress an icy shiver. For her, the plan to assist the boy into the next life no longer existed, and she told Maria so and offered no explanation. Maria suspected a story behind the encounter between the nurse and Gabby, but she didn't seek it out.

Raphael's fever spiked again, and he was wracked by coughing fits, during which green phlegm was expelled. Margarita said that it was unusual for the fever to persist this long, but no two cases were ever exactly alike.

Maria took to locking the outside doors with a slide bar too high for Gabriella to reach, just in case the girl decided to disappear again. Next time they would only have to look for her indoors at least.

The two women returned to the old routine, where one stayed with Raphael while the other took care of things outside. Whenever the nurse was in the room with the boy, Gabby stood outside, hidden behind the door jam, peering in, exposing only one eye at a time, depending on which side of the door she stood. There was no malice in the look, but the particular way the girl stood, half hidden, unnerved the Mexican woman.

On the second day following the small girl's disappearance, the boy became desperate, unable to get enough air into his lungs to sustain himself. Maria was beside herself, and Gabby refused to leave the boy's room, even to eat or go to the bathroom. The small girl sat with arms wrapped around herself, rocking slowly back and forth while staring at her brother. The nurse called Maria into the kitchen and told her that she was concerned about the girl's health, as she refused food or water and became violent when they tried to remove her to another part of the cabin.

"I have seen family members die of grief," she told the mother, "and

I've heard of cases where twins died within minutes of each other, with one perfectly healthy before the other succumbed to illness. I am trying to prepare you for the possibility that you could lose both of your children, and I don't know how to stop it."

"If my babies die," stated Maria calmly, "then they will find the remains of my body beneath the bluffs, for I have sworn never to let another family member make the journey to heaven alone." She strode slowly back into the bedroom to sit, to resume a vigil she had begun so long ago with her loved ones in Mexico.

CHAPTER 30

As they wound their way between stony bluffs and through high mountain passes, ever upward, the air thinned, and the temperature dropped. The atmosphere wavered between springlike sunshine and random chilly episodes of shade, reminding the searchers of the waning winter they had left above a short while ago. Forgotten were the sunbaked days and chilled nights that marked their time crossing the life-leaching sand and dry scrub of the desert below. The brilliant sun played hide and seek with them as they entered the halo of ever-present clouds formed where the pool of hot, dry air, languishing in the bowl of the Mojave basin, rose to touch the moisture-rich coolness of the altitudes above.

The old Indian became distracted and said less and less as they made their way toward the Army post at Three Forks Station, for he was unsure what the reception might be for him there. His last encounter with the U.S. government, before moving into the mountains to be near his only remaining son, was recalled with the copper taste of blood on his tongue from an encounter with three drunken soldier coats. They were escorting a survey team sent by the Bureau of Land Management to assess the mineral deposits on the land surrounding the Grand Canyon, where the Havasu people were confined. The soldiers had been instructed to treat any Indian found roaming the plateaus outside the reservation as trespassers on government land and were to be considered criminals.

These men were unfortunate to encounter this Indian who had already endured more pain than the three of them could deliver, even though they intended to leave him as a bloody example to other would-be renegades. Their casual assault on the lone old man resulted in the release of pent-up retribution uncoiled upon them in a wholly unexpected way. The butt of his rifle used as a club and a sharp skinning knife expertly wielded made quick work of the three fools who had stumbled unwittingly into this fight. The ultimate result of the encounter was a missing ear, a broken nose, a fractured arm, and assorted cuts and bruises, some of which would take considerable time to heal. Had the old man been a little more cautious in the encounter, he could have walked away unscathed, but the satisfaction that he was feeling to have a focus for his repressed rage caused him to throw caution to the wind as he challenged them to do their worst.

He smiled as he rode slowly away from the fight, then winced from the pain of a busted lip. He shook the pocket of his coat and chuckled at the jingle of the handful of copper buttons cut from the uniforms of his fallen foes. He would like to have been there when they woke up to stumble back to camp and explain their battered state and why their pants kept falling to their ankles. Some days are better than others, and this was one of the good ones.

Miguel's anticipation grew, for the road was becoming better defined as other trails joined with the one they followed. The wheels of wagons and hooves of horses and mules deepened and widened what had begun at the desert little more than a rutted path. It led through the foothills and up ravines between mountains that looked like they were holding up the sky. As they trudged ever nearer to the Army post, he wondered what worldly sights awaited them there. He knew that Three Forks was the nearest thing to civilization within a two-week ride of the Strider home, and from its mysterious trading post came all things that he and his brother and sister classified as store-bought. He couldn't have been more excited if they expected to encounter the towers of London or the streets of New York over the next hill. The boy began to lean forward unconsciously in his saddle, causing Dotty to crowd his grandfather's mule continuously.

Occasionally, they met riders going in the opposite direction, most leading pack mules loaded with newly purchased supplies, returning to their winter camps. They saw the curiosity aroused by the makeup of their party in the eyes of the passersby, the old Indian perched stoically upon his homemade saddle, leading the single-file procession of Indians and Mexicans, young and old, on horse and mule, with a travois dragged behind, carrying an injured man. No questions were asked, and no explanations were given as most in these mountains understood the value of minding one's own business.

The never-ending chatter of the young Mexican girl that had accompanied the small troop all day like a comforting melody that echoed off canyon walls and drifted away among the towering pines became hushed and then silent as the misty isolation of the mountains closed in around them. It was as if they were entering a land apart from the world below, and they all felt the lonely separation as the day waned, and shadows crept from behind rocks and trees to watch them pass slowly by. The commotion of birds and squirrels ceased, leaving the woods silent save for the rustling of leaves stirred by cooling air sliding down from the mountain.

At dusk, they camped near a small aspen grove out of sight of the trail. They had pushed hard all day, anxious to reach the Army fort where they hoped to find a doctor to look at the injured man's leg. William had grown silent in his pain, refused food offers, and only took small sips of water. The old Indian and boy carefully lifted the travois from Leah's back and placed it on the ground in preparation to tend to the wounded leg. They had only briefly stopped through the day and then only to water the animals as they passed near streams still fat from storm runoff. Miguel was the first to notice something wrong with his father when he didn't respond when asked how he felt. The boy quickly loosened the blanket wrapped tightly around the man and was immediately aware of the wave of heat radiating from him.

"Grandpa!" called the boy urgently.

The old Indian had just set the hobble on the mule and turned quickly to his son and grandson. Miguel stood holding a corner of the blanket, looking at his father with alarm.

After a glance at the wounded man, the Indian said to his grandson, "Get us a fire going and boil some water." The old man slipped his coat and let it fall to the ground behind him. He placed his weathered hand on his son's feverish brow, then pulled it back as if it were burned.

"I should have watched him closer," he said aloud. "I knew he wouldn't make a peep to let us know he was hurtin. Now he's got his self in some real trouble."

As Miguel started the fire and arranged stones for the pot of water to boil, the Mexican man and his daughter came to offer their help.

Alejandro and the Indian unwrapped the blanket from the man and carefully loosened the straps holding the leather splint in place. One look at the leg in the orange glow of the firelight let everyone know how bad the man's condition was. It was a deep dark purple from hip to heel, and the look on the old man's ordinarily stoic face as he closely inspected his son's leg betrayed a dire diagnosis without a word being spoken.

"I need me a clean blanket," said the old Indian, turning to the Mexican man.

The girl and her father started immediately toward the pack mules, and Miguel looked searchingly up into the old man's face. Instead of finding the solace he was seeking, he was met with the stony countenance of the old warrior, steeling himself to deal with yet another tragedy in a life defined by a succession of tragedies. The boy was tempted to ask the useless question but knew it would only betray him to be the frightened child he was, worried about his sick poppa. He had lately determined to be the man he knew his father and grandfather expected him to be, worthy of joining the clan of men he knew they belonged to. He started to turn back to the fire but noticed Juliet out of the corner of his eye, trotting into the clearing and coming to sit at the foot of the travois, staring down at her master. A short mournful whine escaped from the big hound as she sniffed the injured leg, for even she recognized the seriousness of the situation.

When the Mexicans returned with a blanket, soap, and a box of sulfur powder they knew would be needed, Natalie knelt, facing Miguel. Alejandro stood by the Indian ready to help tend the man's wounds.

"I'm sorry," whispered Natalie in the distracted boy's ear. Surprised, he turned to peer into the young Mexican girl's dark eyes, reflecting the light from the dancing flames.

"There is no need to be sorry," stated the boy.

"But if you hadn't come looking for us, none of this would have happened," she murmured, dropping her eyes.

"Listen," said Miguel, echoing the girl's soft tone. "The blame for my poppa's leg goes to those two men we buried back in the desert, and for whatever their reason, they paid for it with their lives. I'm glad we came to find you, and if he could, I know that my father would tell you the same."

After the ruined leg was washed from top to bottom with warm soapy water, the old man carefully dried and sprinkled fresh sulfur powder into the wound. With everyone's help, they wrapped it with the clean blanket but did not reapply the leather splint; instead, the Indian whittled short flat slats from green aspen limbs and bound the man's thigh.

"The air will do him some good," the old man explained. "I'm afraid the leg hasn't been getting enough blood."

They spent the night at the camp, and the Indian cooked extra food so they wouldn't have to stop on the last stretch of road to the Army fort, for the man desperately needed medicine to control his fever.

Miguel got no sleep that night for worry over his father, who became delirious and spoke disjointed words in his childhood language. The following day the boy asked his grandfather what the words had meant, and the old man just said, "He talked some to your momma, and I heard him say your brother's name, but he was just out of his head."

They broke camp before the sun was even a faint glow on the eastern horizon, determined to reach the fort before the day was done. The old man set a much faster pace than the day before, and when questioned about the possibility of further injuring the man's leg, he simply responded, "If we don't get there soon, then his leg won't matter much."

Though the jostling was severe when they crossed rough patches in the road, William remained unconscious, and the old Indian drove them onward. Sometime in the early evening, their destination came into view. The soldier fort was maybe a mile away when they topped a rise to look down on it. Miguel's first reaction was disappointment, for there was no great wall or even an intimidating gate; the fact was that it looked more like a sprawling collection of shabby cabins with little if any organization other than two rows of barracks separated by a muddy street. The only thing that looked remotely like an army post was a half-moon arrangement of sawn board structures circling a flagpole with an American flag flying atop it.

"Keep them coming," the boy's grandfather said as he handed the boy the lead rope of the donkey he had in tow. He took one quick look at his son on the travois, then whipped his mule into a run with the loose ends of his reins and sped ahead. Juliet, aroused by the commotion, abandoned her post behind the travois and dashed after the receding mule and its rider with a yelp.

Miguel stood in his stirrups and watched the old Indian race toward the Army post down the hill. He assumed that his grandfather went looking for a doctor to help with his father's leg. Before the rest of the troop had covered half the distance to the settlement, they saw the old man emerge from between the twin barracks and come racing toward them through the post gates. When he arrived, he didn't stop but wheeled around, took the donkey's lead rope, and started back toward the Army station. "A doctor is waiting to see your daddy," said the old man over his shoulder, and they all quickly rode the rest of the distance to the fort.

CHAPTER 31

Sitting alone at the kitchen table in the wee hours of the morning, the Mexican nurse felt like a stranger, an unwilling guest to the slow-moving tragedy that was playing out in this home. She stared blankly at the grid of wavy panes set into the top half of the door leading outside, watching as the first blush of morning light seeped in like smoke through the door's glass panes and began painting the outlines of the room. She watched the hulk of the cook stove materialize from the gloom and could now make out her own hands folded on the smooth oak table before her. She had sat thus since snuffing out the hanging lantern late last night, hoping that the darkness might somehow insulate her from the unrelenting sounds coming from the small boy in the bedroom as he struggled to survive the bouts of strangling. In moments of calm during the night, she had prayed to God to strike her deaf before it should start again; her prayers went unanswered, so she sat alone in the darkness, enduring as the mother had the long lonely night.

The seven-day clock's precision workings whirred at the behest of its tightly wound spring, a precursor to the execution of the device's one function, which was to announce the hours of the day. Maria walked into the room to the rhythm of the bim-bam tones of the strike rods blending five times in rapid succession. The chimes seemed to release the sounds of morning, for the voice of a rooster, muffled by the thick log walls, drifted up from the barnyard below. All hopes that dawn would reveal this ongoing ordeal to be nothing but a bad dream faded.

"How is Raphael?" The nurse asked, realizing the absence of sounds coming from the children's room for the first time.

"He's resting," said Maria exhaustedly as she slowly walked to the sink to rewash her red, chapped hands. The lye soap washing ritual she had adopted since the boy became sick was taking its toll.

"Gabriella?" asked the seated woman apprehensively as the mother turned to dry her hands.

With a weary sigh, Maria stated, "She fell asleep at some point; I'm not sure when. After last night, there are few things that I'm sure about."

The nurse looked up into the haggard woman's face for the meaning of her last comment and said with empathy, "May God grant you peace and rest, my dear."

Maria walked slowly to the table and sat down opposite her guest. She deliberately pushed her hands across the oak boards to clasp her friend's folded ones between her own. Margarita looked searchingly into the woman's eyes, sensing her need to express whatever revelation had come to her in the night.

"Please don't be offended," said the exhausted mother, "but there is a thing that I would like to tell you, and if you have an opinion on it, I would very much like to hear it. I have been thinking about it all night, and even though I know it will sound horrible when said aloud, I feel I must say it or go mad."

The nurse sat in silence, searching Maria's face for a clue, but then, "no," she thought, there is only one subject this could be about.

"Before you say a word," said the nurse, "tell me if this is about God?"

"How did you know?" answered the weary mother.

"Because," said Margarita, "there is only one subject on the mind of anyone facing the loss of a loved one. They begin with faith that God will make everything right. After a certain time, they begin to fear that God might not help, and perhaps the fault is with them. When all hope is exhausted, they blame God, or more; they question whether there is a God."

"Then I won't have to explain when I ask," stated Maria, "where is God in all of this? Long ago, when my family was dying, I asked my father that same question. He said only, 'God loves you,' and then he died. Holding his dead hand in mine, I told him, "No, God surely hates me." But last night, I realized I was wrong; God doesn't hate me or love me because there is no God."

After a moment of indecision about how to respond, the nurse began:

"Maria, my friend, you asked for my opinion, and I gladly give it to you. To begin with, it has always been my firm opinion that no voice on earth can tell you with certainty that there is or is not a God. The words can be spoken, but no satisfactory proof can be given. When we are children, our parents tell us that God exists, and we believe in them, but that is not the same as believing in God. That can only come after we have asked the question of ourselves and answered it to our own satisfaction. As much as I want you to believe, the best I can do for you is bear witness to why I believe. In my younger years, when attending University, it was popular to deny God in favor of science. I adopted that belief for a while, but then I would visit my parents and see the joy and contentment they lived with because of their faith. I became jealous of their happiness and finally asked them how they had reconciled all the arguments against their beliefs. What they told me was so simple that I went away thinking, what fools they were to be so easily duped into believing in this religion that my friends called superstition. It took me a while to understand the advice they had given me, which was this:

'You have but to open your eyes and your heart,' they said.

"I believed that they thought my question was insincere, so I asked again, and they replied:

'First, you must decide that you want to believe, for, without that, your heart will never see what your eyes present to you. Wanting to believe comes when you recognize what you want for yourself in others. If you look at nonbelievers and convince yourself they are content; you will likely stop looking. But when you see believers and recognize their contentment and want that for yourself, you need only to open your eyes and look upon all the things about you, ignore the people, and look for one thing that only God could have created. Ask yourself this question, could all that is on the earth, in the sky, and in nature have been created by some great cosmic accident? Find that one thing that could not exist if it weren't for God, and then put your trust in Him. If there is a God, you must believe that there is a reason for everything, and the reason is good.'"

The nurse stood and held one of Maria's hands as she walked around the table. "Come with me; the children will be fine for a few minutes." She led them to and through the kitchen door. Outside on the porch, they walked hand in hand down the steps and picked their way in the growing morning glow across the yard in the direction of one of the many bluffs that Gabriella had been anxious to show her after her arrival. Shortly, they entered the trees and walked through and onto a shelf of substantial flat stones jutting out into space above a sheer drop into the canyon below. This was a place that Maria had seen before but never in the morning darkness, and she was frightened by the black expanse stretching out before her. The eastern sky across the Mojave began slowly filling with blood-red light as the earth's surface sped toward the waiting sun. The effect was dizzying as the two women stood side by side, arm in arm, watching as the world seemed to create itself from the darkness. As the top edge of the sun appeared on the horizon, the entire world around them was bathed in golden light, its warmth pushing the cool air at them in gentle waves. The green of the mountains and blue of the sky emerged from the blinding light stretching out before them beyond sight.

"This is my proof," said Margarita. "Now, you just need to find your own, and your fears about your son can be put to rest, for you will know that God is watching over him regardless of his fate."

Both women caught their breath at the spectacle presented before them, and the nurse said, "Now repeat the words if you can, that there is no God."

The weary mother was overwhelmed standing in the warm light of creation. Had the sky been filled instead with the light of a thousand angels, she couldn't have believed more in heaven at that moment. The stone of doubt she had felt in her heart was gone, and tears streamed once more from her eyes. The two women held each other and imagined they stood looking at the face of God.

CHAPTER 32

The rest of the group followed closely behind the old Indian and his donkey as they all rode through the gates and between the twin barracks, straight up a rise topped with a crescent-shaped collection of buildings flanking a parade ground. A man in Army pants and a white shirt with sleeves rolled to his elbows emerged from an open door and walked to the edge of the plank porch, which provided a raised walkway connecting the first building to the last. Another man in an Army work uniform followed him and stood by as they both waited for the caravan to arrive. As Miguel rode past, leading the mule with the travois carrying his father up even with the steps, the doctor and soldier stepped down and began untying the straps holding the man to his bed. The boy slid from his saddle, wrapped Dotty's reins around the hitching rail, and walked back to steady the mule while his father was examined.

Miguel looked around distractedly to avoid renewing the image of his father's ruined leg that he was sure would be worse today than last evening. He noticed the sergeant stripes on the soldier's sleeve, and gray hair overrunning his beard and the hair below his cap. He was reluctant to look lower than the man's shoulders as his father lay somewhere below that point. Panning his gaze up instead of down, he saw a painted sign above the open doorway advertising the building they stood in front of to be the 'Post Hospital' and another just lower that warned, 'Wipe your feet.' A wooden bench sat beneath a wide glass window, which he assumed was for overflow patients or maybe just for loitering, as a brass spittoon sat handy at each end. The sky had turned red in the west as the sun settled lower into the evening and raced toward nightfall. A third man, who seemed to be a helper, came through the open doorway carrying a litter made of green canvas and two wooden poles with turned handles and little metal legs that held it up off the deck.

Neither the old Indian nor the Mexicans made a move to dismount as the doctor examined the injured man; they sat patiently in their saddles, not sure enough of their welcome to offer help. After some time, the doctor began giving directions to the soldier and helper as to how to proceed in removing William's body from the sled, and the three of them lifted him using the Army blanket that he lay on, placing him on the litter making him groan at the jostling. As the soldier and the helper carried the man inside, the doctor stepped to Miguel and asked him who he was.

"That's my poppa," the boy answered, nodding toward the stretcher as it disappeared through the door.

"Well, son," said the stocky, rough-looking doctor, "your poppa is in a pretty bad way, and I ain't going to lie to you about the prospect of being able to do too much for him. You leave him here with me tonight but come back tomorrow, you can either carry him on out of here, or we will help you find a place to bury him, whichever is appropriate. Your grandpa told me that your poppa fought in the Great War, and that gets him a look-see and some medicine but no more than that." He turned without ceremony, walked up the steps into the clinic, and closed the door.

The old Indian turned his mule around, walked him back even with the boy, and asked, "Well, what's the verdict?"

Miguel hesitated just a moment as he caught up with the day's events and digested what the doctor had just said.

"You take everybody and find a place to camp for the night, and I will stay here with Poppa. Come back tomorrow, and we will sort it out from there." He handed the mule's reins to his grandpa.

The Indian looked down and studied his grandson's face for a moment, then put his moccasin-clad heels into his mule's flanks and led the procession back the way they had come in. The old man rode on without a glance back, but the young Mexican girl allowed her horse to follow along while she held the boy's gaze until they turned a corner and rode out of sight.

The boy watched the small troop make their way past the barracks and out the gate, then he turned to Dotty and said, "Well, girl, I guess we've kind of made a mess of things on this trip, with your momma being killed and my poppa about to die on us."

He pulled the reins loose from the hitching rail and led the young Appaloosa mare to the end of the row of cabins and around back to where he guessed the rear of the clinic was. He located a small tree strong enough to secure the horse, then removed the halter and replaced it with a braided leather lead rope long enough to let her graze and tied the end to a low branch. Dotty dropped her head and began to eat as he removed the saddle and placed it on the ground out of the tether's reach. He then unstrapped his bedroll from the saddle and carried it and the horse blanket back to the bench at the front of the hospital, where he planned to spend the night.

Miguel hadn't been sitting long before the man in uniform who had helped carry his father inside opened the door and stepped out onto the planks of the walkway. Without looking down, a practiced right hand went into his left shirt pocket and lifted out the makings for a cigarette. He stood appreciating the last warm rays from the sun as it hovered above the horizon far beyond the flagpole, and his hands continued to construct the smoke. The boy watched, fascinated, as the man thumbed out a sheet of rolling paper with his left hand, then dropped the thin rectangular packet back into his pocket. With his thumb and first two fingers, he made a vee shape of the paper and deftly tapped in a quantity of tobacco from the bag with the forefinger of his right hand; he then hung the drawstring on his lip to allow the use of both hands to complete the roll. When it was done, he licked the cigarette from end to end, pulled on the hanging sack to clench the string tight, and placed the tobacco pouch back with the papers. He pulled a sulfur match from his watch pocket and reached down to strike it on the arm of the bench, and that's when he noticed the boy sitting there.

As he touched the match to the smoke, he turned, pointed to the space on the bench, and asked, "Mind if I sit?" Without waiting for an answer, he settled on the bench and took a healthy toke on the cigarette.

"Did I hear you say that's your daddy in there?"

"Yessir," Miguel replied.

"I was here when your grandpa come in lookin for help, bein the doc has the only good place to sit when a man has to stand duty. I heard your daddy's name called, so I stuck around to see if it was really him. I knew him for a time in the war, I might call him a friend if I had known him better, but I heard more about him than I heard from him. I imagine you've already heard tell all the war stories you can stand about your pa by now?"

"Poppa, don't talk much about things like that," the boy replied. He was filled with questions, but his Indian half held him back until he knew more about this stranger. He wanted to say, heck, I only learned about him being a marine a few days ago, but he just sat looking round-eyed at the big sergeant.

"That don't surprise me much; I only knew him to say maybe ten words all the time we served together. That long gun of his was a talker, though, and when it said somethin, everybody listened. I was in the Army, and your daddy was a Marine. We were both in Virginia when they organized the 6th Marine Regiment and shipped them to France. I could talk a little German, so they lent me to them, and we all rode over there together. I first heard him called the Injun Marine by some boys tryin to make fun of him, but when we got on the ground over there, them same boys was fight'n over who got to go on patrol with him. They said he could shoot the ears off a gnat after a couple of weeks of watching him kill Huns. They said somebody told him we could go home as soon as he killed them all."

Miguel scooted closer to the man, not wanting to miss a word he was saying as he was painting a whole different picture of his father than any he had ever imagined.

"We come up against it at the Belleau Woods, where the Germans had stopped to regroup on their way to Paris, figuring to end the war right quick if they could take it over. The Frenchie's was runnin for the hills and trying to get us to go with them, and I was inclined in that direction myself, but them damn Marines was havin none of it. Some Sargent Major yelled, 'Come on, you sons of bitches, do you want to live forever?' and the fight was on. They sent your daddy to high ground overlooking the Marne River with a box full of ammo and told him not to let one by-God German get across. After the fighting was over and the Germans was retreating, somebody came into headquarters and said that Injun Marine fella was shot all to hell and gone, but nary a German got past him. When they got around to seeing what had happened, they counted a hundred and thirty dead Germans up and down that river, most shot through the head. Your daddy had three great wounds and all manner of little ones where that Battalion of Heine's tried to shoot him off that bluff. Course he lived, and they gave him a silver star medal over it, but it's still settin in some General's desk in Washington because your daddy never went to pick it up. They asked him in the hospital why he shot so many in the head. He said that after a while, them Germans got plumb stubborn about not wanting to stand out in the open. Some with him said that whenever a Hun would stick his head out, your daddy would part his hair for him. They said he clipped more German hair that day than a Berlin barber."

The boy sat speechless, re-evaluating the man he had lived with all his life, realizing just how little he knew about him. For the first time, he considered that his poppa had lived a whole life before bringing him into the world. It made him sad that his father was such a stranger to him.

The sergeant stood up and threw his cigarette butt into the spittoon, and turned to look the boy over, top to bottom. "You look a lot like him twenty years ago," he said. "I wouldn't worry too much if I were you; your daddy's a tough one," He walked down the steps and headed across the parade grounds toward the barracks.

Miguel had no more visitors to interrupt his lonesome vigil that evening, but just before dark, two men in uniform came up from the barracks, lowered the flag, and folded it into a small triangle. One of them tucked it under his arm, and they both ambled back the way they had come. That was the last activity of the evening, so he sat watching the sun as it melted into a pool across the horizon in the growing dusk. A little before dark, the mournful notes of taps being played on a bugle drifted up from below to fill the air and echo eerily between the buildings. It was the first time the young boy had heard the sad tune, and it made his breath catch in his throat as if it were being played to acknowledge the despair he felt in his heart.

It was a long night, for sleep wouldn't come, and he was afraid to wander inside the fort after dark. He had checked on Dotty several times and found a bucket by a horse trough to bring her a drink, but the grass she was eating was wet with dew, so she only sniffed at the water. About daylight, he walked back around, saddled the horse, and brought her to the front to keep him company until the doctor returned. He assumed there must be another way in and out of the hospital as neither the doctor nor the helper had left by the front door. As the sun gained momentum and lifted off the ground in the east, the fort came alive with activity. Two different men in uniform came to raise the flag as a bugler stood nearby and played a more upbeat tune on his horn. All those in sight stopped, came to attention, and saluted until the last note drifted away. Miguel stood tentatively and saluted, mimicking the soldiers' actions, for he had no idea what else to do. As the tones fell silent, everyone else resumed what they had been doing before, so the boy dropped his hand but continued to stand, fearful of disrespecting a ritual that he had no previous knowledge of.

At about eight o'clock, he stood watching soldiers come and go from every direction. The hospital's front door opened, and the doctor stepped out, hunching his shoulders, then bent to each side at the waist, stretching his back the way Miguel had seen his father do after sitting up all night with a sick calf.

"Well, you're here bright and early," said the doctor. "Are you ready to see your poppa?"

"Yessir," said the boy, afraid that he was being asked to view his father's body.

He followed the man through the door and down a hallway into a room with a dozen beds lining the walls, all empty except for one near a window in the back that held his poppa. He was alive but still frail, given the slowness of his reaction. He turned his head when they stepped into the room and followed their progress as they came to stand by his bed. His face still had the pallor of cold ashes around the mouth and eyes, but not nearly so severe as last evening. Unconsciousness had suggested a nearness of death, as the mind has relinquished all control to external forces and can mount no defense against them. The fact that he was alert made all the difference.

"I was hoping someone might come back to claim me," said the man.

"Well, to tell you the truth," said Miguel, "me and Grandpa flipped a coin this morning, and I lost."

The man tried to show his appreciation for the joke with a wan smile, but something outside the window caught his attention, and he turned his face to appraise the sky instead. He only turned back when he felt his son's arms go around his neck. A thing that hadn't happened in so long that he couldn't remember.

After a long pause, the doctor impatiently cleared his throat, and the boy, embarrassed by his impulsive action, transformed into the young man who had prepared himself all night to continue his journey home to care for his mother, brother, and sister. He stepped back and wiped a tear from his cheek.

"I thought sure I'd find you dead this morning," said Miguel, "the way you looked when they carried you in here last night."

"I was right there with you, son," said the doctor, "but we pumped him as full of penicillin as we dared, and low and behold, he comes back to life. We cleaned him up and put him in a proper cast before he woke up, so I think he can probably travel now without making it any worse. That was a big damn hole in his leg, but it was already starting to heal, so it was too late to open it up and clean the inside. I've got a feeling that there was probably all manner of trash dragged in there by the bullet, and that's what's causing the fever. I'm sending you a pack of penicillin pills, and they orta help keep the infection down. After that, if the fever starts up again, all you can do is pray that your body is strong enough to stand it off."

The room fell silent again, and finally, William said, "Thank you, doctor; I know you didn't have to take me in, but I do appreciate it."

"Well, Sergeant Baker spoke highly of what you did in the war, so I guess this is the least the Army can do. I sent Sam to bring you some breakfast, so the two of you just sit here til he gets back. Me and him set up all night, and I'm just running on coffee, so you will excuse me if I don't stay around to chat. Sam will fix you up with the pills; I'd wait five or six weeks before I took that cast off."

The doctor walked out with a slight shuffle, as a man might who isn't used to going without so much sleep. He was met at the door by the helper Miguel took to be Sam with a covered tray. The young man carried the food over and sat it on a small table that he pushed next to William's bed.

"The rest of your folks are all parked out front," said Sam, "and that old Indian is drawing quite a crowd. Sergeant Baker is trying to keep a fight from breaking out, but it might not be bad if somebody went out there to have a look-see."

"Poppa, you eat your breakfast, and I will go handle this," Miguel stated and marched confidently from the room. William watched him go, recognizing the change in his young son.

Outside, the boy found a scene of pandemonium, with Sergeant Baker holding several soldiers at arm's length away from his grandfather's mule. The old Indian sat perched as if he were alone in the middle of the desert, watching the sunset.

"Grandpa," called Miguel from the edge of the wooden platform, "Poppa's ok, and if you leave the mule with the sled here, we will meet you outside the gate in a few minutes."

The old warrior smiled his big toothy smile, tossed Leah's lead rope over to him, then guided his tall mule through the gathering of soldiers and scattered them like a flock of chickens. The Mexicans followed along and seemed relieved to be leaving.

Sam had filled an envelope with the penicillin pills that the doctor had promised and instructed Miguel to give his father one every four hours day and night until they were all gone. He said that if the fever started up again, the infection was returning in his leg, so to crush a couple of pills every two hours and give it to him stirred into water. That way, the medicine would get into his system faster and maybe have a chance to fight it off. He bid them good luck and a safe return home.

With the help of the sergeant and a couple of the other soldiers, William was settled on the travois and strapped in. After speaking to the big sergeant for a few moments, Miguel led the mule slowly down the hill.

CHAPTER 33

The boy had no trouble locating their party outside the gate as they had only traveled about fifty yards beyond the boundary of the Army post and stopped in an open field. They were all still mounted and had maneuvered their animals around to face the direction from which he was coming, expecting a parley to catch them up on the latest developments.

"Well, Mr. Strider, what's the plan?" the old man asked, smiling, as the boy rode up leading the mule.

"Poppa's fine for now," Miguel said. "They filled him up with medicine which brought his fever down. The doctor doesn't know if it will stick, but he gave us enough pills to get him home. He's mighty weak, but we got some soup down him before he went back to sleep, and he doesn't seem to be hurting too bad."

"What about Natalie and myself?" asked Alejandro. The Mexican father was unsure of their position now that they had reached the edge of civilization.

"I talked to the sergeant about your situation before I left this morning; he knew who you were and said that if you wanted, you could stay on at the post and wait for someone going in the direction of San Francisco. The thing is that a Mrs. Ortiz and two troopers came by a while back looking for you or my Pappa, and they steered them on to our place up the mountain. Said the troopers came back by on their way home, saying that the woman had decided to stay with my mother and wait for us all to return."

Alejandro said with trepidation, "That would be my wife's sister; she must have come looking for us."

"Then I guess you have the choice to either come with us and get her or stay and wait for one of us to bring her back to you," Miguel offered.

After a long moment of indecision, the Mexican man said, "We are already in your debt for saving our lives, but I would consider it another great favor if you would allow us to help get your father home where we might meet up with Natalie's aunt."

"Happy to have you along," replied the boy, and he stole a glance at the young Mexican girl who rewarded him with a shy smile. "We might as well get started then," and he clucked to Dotty and raised his reins to start her forward. This time Miguel led the way.

Shortly after they left the valley of the Army post, Natalie urged the assassin's horse that she rode up next to Dotty and resumed the dialogue she had abandoned two days before.

They traveled the sandy road that continued up the mountain but stopped every few hours to allow William to rest, take water and medicine, and ensure the fever hadn't returned. They made camp soon after the evening shadows began sliding down from the peaks above to collect in the ditches and depressions along the trail.

Camping had become a routine for them, so all was settled before darkness fell. The old man cooked while Alejandro and his daughter built up a stock of firewood for the night. William was resting peacefully by the fire after drinking a quantity of thin broth. Miguel had caught him up on events, beginning after they had left the prospector's cabin. He remembered riding the travois that morning under the bright warm sun, but everything else was a mixture of pain and nightmares. He had recognized the sergeant as they prepared to leave the post but was too weak to do more than acknowledge his hello.

After his father was asleep, Miguel sat staring into the fire, drinking a bitter cup of coffee, lost in his thoughts.

"What are you thinkin," asked the old Indian as he tended the pot of stew that he was brewing for their supper.

Thankful for the chance to share some concerns, the boy asked, "Grandpa, what age does a boy figure to become a man?"

"Well, sir," answered the old Indian, "there ain't no age set to a thing like that. Somewhere along the way, every boy runs up against a thing that calls for him to take the reins and start steering his own life. He has two ways to go: beg off or step up. Neither path has a way back to where they started."

"I guess I'll know when my time comes then," said Miguel uncertainly.

"Grandson," said the old man proudly, "that you didn't notice when it happened to you speaks well for your prospects as a man. I'm here to tell you that you're already a mile down the good side of that road."

Miguel slept well that night for the first time in days, as it looked like their fortunes were changing for the better. That and the fact that he had slept not a wink on the hospital bench the night before. His grandfather gladly accepted responsibility for his father's medicine and watching over him.

The following morning William was able to sit on the side of the travois, which they had propped off the ground on rocks the night before. As they all ate breakfast, the mood was lite, and there were jokes all around as the group relived their experiences at the soldier fort over the past two days. It began with Miguel asking his grandfather what he had done to upset the Army soldiers outside the hospital the previous morning.

"I don't know," said the old man. "I think it was just them soldiers being soldiers."

"It might have had something to do with him asking them if they wanted to buy some brass Army buttons," said Natalie. "They wanted to know where he had stolen them, and he just laughed like it was a joke."

The old man just humped his shoulders as if he hadn't a clue.

Two days of traveling and several forks in the road led them through canyons, between mountains, and around great boulders strewn along the trail that had at some time in the past, dislodged from the ledges above. The sight was so common that the Mexican girl asked Miguel if he had ever seen any of these big rocks fall. The boy said that he had not seen them, but you could sometimes hear it happening at night in their cabin.

The going seemed painfully slow as Miguel began to recognize views out across the desert that told him they were closing in on his birthplace. The weather cooled as the altitude increased, and the trail became narrower as the distance from the Army post grew. You could still see the evidence of ruts made by iron-rimmed wagon wheels that had traveled this way not so long ago. He figured they were made by the soldiers he was told about coming and going from his home.

The anticipation grew as they passed places that he had seen before, and when they started up the last incline before the trail leveled out and led to their cabin, he wanted to race ahead, but for the mule's lead rope holding him back, he would have done so.

Miguel called out as they came to the yard gate, but even though the day was bright and warm and he half expected the twins to be out playing, the scene around the cabin and barnyard was as silent as a cemetery.

CHAPTER 34

There should have been chickens squawking and scratching in their pen. There should have been chickadees and sparrows and bluejays fussing in the trees. There should have been a cow lowing in the pasture and squirrels barking at such a rude intrusion as theirs into this isolated world. In short, there should have been the sounds of life celebrating the coming of spring in these mountains. Instead, there was a hush that made the travelers conscious of how intrusive their squeaking leather and clopping hooves and dragging timbers were to the scene. They stopped still outside the yard gate and quieted their breaths, waiting for the spell to break that seemed to be smothering this place. It was like coming late to a funeral and finding oneself alone in a slumbering garden of tombstones. Even the dog recognized something was amiss, and she sat waiting in the lane with the others for some sign of welcome from the homeplace.

Miguel's voice, as he called out, echoed hollowly across the vacant house and barn yards until it was lost among the trees in the silent forest beyond.

Moments passed before the door to the kitchen opened, and a woman stepped out onto the porch. At first, the boy thought it was his mother; strange that the two little ones weren't skipping and hopping at her sides and calling out a welcome home to their father and brother. By now, Raphael should have been scaling the gate to the yard, all the while yelling the news of the home front and demanding answers to questions fired at them of their trip into the desert. Instead, the woman took several lone, unsure steps toward them, then stopped and waited with her hands twisted into the apron that Miguel recognized as his mother's.

Natalie, who rode closest to the gate latch, slipped from the saddle and led her horse to and through the pole gate and into the yard. She stood out of the way, holding the reins with one hand and the gate with the other to allow the procession to ride through.

Miguel urged Dotty forward, leading Rachel, who was still pulling the travois, up to the porch steps to accommodate the unloading of his father. Even though he recognized every board, log, and stone, it felt more like they had arrived unannounced at a stranger's house than having returned to their own home.

As he rode past the strange woman on the porch, he noticed that she was ignoring him and his father in favor of searching the faces of their two Mexican companions bringing up the rear. He felt the moment when she recognized that there were only two instead of the four that she had anticipated seeing. Her family relationship with them was apparent, and the boy twisted in his saddle, trying to glimpse their reaction to seeing her. What he saw in Alejandro's face was reluctant anticipation; he guessed a result of the questions sure to be asked. Natalie was smiling, but he sensed an air of apprehension. The boy was too young to recognize it, but what he saw was the guilt that is sometimes experienced by the survivors of such a tragedy as theirs.

The kitchen door opened again as Miguel reined in Dotty and stepped from his saddle to the ground. He looked up at the doorway to see a woman with unkempt hair and tear-swollen eyes peering out at him from within his mother's haggard face.

"Momma?" the boy muttered in disbelief, for he could not reconcile the image that confronted him. This was undoubtedly his mother but not the same one whose stern, disapproving look had ushered him and his father into the timber as she stood sentinel on the morning of their departure.

As if compelled by irresistible gravity, mother and son met in the middle of the porch and locked in a desperate embrace. She wept tears of relief, dread, and hopelessness all mixed up together. He felt a swell in his chest that ached at the pain he imagined it must have taken to transform his clear-eyed, stone-willed mother into this shattered visage of a woman.

After a few moments, Maria pulled back to arm's length and looked tearfully into her eldest child's face. She touched his cheek to assure herself that this was indeed the same son whose coming she had desperately prayed for. But she recognized that the boy who had ridden away only days before was now returned a different person entirely. The evidence wasn't in a physical change but in the eyes, where she searched for the boyish innocence of old, only to find it missing, replaced by an unmistakable reflection of the disappointing world he had just returned from. Her worst fear was that he would see things that could not be unseen, and they would change him forever.

"Everything's all right, Mother!" Miguel reassured her, "We are home now."

"Yes," said Maria gravely, "you are home now."

The boy could not begin to guess what thoughts were hidden behind his mother's eyes.

With a silent gesture guiding his mother's gaze, Miguel glanced back at the travois. There, his father was making a feeble attempt to free himself from his bindings so that he might welcome himself home to his wife. Seeing this, Maria released her son and stepped haltingly down to her husband's side. She knelt on her knees to offer herself, for better or worse, to the father of her children.

"Oh William!" the woman confessed through tears, "Raphael has rabies, and I am afraid he is dying."

The old Indian sat silently atop his tall mule with an expression of concern at the foreboding he sensed surrounding their peculiar reception. Juliet had quietly found her way to the bed of straw beneath the porch treads and lay peering timidly out from her hidden advantage.

Having heard his mother's words, Miguel turned in stunned disbelief and walked determinedly through the kitchen door, looking for his absent siblings. Seeing no sign of either of the twins in the kitchen, he turned toward the bedrooms, and there standing in the doorway, was Gabriella. If he hadn't recognized the blue cotton dress that his mother had made for her last birthday, he would have assumed that the child belonged to the unknown woman outside. The slip of a girl was gaunt and drawn with dark circles under her sky-blue eyes. At first, she stared at him as if he were an intruder until he whispered in disbelief, "Gabriella?"

The young girl seemed to wake as if from a trance and rushed at her brother with a force that staggered him back as he lifted her to him and felt her tiny arms encircle his neck.

"Oh Willie, you came home!" she sobbed into his ear as she pressed her tear-stained cheek hard into his. Theirs was the desperate embrace of lost children finally made whole with their finding.

"Gabby, where is Raphe?" asked Miguel cautiously.

The girl released one arm, pointed to the bedroom door without looking up, then resumed her grip on his neck and spoke with a tear-choked voice, "He's in there."

Miguel carried his young sister back into the bedroom she had emerged from to find his brother. The room was as dark as night save a flicker of light from a lantern sitting on the chest of drawers against the log wall. A candle would have thrown more light as the neglected globe was soot blackened from the tiny air-starved flame. The boy stood holding the small girl gripped around him with arms and legs as if she might never let go.

He walked with his young sister to the dresser where the lantern sat smoking. He noted the fragile feel and slight weight of her body, more akin to a shock of dried corn stalks, he thought, than a person. He reached around the girl and felt for the knob that turned up the wick on the lamp, and slowly the flicker became a flame. The room took on a buttery glow as light escaped through the darkened glass. Miguel turned back to Raphael's bed and saw the boy lying as still as death beneath one of his mother's favorite quilts.

He carried Gabby to her bed, where he sat opposite his silent brother and whispered to the girl, "Has he been like this long?"

"Just a few days, I guess?" the girl choked, looking up to stare into the eyes of the brother whose existence she had begun to think she might have imagined.

"Tell me what happened then," the boy implored.

"It was Mary Magdalene that gave him the rabies," she managed, "and it was wolves that gave it to her."

Miguel extricated himself from his sister's grasp, sat her on her bed, and then moved to sit next to his brother. He laid his hand on Raphael's forehead, felt the heat of his fever, and heard the deep rattle of his breath. The pallid complexion and lifeless face of the boy lying next to him bore little resemblance to his last memory of his brother. He looked back upon his small sister and was alarmed to see the same shadows there that were apparent on his brother's. Tears filled his eyes and streamed down his face as the horrifying reality that his mother had spoken of was confirmed. Not only was Raphael dying, but he saw that his baby sister's life was in real jeopardy as well.

The boy muttered to himself, "How can so many things go so wrong in so short a time?" When he and his father had departed, all the world seemed bright, but they had returned home to find only darkness.

CHAPTER 35

After wiping his tears and steadying his breath, Miguel stood and reached for his sister's hand, "Come on, and we will go outside and see Poppa," he said, but the girl quickly pulled back and shook her head no. Having welcomed her older brother home, she was ready to resume her solitary vigil watching over her dying twin.

Miguel understood his sister's reluctance to leave, and he brushed her cheek before walking down the hallway into the kitchen. Just before stepping through the door outside to help his father into the house, an old habit was unconsciously triggered, and he looked up to where the big shotgun forever hung on wooden pegs above the door. The empty pegs he saw now had ever meant only one thing: something was about to lose its life for committing a trespass against the homeplace.

Through the wavy glass of the partially closed door, he could see the distorted image of his mother, shotgun held to aim, leaning forward against the big gun's impending recoil, only moments from firing.

Thoughts faster than light flickered through the boy's mind; what or who could his mother be preparing to shoot? Was it some rabid animal that had wandered up? A picture flashed of the people waiting outside; she had just embraced his father; the Mexicans were unknown to her before today, then the smiling face of the old Indian came to mind. The pieces slipped into place, his father's failure to tell his mother about visiting the old man, the thirteen years he had lived without meeting his grandfather, and the warning to him by his father not to reveal their encounter. The focus of his mother's aim became all too clear.

In a panic, he jerked open the door, stepped out onto the planks, and yelled, "Grandfather!" but the world exploded at that moment. A blinding cloud of rolling white smoke filled the air, and he knew that both barrels of the mighty gun had been unleashed. Like thunder, the blast echoed between mountains until it was lost in the canyons below.

The scene the boy had missed while he searched for his absent brother and sister was his mother rising from the ground when she realized that he had entered the house. As she stood gazing after him, her apprehension grew, anticipating his reaction to seeing Gabriella's pitiful condition, the result of a child unable to cope with her twin brother's pending death. Miguel had forever been the protector and hero to his two much younger siblings, who had from birth been his only friends and he theirs. She knew that her son's only reservation about going on this accursed hunt with her husband had been his concern for the loneliness that he and they might feel in his absence. Now he would see that she had failed to keep her promise to hold the little ones safe while he was away, and his disappointment was dreaded even more than her husband's.

Shortly after Miguel had entered the house, the old Indian had urged his mule up to the travois. Maria turned at the sound and was transported back to her youth when a wagon had pulled noisily up to her father's house in Mexico. She and her sister played in the yard when this same man drove that wagon up to their gate. She could still see her father smiling, welcoming the strangers bringing death to her village.

Uncontrollable rage gripped her as she recognized the face of the man that she held responsible for the death of her father, mother, sister, and brother. How could this be? she was stunned and confused. She looked again at William; seeing the two men so close together caused a sickening feeling, for she saw a father and his unmistakable son.

William had followed his wife's gaze and realized his error in not trying to prepare his wife for this meeting. His only excuse was the fever that once again raged within his body, a fog that clouded his judgment.

Maria scanned the faces of all those around her, and recognizing no allies, she turned quickly and marched up the steps and into the kitchen. When she reappeared, she was cradling the gun that hung forever ready above the kitchen door. As she stepped back onto the porch, she leveled the gun at the old man and squeezed the triggers. Nothing happened, and she realized she had forgotten to pull back the gun's hammers in her haste. She calmly lowered it again, still looking with hate at the old Indian who sat patiently waiting; she pulled back the hammers one at a time and raised the gun for a second time. As her fingers tightened on the triggers, a familiar voice behind her called, "Grandfather!" Her son's voice, strained and hoarse with emotion, caused her to hesitate for one crucial moment.

Miguel watched as the air slowly cleared, and sitting atop his feather bed camel saddle sat the old Indian as calm as he had been amid the crowd of angry soldiers at Three Forks Station. How could it be, at this distance, even Gabriella could not have missed the mark? He looked to his mother and saw the gun pointed up to the heavens, explaining why the old man still drew breath. As he had done at the gate to the yard so long ago, Miguel tiredly walked to his mother and lifted the heavy gun from her hands. It was as if the gun was holding the woman, for when he took its weight away, her knees folded, and she sat heavily down.

Maria was stunned that as the moment of reckoning she had envisioned countless times had come and gone, the man she blamed for her family's death in Mexico still lived. He not only lived but seemed casual about the fact that her attempt on his life had only been thwarted by Miguel's sudden shout. Without a doubt, this was the same man who had driven the wagon that delivered the Spanish Flu to her village and doomed them all, save her, to an untimely death. Now, having all the pieces to the puzzle, she knew why William had arrived so unexpectedly at the side of her deathbed all those years ago, the grand lie of omission become all too apparent.

The old Indian felt nothing but disappointment at the woman's failure to execute her obvious intent to end his life. For all practical purposes, a life that had ended in Mexico all those years ago. He had thought that his decision to abandon the land of his ancestors would be his ultimate sacrifice, and in a way, it had been. While he had an enemy to fight, he fought, but when that enemy no longer seemed even to notice that he was alive, he saw the hopelessness of the struggle. He knew that his son's wife blamed him for her family's deaths because William had told him so, but the reality was that none in his family were ill the day they arrived in her town. Only after his wife was recruited as a healer by Maria's father to tend to a sick child did the disease begin striking his loved ones. When his wife became ill, he attempted to escape with his family into the country, but they carried the sickness with them by then. Strangers In a far-off land, he and his children placed a wife and mother into her grave; then, one by one, he laid his children in the cold earth near their mother. When the last of them was buried, he abandoned all but the mules and rode slowly back to his home in the canyon. Only after a long period of mourning and remorse did he go looking for his one remaining son.

By the time William learned the fate of his family, he and Maria were man and wife. His father had come to him alone on the mountain and recounted to him the tragedy in Mexico, and in doing so, he mentioned the name of the village near where his mother, brothers, and sister were buried. After hearing this, William realized his wife's connection to his father and family, and he reluctantly revealed to his father her belief that they had brought the sickness to her village.

William argued for setting the record straight, but his father had replied, "With no one for her to blame for their deaths, sooner or later, she will begin to blame herself." And so, in the end, William had agreed to let the lie stand; after all, who would know better than this old man the consequence of losing a family?

CHAPTER 36

Miguel leaned the now harmless gun against the wall of the house, and Margarita rushed to the side of his mother, and after helping her up, guided her to the kitchen door. The boy's expression was a study of troubled thoughts as he looked around at the startled faces of his companions. Having no explanation for his mother's actions, he walked to the travois and began loosening the straps that held his father. With the help of his grandfather and Alejandro and Natalie, they lifted the man on his blanket, carried him into the house, and placed him on his bed.

The old Indian eased out of the bedroom as quickly as his son was settled and walked silently through the kitchen to get outside. He was sure that this place would offer no welcome to him, and besides, he knew that the horses and mules needed to be tended to before he began his long ride home.

Alejandro and his daughter took the old man's exit from the room as a signal and politely left the boy alone with his father. As they entered the kitchen, Margarita looked up from where she sat with the badly shaken Strider woman. A glance between the three reminded the father and daughter that there remained a chore of work to be done. Margarita would have to know the details of their escape from their hostile homeland, and the tragedy in the desert remained unresolved.

William welcomed the feel of his bed beneath him, but after a short moment of relief, he opened his eyes and looked intently into his eldest son's face. The questions he saw needed answering, but now was not the time.

"Tell me about Raphael," he said weakly and moved his hand slightly toward the boy, seeking physical connection to his son, who had recently taken on a man-sized burden. He was aware of the extraordinary relationship that his children had with each other, having been raised so isolated in these mountains, and was anxious to know the boy's mind.

Miguel took up his father's hand and immediately noticed its heat. Though this familiarity would have been unimaginable a few weeks ago, he laid his other hand on William's forehead. There he got confirmation that the fever was back and with a vengeance. He knew he needed to make up the strong dose of penicillin the medic had described, but first, his father should know about Raphael.

"I could barely tell that he was breathing," Miguel said slowly, "and his fever is almost as bad as yours."

"They said he had rabies?" the man queried.

"That's what Gabby told me; she said it was Mary Magdalene who gave it to him, something about wolves too?"

After brief contemplation, William said with finality, "Go tell your mother to come here to me."

Even through the weakness, the boy recognized a tone in his father's voice. He was a bit bewildered as he had never before heard anything from his father that sounded so much like a command to his mother. He released the man's hand and turned obediently toward the kitchen.

"Momma, Poppa wants you," the boy said as he stepped into the kitchen. All present turned and looked his way, including Maria, but she failed to rise. A look of apprehension crossed her face, and she hesitated.

"I think he wants you now," Miguel said. The words had an edge of accusation, for the boy was still upset over the shooting incident.

The boy's mother almost automatically snapped back at him, but these were untested waters. William had never given her an order before, and Miguel had never dared to use this tone with her. Guilt and circumstances dictated caution to the woman, so with a look meant to tell the boy that this would be revisited, she rose, ready to comply with her husband's request.

Maria brushed her cotton apron straight and tucked a strand of wayward hair behind her ear, and then with head held high, signaling a certain amount of defiance, she walked past her son toward the bedroom where her husband lay.

"Sit here on the bed," William said to his wife politely as she entered, leaving no room for discussion.

The woman sat close enough to the man to notice the heat radiating from his body and started to comment on it but held her silence, waiting for him to set the tone for this conversation. She anticipated questions about Raphael and was fully prepared to justify her attempt upon the old man's life. Still, she was more than surprised when instead of admonishing her, he gave her a simple command.

"I want you to go outside and make peace with my father," he said without passion.

She stared at him with disbelief, then said accusingly, "But you've known all along what he did to my family, and now you want me to forgive him? I don't think that will happen, not in this lifetime!"

"I know that you believed that he was the cause of the death of your family," said the man, "but even if it is as you say, the facts are that the same sickness that killed your family also killed his. So, what good is it to try to place blame? It will bring none of the dead back to life."

"I don't understand how you could have deceived me from the beginning," Maria defended. "The only reason you were in my village was that you knew your family would be there. You let me believe that you had found me by chance, and I never questioned you about it."

"You are right, I was there looking for my family, but my search ended when I found you. I came because of a letter sent to me by my mother while I was overseas. I had only a rough idea where they were going, and yes, it was simple fate that brought me to you. I planned to take you to safety and then return to my journey, but you were so weak, and every place we went, they turned us away, so I finally brought you back here and abandoned my search. By the time my father came to these mountains, you and I were already married. On his advice, I let you go on believing that strangers had destroyed your village instead of the truth, which is that your village, just as likely as not killed them."

Maria looked at her husband, and her thoughts whirled at his unexpected declaration. "I am sorry for your family," she said, "but this is the man I have hated for most of my life, and I can make no promise to forgive him now."

"I ask no forgiveness for him," said the man with a firm voice, "but I tell you this, go and bring him into our home that he may know all of his grandchildren, for if what I am told about Raphael is true then this may be his last chance to meet him. He has stayed away all of this time only as a kindness to you, but now it is time to make it right with him."

"I have told you my feelings," said the troubled woman, "but now I will do as you say." She rose, prepared to leave, when a thought occurred to her, "What do you know about Raphael?" she asked.

"Enough," said the man, "my mother was a healer, and my father knows many things about the sickness Raphe has. Bring my father to see him; he may know something that will help."

Maria thought, "I will do as you ask, but you can't make me trust that old man."

Maria left her husband alone, and he closed his eyes and pulled his cover tighter against the shiver he felt from the fever. He knew his condition was getting more severe because he could no longer feel his leg, but there was too much to be dealt with to worry about that now.

"Where is the Indian," asked Maria as she looked around the kitchen. The Mexicans sitting together at the table stopped to look back at her but said nothing.

"He's out there," Miguel said, pointing through the open doorway. He had just placed the shotgun back on its pegs and stood aside to let her pass.

The boy's mother stepped out onto the porch treads and spied the Indian at the barn removing the straps that held the travois to the mule. He had led his grandson's horse Dotty and the mule from the house and intended to put them up in the barn lot before departing. The woman walked down the steps and started toward him, but he continued disconnecting the drag poles from the sawbuck tree even though he sensed her coming.

Miguel followed his mother through the door but stopped to wait on the porch. He had retrieved the bag of medicine from his saddle before the old Indian took his horse and intended to prepare a dose for his father. At this moment, though, it seemed more important that he stand by in case of more trouble between his mother and grandfather.

When she neared the old man, the woman stopped and waited until he looked up and acknowledged her presence.

"I know who you are," she began, "but my husband says I have judged you unfairly. At any rate, the past is the past, and your son wishes us to put all those things aside and try to make a new start. I am willing to try if you are."

Having made her offer, she stood silently by, waiting for his reply.

Though she saw no change in the Indian man's demeanor, she heard him say, "For more than ten years, my son has been the only reason I have kept this body from the grave. Now in these last few weeks, I have come to know the son of my son, and that knowledge has made up for all of the sadness of those years. I believe that if I can know his wife and other two children, then the family I lost will be partly returned to me, and maybe in some small way, so will yours to you."

The man's words unexpectedly touched her, and she said to him, "Come to the house when you are finished, and you may meet my other children."

Miguel wasn't sure what had been said, but when his mother turned to come back to the house, her frown had softened, but when she passed him on the porch, their eyes did not meet. He turned and followed her into the house; when she continued on to report her actions to her husband, he walked to the cabinet where he had left the bag of medicine and emptied its contents to inventory the remaining penicillin pills.

The Mexicans looked up as the two entered the kitchen but quickly returned to the serious conversation they had been having. Shortly after that, Margarita rose, walked to the door, and went outside; Alejandro and his daughter eventually followed.

CHAPTER 37

When Maria returned to the kitchen from the bedroom, she paused for a moment to look at her son, then proceeded to the table and sat down. Miguel watched, unsure what to do, but when she looked up at him, and he saw in her eyes the mother that he expected to greet them that morning, he walked over and sat down across from her.

They were both anxious to speak, and each tried to begin, but the boy quickly fell silent to let his mother proceed.

"I want to explain," she began, "what you saw out there between that old man and me. His showing up here is absolutely the last thing in the world that I was prepared to deal with, but that's no excuse for the way I reacted. I don't know what your father has told you about him and me, but I expect that it is very little, if anything. I swear that man lives by a code of silence that is sometimes maddening to me; before I go on, I want you to tell me what happened to your father's leg and how bad it is."

Miguel told her how they were ambushed by the same two men she had confronted at the yard gate not so long ago. He told her how his father was shot, how badly his leg was broken, how his grandfather had cleaned and splinted it, about the fever and the hospital at Three Forks Station, where they put the cast on and gave them the penicillin. He told her how the medicine had helped, but the fever was back and how little of the medicine they had left. By the end, the boy was dangerously close to tears, and she could tell how fearful he was for his father.

Maria wasn't sure who she felt the sorriest for, her husband for being so severely injured or her young son who had been there through it all, for as he was describing the details to her, his face had reflected each raw emotion as if in the telling he was reliving the ordeal again. It broke her heart to see her son in so much pain.

"Margarita, the woman you saw is a nurse," said Maria, "and I'm sure she'll be able to help with your father. Don't worry yourself too much about him; he's strong, and I'm sure he will be all right."

The old Indian walked through the door and stood silently, waiting for the boy's mother to direct him as she would.

Maria rose and told her son that they would continue their discussion later, then motioned the Indian to follow her as she walked down the hallway to the children's room.

Miguel took the opportunity to prepare a dose of medicine for his father.

Gabriella sat with her legs crossed and feet tucked beneath her as she watched her brother take his silent breaths. She knew that at some point soon, this barely visible movement would come to a halt, and she fully expected to see him float up on his way to heaven, this per her mother's somewhat misunderstood Bible teachings. She had sat thus both day and night for more than a week, waiting expectantly for the event, fully anticipating to follow along with her brother whenever he left.

The girl's mother and the old Indian man padded into the room. Once inside the doorway, the Indian man saw the tiny girl for the first time, her hair a tangle, for she refused to leave her brother long enough for a bath or grooming. The sky-blue eyes he recognized from the face of a long-dead sister. The girl's twin was lying on his bed and could have easily been mistaken for dead if judged by his pallor and the almost complete absence of breath.

"Gabby, this is your grandfather," the woman announced, lacking an idea for a more subtle introduction.

Gabriella was genuinely stunned at this declaration, for she had only ever heard of one grandfather and knew that he had died long before she was born. She turned to look up at the man standing before her and thought him to be a much older replica of her father. His face was ruddy and weathered, and his buckskin clothes fascinated the girl. He wasn't as tall as her father, but there was no mistaking the resemblance. Her gaze was drawn to his face the same way it always was with her poppa. Deep lines of age told of advancing years, but his black eyes were her father's eyes. His hands were smooth and firm, and those also were her father's hands. And she noticed that these hands were holding something, and when she looked, the man dropped a leather string to let it dangle before her. She saw that it was a necklace, and attached to it was a small figure of a running horse carved from white bone. She reached out for it, then stopped to look up at her mother for permission, which she got with a nod, then took it and drew it closer for inspection.

"Is it for me?" she asked timidly, and the old man smiled a contented smile.

"I made one for your brother too; maybe you could hold on to it for him," the man said kindly and handed her a second necklace with a carving of a buffalo attached.

As she clasped both gifts, the girl looked again at the boy lying in bed across from her. Silent tears began to leak from the corners of her startling blue eyes and flow down her face.

"I'm sure he will like it, sir," the girl murmured in her small voice, "if God will let him wake up before he takes him to heaven."

At this, the old Indian swallowed hard, reached down, cupped the girl's tiny chin in his big soft hand, and turned her face up toward him. With the pad of his thumb, he wiped the tears from her cheek.

"With a good sister like you to watch over him," said the grandfather, "I'm sure he will be fine until God decides what to do. Would it be ok if I visited with him for a while? Your mother might take you to get something to eat?"

"I guess so?" replied the girl tiredly, "but you will have to call me if you see him start to leave."

The old man looked to the woman for her approval, and after a moment of hesitation, she again nodded.

After the mother and daughter had left the room, the old man retrieved the lantern that sat on the dresser by the wall and turned the wick up high enough to chase the shadows from the room; he then placed it on a chair that had been pulled up to the foot of the boy's bed. Reaching for the covers, he pulled them down and thoroughly searched the boy's body; he wanted to find where the infection had started.

The boy groaned as the cool air caused a fever chill that stirred him slightly. Working quickly, the old man inspected both legs and arms, then rolled the boy over to his side to look at his back. Finding no unhealed wounds, he turned the boy back over and tucked his covers tightly around him; he then forced open the boy's eyes and lips but still could find nothing indicating a case of the moon madness.

It wasn't sure that the lack of wounds disproved anything, but it did call the diagnosis into question. Over the years, the Indian had seen many people die of the disease, and in all cases, the sickness had originated from the site of a severely infected wound. He had been exposed to several victims who died of the disease and knew it was hard to catch it unless there was a bite.

The old man stepped from the bedroom into the hallway and went to the room where he had helped to bring his son. He was pretty sure that the woman had been coerced into agreeing to let him meet the children, and despite her cordial manner, he had felt the icy hatred in her stare. Better to share his concerns with the boy's father, he was sure, and leave any needed actions in his hands.

William lay with his eyes closed tightly with a grimace of pain on his face.

"Son," the old man said when he entered the room.

The man opened his eyes and forced the tension from his face before responding with a questioning look.

"I don't think that boy in there has the madness," the old man stated.

William asked, "What do you think is wrong with him then?"

"I would say that boy has the lung fever," came the reply.

The man thought for a moment, recalling the hundreds of cases of pneumonia that were such a common malady during his time in the war and the medicine that the medics had used to cure it, Penicillin, just like the doctor had given him at Three Forks Station.

"Do you still have any of the medicine they gave me at the Army post?" he asked.

Standing in the doorway, Miguel answered, "We have a few pills left, but it's not much." He held a spoon full of crushed pills and a glass of water up to show the two men the dose he had intended to give his father.

"Take it to your brother," William said weakly.

"But Poppa, you need it as badly as Raphael does," and he stepped closer to his father's bed. "I can make up some more for Raphe," he urged.

"No, you do as I say now," he bade his son.

Miguel looked from his father to his grandfather for guidance, but the old man's face gave no clue about his opinion on the matter.

"But if I can't wake him up, how do I get him to swallow the medicine," asked the boy, showing his distress and uncertainty over the wisdom of his father's decision.

"You mix a little water in the powder to make a paste, then use your finger to put it under his tongue," the old man suggested. "I have seen your grandma do that sometimes when doctoring sick people. If you want, I can show you."

After a last glance at his poppa, the boy turned, and he and his grandfather left the room.

William closed his eyes again when they were gone, slipping into unconsciousness.

Miguel and the old man walked the few steps to the room where the young boy lay unaware of anything happening around him. The Indian took the spoon from his grandson, dipped one finger into the glass of water, and stirred it into the powdered penicillin until it became a thick goo that clung to his finger. He asked Miguel to open the small boy's mouth and swiped the medicine paste beneath the boy's tongue and into his cheek.

Raphael stirred slightly, and they saw that he was attempting to swallow the chalky concoction. The old Indian dipped his fingers again into the water, then let it drip into the boy's mouth. Using this method, they got all of the medicine down his throat.

"Do this again every couple of hours til you run out," he told the boy.

"But what about Poppa?" the boy asked with concern, "there isn't nearly enough for both of them."

"Do what your poppa told you." said the old man. He then turned and walked out of the room.

CHAPTER 38

The Strider home, isolated on a shelf of land deep in the heart of the Sierra Nevada Mountains, which had only a few short weeks ago been a sanctuary to a happy, humble, frontier family, had now become a place overflowing with unintended tragedy. Shadows of death collected in the dark recesses like vultures waiting for a meal. A young boy was tenaciously clinging to life, one breath at a time—a tiny girl willing air into a brother's congested lungs. A father, weakened and fading, trying to create a chance at life for a dying son. A mother was waging her latest battle in a lifelong war to maintain sanity against a world conspiring to destroy it. A woman was trying to reassemble a family splintered by the aftermath of a terrible war. A husband, desperate to survive, trying to understand how an act of love had been twisted by fate into a heinous crime. A daughter clinging to a sliver of hope for a normal life while adjusting to ever-changing circumstances. A forlorn grandfather hoping to reclaim a portion of his shattered life in the offspring of his only remaining son. A young, innocent boy whose eyes were being painfully opened to the realities of manhood.

Margarita had long ago forced herself to accept the inevitability of receiving the worst possible news from the returning searchers who she now knew had been sent into the desert, not for rescue, but to locate the bodies of the loved ones she came seeking. She wasn't sure which had shocked her most, the sight of her brother-in-law and niece riding in with the rescuers or the place at their side left vacant by her sister. She hadn't allowed herself to rush to them as she might have, for dreading confirmation of the thing she already knew in her heart. Now sitting at the kitchen table, looking across at Alejandro and Natalie, who looked back at her in awkward silence, she steeled herself to hear the dreaded words she knew would be spoken.

Alejandro finally began, "It is my painful duty to report to you that your sister, my wife, has perished in the desert known as Mojave."

The facts stated so simply by this man who could not seem to look her in the eye stirred within her a certain amount of rage. She knew him only from letters written to her by her younger sister Camila, and her own witness was now proving the descriptions she had read.

"Do not take this as an accusation," said Margarita accusingly, "but only as a sister's wish to understand the circumstances of a loved one's death. How is it that you and la chica were able to survive the ordeal when others in your family perished from it?"

Alejandro had been rehearsing answers to this and many other questions as they had ridden into these mountains. He had foreseen this very conversation, although, in his mind, it had happened at a much later date somewhere in San Francisco. For him, it was unfortunate that the pressures of the moment were affecting his judgment, and the guilt that he had thought reconciled within himself now came rushing back with a vengeance, causing him to blurt out an answer, not to the question asked, but to the one that had been haunting his dreams.

"I am confident in telling you," Alejandro said, trying to suppress the quaver in his voice, "that your sister felt no more pain at the moment of her death than did her own son, Mateo."

Both the woman and girl stared at the man in shocked silence.

Finally, Margarita leaned in and spoke in carefully measured tones, "Please, explain these moments of death that you speak of amid this ordeal lasting many weeks."

"What I meant to say," stuttered Alejandro, realizing his mistake, "was that Natalie and I were lucky to have survived. We were without food and water for many days, and the sun was so hot that one could hardly breathe."

"Yet you survived where they did not," the woman demanded.

Alejandro was at a loss and so turned to his daughter, hoping for help, but all she offered was, "Father, you know that I was not even present at the time of their deaths."

This only caused more confusion on Margarita's part.

At this point, Maria and Miguel reentered the kitchen from the porch, having sought out the old Indian. The three Mexicans' discussion had taken such a turn that Margarita was unwilling to continue it in front of their hosts. She rose and walked outside, where she intended that they continue their conversation in private.

Alejandro hesitated but then ducked his head and followed his sister-in-law's lead, exiting behind her.

Natalie sat watching them both leave, then finally, reluctantly, the young girl who hadn't wanted to hear her father speak the details of her mother and brother's deaths followed the two out onto the porch.

These departures went virtually unnoticed by the mother and son as one walked on to the bedrooms and the other, distracted by his mother's demeanor, busied himself at the cabinet.

Outside on the porch, the inquisition began in earnest.

Margarita stood with arms crossed, protectively hugging her shoulders, her unfocused gaze attempting to probe the past as her fury mounted, waiting for whatever explanation this guilty man had to offer.

Alejandro stopped at what felt like a comfortably safe distance from his dead wife's sister and waited for her to collect herself enough to allow him to speak the truth as only he knew it. He was fully aware that his words would be perceived as those of a criminal trying to justify the murder of his children's mother, but there was nothing to be done for it.

Natalie stood apart from her aunt and father, the last two members of her immediate family that she feared was about to grow smaller by one before this conversation was done. Previous to this day, she had contented herself to know as little about her mother and brother's deaths as possible, hoping to cloak herself in ignorance of a thing that her mind would not accept.

The Mexican woman turned to face her brother-in-law without altering her defensive posture. Nothing she could imagine that he was about to say to her would lessen her pain over losing her sister, for the cryptic message he had conveyed by mistake brought all manner of bazaar images to mind.

The man looked at his daughter before beginning. "Do you remember Natalie, when your brother collapsed of exhaustion, and we all stopped to rest? I am sure your mother would have never said the things she did under any other circumstances than the delirium she felt at having had no water for so many days. She begged me to take up the gun to end their pain and suffering as I had promised. She said that at least that way, we would meet God together instead of dying one at a time strewn out across the desert. When I refused, she took the gun up herself. She would have killed you, Natalie, had you not run away into the desert. She fired the one bullet in the gun as you ran and then demanded that I give her the others I had saved for this purpose. I took the bullets, dropped them into the sand, and scattered them. As your mother crawled in the dark to recover them, I took the gun and threw it as far away from us as I could. Finally, your mother collapsed, crying over Mateo's body, vowing to end at least his suffering. Before I could stop her, she had taken up a stone and brought it down on his head. I don't believe the blow ended his life, but I knew that he would soon die in his condition. I took up his body and walked in the direction we had been traveling, and your mother followed us. I called your name in the darkness, but you did not answer. When we came to a hollow place with huge boulders, I could go no further. I lay my dead son down against the side of a bank, and your mother lay with him. Through her grief, she begged me to do for her what she had done for him. She sobbed in the darkness, asking me again to fulfill my promise; in the end, I took up a stone, and she wept no more."

When Alejandro had completed his speech, the three Mexicans stood in stunned silence, for what could anyone say after such a tale of woe?

Margarita's first thought was 'Murderer!' as she envisioned the scene of her young sister's death. The sister, she realized, who had just executed her son. Another realization crept into her mind; she had been only moments away from committing the same act she was about to accuse Alejandro of. Had the small blue-eyed girl not seized on her leg a half second before she plunged the needle, she would be guilty of his crime. She could derive no solace from the fact that she hadn't completed the act of her intent, for isn't the sin committed by the heart and not the hand? Has there ever been an instance throughout history where God would forgive the taking of a life? No, she concluded, 'Thou shalt not kill,' says the commandment, and doesn't it mean, 'Thou shalt never kill, even in your mind?' Her self-righteous thoughts melted away.

The Mexican woman turned back to the man she now neither hated nor loved and placed a sympathetic hand on his shoulder. Looking at Natalie, she took a halting breath and said, "I don't know how God will view these things that have passed between this family, but to condemn this man, is to condemn my sister, and that I am not prepared to do."

Wearily she made her way back into the house, leaving the father and daughter to sort out their feelings without further consideration from her.

CHAPTER 39

The old Indian left the bedroom, walked down the hallway, and into the kitchen, where Maria and Gabriella sat at the table. The young girl was holding a fork she was using to eat a fried egg, and as he entered the room, she looked up and raised her left hand from which the two necklaces dangled by their strings, a signal that she was still minding his gifts. He smiled warmly back at her but didn't stop, and proceeded through the door and onto the porch. There he saw the two Mexican women standing on opposite sides of the Mexican man listening intently to what he was saying to them. Alejandro took a moment to glance up at the old man, who had only once before seen such a look, in the pleading eyes of a man with his head in a noose searching for a friend in the crowd.

The old man walked to where his mule was tied, pulled himself up onto the saddle, put his heels to its ribs, and steered it toward the gate. As he rode away, he glanced back at the cabin and saw Gabriella standing in the doorway. The old Indian raised a hand in farewell, but this only confused the girl, for she had come to invite him to join her vigil over her brother. When it became apparent that he was leaving, she quickly took a step forward, raised the hand with the necklaces, and murmured, "Goodbye, Grandpa," but by then, he had reined his mule toward the lane and was riding slowly away.

Miguel sat with his brother until Gabby reentered the bedroom and silently took up her post again. By then, he felt sure that the boy wasn't going to choke on the medicine paste that he and his grandfather had administered, so he went to check on his father. The man seemed to be resting peacefully, so he walked back to the kitchen. Maria and Margarita were both sitting at the table talking as he entered.

"Where's Grandpa?" asked the boy, unsurprised to see that he was not with the women.

"He is gone," said his mother matter-of-factly.

"Do you mean that he has gone outside?"

"I assume he has gone back to wherever he came from," she answered casually.

"Well, did he say anything?" Miguel asked incredulously.

"He walked through here a few minutes ago, and then we saw him ride off on his mule; that is all I know," his mother stated.

The boy stood open-mouthed, looking at the two women, "Did you know?" he asked with disdain, "that Grandpa doesn't think Raphael has the rabies? He thinks he has a bad case of lung fever instead, so we gave him a dose of Poppa's penicillin." Before either of the women could protest, shaking his head in disbelief, the boy walked to and through the open door and out onto the porch.

Alejandro and Natalie were standing together talking when he came out, and they both stopped and turned toward the boy.

"If you are looking for your grandfather," Natalie said. "He left without saying a word; he didn't appear as though he intended to come back."

This was a surprise and a disappointment to the boy, as both his father and brother lay dying in the house, and he would have expected his grandfather to at least stay and do what he could to help them. Instead, he had left them alone without so much as a by your leave.

"Mother did this," the boy thought, "and I will not forgive her, no matter her reasons."

He started to go after the old man, but what would he say, "Don't pay any attention to my mother trying to kill you? She didn't mean anything by it?"

He turned around and walked back through the kitchen without even a glance at his mother, entered the bedroom, and sat stiffly with an arm around his small sister.

CHAPTER 40

The man's condition worsened, but the boy's improved despite Margarita's insistence that the penicillin would not affect the rabies she had diagnosed. Miguel doggedly complied with his father's orders to give the medicine to his brother and withhold it from himself. There was a fight over the remaining pills, but the boy would not be budged from his convictions.

"It's the Indian in you that makes you so stubborn," Maria accused at the end of one of their arguments over the pills. "You will end up killing them both, and if that happens, you may kill me too!"

Miguel wavered, for sometimes his father was delirious, and the boy was reminded of what he had told him about lost people going insane and doing crazy things, but in the end, his Indian stubbornness did not crack.

When it became undeniable that Raphael was improving, the battles over the pills ceased, but all too soon, there were no more pills to fight over, and the young boy's fever began to rise again.

The nurse and Maria had been attempting to control William's body temperature by using cold well water and wet compresses. To a small degree, it was helping, but the man continued to grow worse as the infection in the leg raged. When it got so bad that Margarita was afraid that his temperature was getting fatally high, they would send Alejandro for buckets of cold water and dowse the man, bed, and all until he cooled back down.

Miguel and Gabriella were assigned to watch their brother, who would regain consciousness from time to time, and when he did, he was apt to be taken with coughing fits and strangulation as the congestion in his lungs had already begun to loosen. It became the routine that one of them stay awake while the other rested to be prepared at a moment's notice to assist him thru these ordeals. If Gabby were on watch, at the first sign that her twin was waking, she would shake Miguel until he came to her assistance.

The Mexican man and his daughter helped where they could, but for the most part, they were ignored by the others, who were doing their best to keep both patients breathing.

Margarita came into the children's bedroom and asked Miguel if he knew where there might be willow trees; he said that he did, for they were all along the streams that ran between the mountains. The boy wanted to know why, and she told him to make willow bark tea. They used it in Mexico during the war when there was no medicine to help with fever.

"I could ride to Three Forks for more of the pills," suggested the boy, "but I'm not sure if I could find my way there and back."

"We couldn't spare you anyway," the nurse responded soberly. "We need you here, for Gabriella won't respond to anyone but you, and we certainly don't need another patient on our hands. But what of Alejandro?"

"We might send him for the willow limbs," Miguel concluded, "for he would have less chance than I would of finding the Army station. No, I will give him directions for the willows."

The Mexican man was overjoyed at the prospect of having a helpful duty to perform, and Natalie volunteered to accompany him.

"It should only take a few hours to get there and back," said Miguel, and he gave them instructions and scratched a crude map in the sand. "Take the pack donkey and some of the supplies left from our trip coming here. It is best to be prepared when traveling in these mountains because you never know when an emergency will delay your return. My mother warned of an outbreak of hydrophobia in the area, so don't take any chances with animals that seem too brave. Be certain to take a gun, and I will send Juliet along with you; she will warn you if there is danger."

Riding the mountain horses taken from the two assassins and leading the donkey, Alejandro and Natalie set out to retrieve the medicinal tree bark that the nurse had requested. They were both relieved to be away from the stifling pall of the cabin and grateful to be doing something to help the family of their rescuers.

Miguel knelt before they left and spoke privately to the dog; he asked her to take care of his new friends and to look out for the girl especially. Juliet twisted happily at the attention, and as if she had understood every word from the boy, she ran to the yard gate to wait for them to catch up.

After watching the Mexicans depart, the boy filled a well bucket with fresh cool water and returned to the house. Before taking up his station with Gabby again, he took the water to his parent's room and watched as the two women renewed the wet compresses. He could see his father's face beneath a folded towel for a moment, and a reassuring wink from a red-rimmed eye heartened the boy. He could only guess what that small gesture had cost the man, for his life seemed to be slowly draining from his body. It caused tears in his tired and bleary eyes, so he turned away.

CHAPTER 41

As the Mexican father and daughter urged their horses along, they were made curious by the bones of Mary Magdalene lying bleached by the sun below the bluffs. They took this time alone to express their thoughts about the Striders and the future.

"I think I could get used to living in a place like this," said the girl, looking up at the tall mountains, noticing, as she had on the trip up, the grandeur and scale of this land of high places.

"One could do worse," said the father, enjoying the silence and solitude settling around them. He glanced at his daughter and wondered if her words might have more meaning than just a comment on the country.

"We may never be able to repay our debt to these people," Alejandro stated frankly. "They are most likely to lose the father, and it will be at least a few years before Miguel can provide them a living. Had I the skills, I would offer to stay on and help them through this time, for we owe them our lives and more, but I fear that I would only be another mouth to feed in my inexperience."

"Do you think the grandfather will ever return to help his family?" asked Natalie.

"He is a good and kindly old man," replied Alejandro, "but with the woman's actions when she first saw him, I think there must exist a terrible history between the two."

"If we were to go to San Francisco with my aunt, do you think we could send them enough money to sustain them?" the girl asked.

"Perhaps, but we don't even know what the future holds for us there, so it may be difficult for us to fulfill such a promise that would jeopardize them should we fail," replied the man.

"Perhaps then, you could go on to San Francisco," the girl stated hesitantly, "and I could remain and help while you find our place there?"

"We will consult with your aunt about the possibilities," Alejandro responded, "but today, let us concentrate on our task."

Silence fell on the small party as they each contemplated the future.

Happy to be on the trail again, Juliet led the way through fields and valleys between the towering mountains where they had traveled only days before on their way to the Strider home. The warmth from a sun that seemed to follow along with them made the air comfortable and pushed the chill they had felt above out of the protected valleys they rode through. They made their way toward the canyon floor, where the boy had said they would find the trees that were the object of their quest.

Their journey had been all downhill from the plateau above, and they spotted the stream where they were to find the willows in less than two hours. The man recognized that continuing on this path would eventually lead them to the road they had traveled, coming from the Army Station.

"If I weren't afraid for your safety, my daughter," said the man, looking beyond the stream, "I would ride on to the Army fort and bring back more of the medicine."

"You should do it!" said the girl enthusiastically, "you have the donkey and supplies; I don't know why we haven't thought of it before; what better way to pay for our rescue than to rescue them right back? I will return with the willows and let them know where you have gone. It will at least provide hope where now there is none."

"Do you think you can safely make the return journey by yourself?" asked the father, excited by the prospect of doing this unselfish thing that would never have occurred to him in his previous life.

"Of course," said Natalie, "I will have the dog to protect me, and it is only a couple of hours' ride back the way we came."

"Then let us collect the branches before I begin; we should trade horses, for yours is younger and stronger, and I will need to make as much haste as is possible. With luck, I will need two days to get there and two days back. You will tell the family to keep their faith until I return."

With the axe they had brought for the job, they gathered the number of young, healthy limbs that could easily be secured behind the girl's saddle. When all was prepared, they embraced, feeling the joy and excitement of their mission that they hoped might turn the tide in these desperate hours.

Alejandro crossed the stream leading the donkey and looked back with a wave and the entreaty, "Estar a salvo mi paloma" (be safe my dove), to which Natalie replied, "Para estar seguro papá" (to be certain papa). At that moment, she felt pride in her father for the first time. Perhaps they would have said more had they known that these words would be the last to ever pass between them.

After the man galloped out of sight, the young girl turned her horse and called out to Juliet, who sat waiting for the signal to lead them home.

CHAPTER 42

When Natalie rode into the yard and stopped by the porch, Miguel was waiting at the kitchen door. He had asked the nurse how to process the willow bark into a medicinal tea and had assembled everything necessary to accomplish the task. He had estimated the time it would take Alejandro and his daughter to make the round trip to the location he had directed them to and had only missed the mark by a few minutes. Juliet leaped up on the porch and went to the boy for a pat, having done her duty by bringing the girl safely home.

"Where is your father?" the boy asked the girl when he noticed she was alone.

"He decided that he should ride on to the soldier fort for more medicine," the girl replied, expecting a grateful response to what she regarded as a brave and thoughtful idea.

"I agree with your father that we need the medicine," said the boy, "but if he gets lost out there, he could easily die. My father says it only takes one wrong turn in these mountains to send a person around in circles. Hundreds of miles of valleys look the same, and it can be impossible to tell which direction you are going. I wish he had talked to me before deciding to go."

"I didn't realize that it is as dangerous as you say," she said. "Do you think it might be possible to catch up with him? He has only been gone a few hours."

After considering the thing, Miguel replied, "Let me show you what to do with the willows, and then I will try to find him. With luck, I can catch up to him before he gets into trouble. I had already decided to go when you got back, even though my mother will throw a fit when she finds out. I don't think my father will make it without more of the medicine."

"Then I will ride with you, for it was I who urged him to go," said the girl.

"No, you won't!" said Miguel with finality, "because there is a good chance that I might get lost, and I won't take that risk with you along. Please wait until I'm gone and tell my mother where I'm going. Tell her I said that I'm sorry, but I just had to go."

To Miguel's surprise, Natalie said, "Don't worry, I will make sure she knows."

The two unbundled the willow limbs, and while Miguel stripped the bark from the branches, Natalie kindled a fire in the stove to boil the water. Miguel chopped enough fresh bark into thumbnail-sized chips to make two small mounds. He then raked the piles from the table into a tea kettle, measured four cups of water, and poured them on top.

By this time, Natalie had a good fire going, and Miguel went to the cookstove, removed one of the round metal firebox lids, and placed the kettle over the hole so that the flames would quickly boil the water.

"The nurse said to let the bark boil for about ten minutes, remove it from the flame, and steep until it cools. After that, strain the tea into cups and take them to the nurse; she will know how to get my father and brother to drink it."

Miguel left the girl tending the boiling mixture and began gathering the supplies needed for the trip. He would take extra just in case something happened to the supplies he knew the man was carrying with him.

After saddling Dotty and rigging the mule, he loaded the supplies and filled two canteens from the well. As he rode by the house on the way out, he warned Juliet to stay and trusted she would obey. He stopped at the porch long enough to catch the girl's attention, and when he saw her pouring the liquid through a dishcloth into the cups, he waved goodbye. She sat the pot down and acknowledged his wave, and as he turned toward the gate, she hurriedly carried the two cups to the bedroom where the nurse was tending to William. Maria was sitting in the children's room with Gabby and rose when she saw Natalie pass the door carrying the cups. She followed the girl into the bedroom, where her husband lay to help administer the tea.

"Do you think this will help with the fever?" Maria asked the nurse as the young girl left the room.

"Well," said Margarita, "I've read where they have been using willow bark tea for thousands of years, and my husband had me make it by the buckets full during the war. We used it to treat everything from fever to headaches, and all I know is that it helped some, and even when it didn't, it did no harm."

Natalie went to the kitchen, took the note she had written from her pocket, and placed it on the table beneath the bowl of matches where she knew it would be noticed. She grabbed the small bundle of food she had gathered into a flour sack and dashed out the door. She went to where she had tied her horse and mounted, then urged it down the lane after Miguel.

Later, as Maria was taking the empty cups to the kitchen, she saw the note; she returned to the bedroom where the nurse was, carrying the message left by the now absent girl.

"Miguel and Natalie are gone," said Maria in despair. "They went looking for the girl's father, who the note says took it upon himself to try to ride for more medicine. Miguel thinks that if they don't find him, he will most likely become lost and whether they are successful or not, they will still go on to the soldier fort for the medicine. I don't understand why he took the girl with him."

"If my niece is anything like her mother," replied the nurse, "your son probably had no choice in the matter."

CHAPTER 43

Miguel tried to ride quickly but found it a battle to get the still-tired mule to move faster than an awkward trot, and if he forced the issue, she resorted to delaying tactics, like going on the wrong side of bushes and trees. Untangling the lead rope from briers and limbs cost him twice as much time as the faster pace was gaining, so in the end, he slowed to a quick walk that she seemed to find acceptable. Since he found himself going nowhere fast, he spent the time trying to retrace from memory the route that had brought them home from Three Forks. It was difficult, though, because images of his sick brother and father kept inserting themselves into his mind at random intervals causing him to stray from his mental map. The possibility of losing one or both of them led him to contemplate how it would change his world. He knew that if his brother died, it might kill his mother, for she had told them stories about when she had lost her family in Mexico and how she had laid down to die and would have too if their poppa hadn't come along to save her. If his father died, he knew it would be up to him to provide for the family. He was sure he could hunt to bring meat for food, but what about all the other things like flour, sugar, and bullets that had to be bought or bartered for? It wouldn't take long to run out of items on the home place to trade. As far as he knew, there wasn't another permanent settlement this side of the Army fort, so a paying job was out of the question, and besides, what kind of skills did he have to sell anyway? He thought of his grandpa but wasn't sure if he was likely to ever see the old man again after the shooting incident. No, he decided, his father had to be saved at any risk, and regardless of what happened to Natalie's father, this trip was the first step in making that happen.

He rode along, lost in a world of what ifs and maybes, until the sound of a running horse broke through his fog of depression. Turning in his saddle to locate the source of the sound, he was stunned to see Natalie approaching fast, her lengthy hair streaming, and she had a look of intense concentration and concern on her face. When she saw him ahead and realized she wasn't lost, a broad smile broke out on her dark face, and her eyes went wide with joy. The boy noticed that Juliet had accompanied the girl, and he gave her a look for having disobeyed his orders to stay home, just as the girl had done.

"There you are!" she gushed as she rode her horse alongside Dotty. "I was afraid I might have missed you." She spontaneously leaned across the divide between them, wrapped her arms around his neck, and held him tightly for a moment. When she sat back in her saddle, he could see embarrassed tears in her eyes and knew the fear and worry she had been experiencing. The scolding he was preparing to give her for following him gave way to a feeling of elation at being in her company once again.

"I won't even ask what you are doing here," he said with a forgiving smile. "What did my mother say when you told her I was gone?"

"I have no idea," said the girl as if the joke was on him. "I wrote her a note and left it on the kitchen table. If I had stayed to tell her, I do not doubt that I would be tied to a chair right now."

"You're probably right," said Miguel. "I guess it would be a waste of time to try to talk you into going back?"

At this, the girl lifted the flour sack to show him the provisions she had brought for herself, and the subject was closed.

As they resumed the journey, the girl endured the silence for less than a minute before she was compelled to fill the void with the one-sided rambling dialogue that she had employed on their ride up the mountains; for her, quiet encouraged dark memories that she wasn't yet prepared to confront.

For the boy, the girl's chatter relieved the necessity for him to try to come up with something intelligent to say to her, a thing he knew from experience could take the better part of a day, and the best part of this day was already over. Her familiar presence also served to dispel the gloomy mood of self-doubt that the boy had been struggling with. Now he was feeling brave and determined instead of frightened and alone.

When they reached the stream where the willow trees grew, Natalie showed him where her father had crossed. This is where the tracking would begin. Juliet seemed to sense that they were looking for the Mexican man and bound ahead, following his trail.

The heavy horse carrying the girl's father, leading the small donkey, left a clear enough trail down the grassy hollow between the mountains. The stream followed the same geography as the trail, seeking its winding path toward the foothills. Miguel spotted the two parallel scars in the grass left by the travois poles as it was dragged up this pass on their way home, reassuring him that they were on the right track. He hoped the girl's father had seen the same and would determine to follow them to the fort. The only worry now was a hard rain like the last one they had experienced, which might wash away all signs of their previous passage.

They pressed forward, hoping to overtake the Mexican man before nightfall, but were destined to fail since the evening shadows were already marching across the valley. As the last rays of direct sunlight climbed the mountain's eastern slopes, the boy guided them toward the stream where they would camp.

Natalie gathered firewood while Miguel unsaddled and hobbled the animals for the night. The routine was familiar to them both from their recent journey, but something about being just the two of them in this wilderness made it seem like they were the only people in the world, and for all practical purposes, they were.

The boy built a fire and then took the coffee pot to the clear mountain stream to fill it with water; the young girl selected three equal-sized stones and arranged them at one side of the fire the way she had seen the old Indian do when he had cooked for the rescue party. She removed a skillet from one of the panniers, placed it on the stones, scooped a dollop of lard from a tin, and then left it to heat. From her sack of supplies, she pulled out a smaller bag of flour where she had stowed four eggs, fished them out, blew the clinging powder from their shells, and sat them to one side. She then took two potatoes from the sack with a paring knife to peel them, then sliced them into thin slabs, and dropped them into the sizzling grease of the skillet.

Miguel came back and knelt by a pannier and pulled out a tin of coffee; he measured out a small fistful of grounds and dropped them into the pot with the water. While there, he tossed a couple of the biscuits that had remained in the pannier from the rescue mission to the dog. The biscuits were just a token, for he knew the dog's main diet on these trips was fresh rabbit. He then returned to the fire and pushed the pot into the hot coals to boil.

Looking over to the girl, he said, "Save me one of those eggshells after you break it, and I will use it in the coffee."

The girl looked back, gave him a twisted smile as if he had made a joke, and said sarcastically, "Well, Mr. Strider, I may be just a dumb girl, but even I know that you don't put eggshells in coffee."

Sierra Sunrise

He smiled and said, "You just save one anyway, and we will see." He walked over and handed her a wooden spoon to stir the potatoes, "Here," he said, "this will work better than that knife."

Natalie shook her head but took the spoon and made room in the pan for the eggs. She then took them two at once and cracked them into the pan.

"Ok, here are your eggshells," said the girl, handing them to him and waiting to see what he would do with them.

Miguel took the shells, pulled the boiling coffee pot from the coals, and lifted the lid. He crushed the eggshells into the pot, replaced the cover, and then sat it on the ground to cool. Then he arranged their saddles a few feet apart near the fire, went back to the pannier, and pulled out two tin plates, cups, a pair of U.S. Army issue metal forks, and a wool blanket. Coming back to the fire, he spread the blanket between the two saddles and placed a set of dinnerware by each saddle. He then broke short lengths of dead limbs to put the skillet on to protect the blanket. While the boy retrieved the coffee pot, Natalie carried the heavy skillet over and sat it on the limbs.

Miguel poured them cups of hot black coffee and set the pot aside. "Now," said the boy, "you tell me what you think of my coffee, and I will tell you what I think of your cooking."

The girl picked up her cup and, by the light of the fire, inspected the liquid inside. Finding no apparent chunks of eggshell, she took an experimental sip.

"I don't drink much coffee," she said, "but this isn't half bad. I find it usually too bitter, but this is quite good, and so far, there are no coffee grounds. Is it possible that a mountain boy has found the secret to good coffee?"

"No," replied Miguel, "I saw my mother slipping egg shells into the coffee pot at home one time and asked her why; she said there is something in the shells that makes everything settle to the bottom of the pot, and the egg soaks up the bitter taste. She told me she sneaks them in to keep Poppa from learning her secret. She said it's just a woman's way to keep a man under control."

"Very clever," said the girl, "I think your mother and I might have a lot in common."

Miguel sat on his saddle and Natalie on hers, and she spooned the food from the pan into their plates. The boy, in his usual manner when it came to food, became silent and began scooping the potatoes and eggs into his mouth. The girl watched for a moment, then said, "Well, what is your verdict on the food?"

Startled at the question, Miguel looked up with his fork halfway to his mouth, "Well," he said, "I've et worse," and then smiled an embarrassed smile. The girl seemed to be satisfied with his answer.

As the girl talked and the boy listened, they finished their meal. The sky above the mountains seemed to glow, contrasting with the darkening shadows surrounding them as the last rays of sunshine passed overhead. There was a chill in the air as the day's warmth lifted like a blanket, and the coolness of the mountains slid down upon them and pooled in the meadow like cold spring water at the bottom of a pond.

As the day's glow finally left the sky, they sat there staring up at the narrow band of stars between the two tall mountains. The boy recounted the story his grandfather had told him about the village at the bottom of the canyon in Arizona. He wondered how often his father must have sat like this as a boy, staring out into the universe, feeling safe and apart from the world above. The boy didn't say it, but he felt a new kinship with that man of few words, who possessed infinite patience but had shared little else of himself. These mountains were the boy's home and sanctuary, and now he understood that these feelings were in his blood, inherited from his ancestors.

"Do you think we will be able to find my father?" asked Natalie, with a shiver that was only partly due to the cooling temperature.

"We will find him," replied Miguel solemnly, "just ask Juliet if you don't believe me." The dog raised her head at the mention of her name, then settled down by the fire to resume her nap.

CHAPTER 44

The willow bark tea helped to control the fever, but it was no substitute for a cure for either the man or the boy, and the two women and one small girl were kept busy tending to their needs. Maria and Margarita spoke little as the mother of the ailing boy took out her frustration and feelings of helplessness on the nurse's misdiagnosis of rabies. She realized it would have made no difference in the boy's treatment, but that didn't stop her resentment. Then too, she remembered that she had all but accepted the woman's offer to end her son's life, and she channeled that guilt toward Margarita as well. For the nurse, the loss of a sister and nephew, the mistake about the boy, and her stubborn refusal to accept the truth about either filled her with shame. She just wanted to be home with her husband and to put all that had happened in the desert and these mountains far behind her.

Raphael had good moments and bad. He could be taken with coughing fits that sounded like his lungs were being ripped apart, ending with gasps for breath that were almost unendurable to hear. At other times he would whisper to his sister, words that she finally recognized as memories of random childish conversations that they had shared. She stayed through the pain and the rambling dialogues because, as she told her mother, "I am his only sister, and I have to watch out for him."

The high fevers had taken their toll on William; thankfully, he was asleep or unconscious most of the time. On occasion, Maria would look up and see him silently watching her through wet glassy eyes, and when she spoke to him, he would respond with a wan smile but never with words of despair, which she knew he would never do.

The women took turns with the man and the boy and the chores about the place. They had a duty to the animals, even though it was time begrudged away from their patients. They each counted the seconds, minutes, hours, and days, for the clock ticks slowly for those waiting for a loved one to choose life or death. Maria found herself in quiet moments making involuntary bargains with God; Take the boy but leave the man, take me and leave them both, take us all and have done with it! Sorrow became anger, and anger became fear, and fear became sorrow.

Outside these rooms, she knew that the rest of the world was still turning. The sun came up, the sun went down, birds flew, and grass grew, but inside the cabin, time stood still. They all waited breathlessly for the spell they were under to break; whether for good or bad was no longer the question; they were reduced to waiting for the when.

CHAPTER 45

The young boy and girl were up with the sky's first glow as the sun's rays teased the darkness above the sleeping earth. Stars winked out, and faint ghostly shadows appeared beneath the trees as day awoke between the mountains. There was no breakfast for these two this morning, as their goal for the day was to overtake the Mexican man before sundown. Miguel saddled the animals, and Natalie loaded their camping gear into the mule's panniers. She extinguished their campfire with water from the stream carried in the coffee pot and smiled when the egg shells fell with the water. They both mounted in the still gray light, noticing how the chilled spring air revealed their horses' breath and made wispy clouds appear above the surface of the fast water racing toward the sea.

"Juliet, find the man," the boy ordered when they were ready to ride. Miguel had traded the mule's lead halter for a bridal and bit which would give him more control over the animal when it came time to quicken their pace. The dog led at a conservative lope, slow enough to maintain the scent trail and a comfortable gallop for the horses. The mule followed at a stiff-legged trot, but a couple of sharp jerks on the lead rope convinced her to match their horses' stride.

As they progressed through the winding canyons ever downward, Miguel noticed that the trail they followed meandered as if the man were casting about to find the path. It was obvious that he had either not seen or recognized the plain signs of their previous passing. When the walls between mountains narrowed, and there were no alternate routes, the boy urged them along faster, attempting to narrow the gap between them and the girl's father. He knew the dog could pick up the scent trail when the canyon they followed became two.

The sun had just peeked above the eastward mountains when they came upon the man's cold campsite where he had spent the night. Pausing a few moments to read the signs of the man's passing, Miguel noticed where the man had tied the horse and donkey's reins to a small tree instead of hobbling them for the night. The stream, which would have watered the animals had he camped near it, was far across the valley. The stripped branches told of the animals pulling loose from their tethers sometime in the night and then making their way toward the creek. Upon closer inspection, he saw the man's boot tracks clearly on top of the hoof prints as he followed after them across the meadow. There were no signs of a fire or camping gear, which could only mean that the man hadn't unloaded anything for the night. He had probably ridden late and stopped to roll up in a blanket on the ground.

"We should hurry," said Miguel. "It looks like your father is on foot, and that is not a good thing in these mountains."

The girl didn't ask, and the boy didn't take time to discuss why it worried him so much that the man was without a horse and, as far as he could tell, without his gun. Not only was there a danger from rabid animals, but there were things in these mountains, human and otherwise, that would not hesitate to attack a man alone and unarmed.

They crossed the valley toward the stream, and Miguel silently questioned whether he should have brought the shotgun instead of his father's long rifle. His decision was based partially on his admiration of that gun and the fact that he knew his mother's skill with the other, and she did remain the sole protector of the home place. He knew that even a near miss was often good enough with the shotgun, but the rifle relied entirely upon accuracy. He hoped he wouldn't be tested again like before with the assassins, for he was pretty sure that beginner's luck had seen him through that situation.

They saw where the animals had drunk at the stream and wandered about in the dark, looking for forage. The man's footprints stopped at the water's edge, then went one direction, then another, looking for his animals. Finally, the man must have made his best guess at a direction, for the horse and donkey tracks crossed and recrossed in a confusing pattern that would have taken an experienced tracker to decipher. From his own experience and watching and listening to his father and grandfather on the trail of the Mexicans, he had gleaned enough technique to know that intuition played almost as important a part in tracking as the signs. When there were no visible clues, he asked his father, "How do you follow a trail when there are no tracks?"

His father had told him that it is essential to put yourself in the mind of your quarry and try to anticipate the decisions they will make. Of course, his father's actual words had been, "You just gotta think your way through."

Miguel was sure that the man wouldn't go on without his horse and supplies, and since he had no tracking skills, his movements might be random. He was confident that Juliet would eventually decipher the trail. Still, instead of waiting, he rode back away from the trees lining the stream and surveyed the surrounding area looking for an accessible high point from which he might spot the man or his animals. He located a promontory overlooking the creek that seemed accessible by foot and called Natalie to follow him. They rode up the mountain base as far as possible, tied their horses, then climbed.

During their ascent, all the boy could think of was how much time was being wasted looking for the girl's father when the important thing was the medicine and getting it back before his brother and father died from the lack of it.

When they made their way up to the overlook, Miguel used the magnifying sight on his father's rifle to scan the stream bank for signs. Natalie shaded her eyes against the fully exposed sun and searched the valley for movement. Suddenly, she grabbed the boy's arm and pointed. It was too far away to make out clearly, but something was weaving its way through the tall grass and bushes further down the canyon. As the boy swung the rifle around to focus on what the girl had seen, he realized immediately that it wasn't his companion's father. What he saw looked more like a man wearing a fur coat. It reminded him of the men they had passed on the trail from the soldier fort, mountain men of differing descriptions, wearing clothes made from the skins of animals. Scanning further along, the shape of another man came into view. This one, thankfully, was the girl's father, still on foot and moving slowly toward a grove of trees at the end of the valley. It became apparent that the first man was tracking the second, for Miguel saw flashes of the brown coat moving quickly along Alejandro's line of travel. The following man moved into a clear space in the foliage, and Miguel gasped, "Oh my god, it's a bear trailing your father!"

In a panic, Natalie demanded, "Well, shoot him!" for the bear was quickly closing the gap.

Miguel looked down at the range settings on the complicated sights; his father had told him once that up to two hundred yards distance, an experienced marksman could use the rifle to hit just about anything he aimed at reliably. The boy knew that the bear was well over five hundred yards away. The chance that he could hit the moving animal from this distance would be more than a miracle.

"I may not be able to hit the bear," said Miguel, "but maybe I can warn your father or scare the thing away." At this, he ratcheted a shell into the chamber, brought the long gun to his shoulder, elevated the muzzle to twice what the sights allowed, and fired. The rifle's report echoed down the valley, bouncing from mountain to mountain until it was lost in the distance. They saw the bear hesitate, but it did not stop its charge. He worked the bolt again and fired a second shot. As the two moving bodies became one, the boy fired a third and final round. Juliet, who had continued trying to unravel the confusing trail of the man until the shots rang out, began scrambling up the steep slope to find the boy and girl.

Miguel turned and looked into the girl's desperate face, and together they skidded to the base of the promontory, almost colliding with the dog. They mounted the horses and dashed down the valley toward the grove of trees, but before they had covered half the distance, they heard shots being fired in rapid succession, then all fell silent save the sound their horse's hooves made on the grassy ground. A hopeful look passed between the two as they continued to ride. Perhaps the man had killed the bear, but when they arrived at the scene, their hopes were dashed as it was apparent they were too late. The bear had caught the man from behind despite their efforts to warn him, and the massive amount of blood on the man's head and body told his fate. It puzzled Miguel, however, that there were no signs of a gun to be found, yet the bear lay dead at the man's side. Juliet skidded to a halt when the scent of the bear hit her in the face as she entered the clearing, and she stood with hackles raised and a low growl rumbling in her throat.

Natalie slid from the saddle and ran to her father, stopping short and staring down at the body. She was obviously in shock at seeing the severity of the wounds. Miguel hurried over and checked the bear for signs of life. Only when he was sure it was utterly dead did he lay down his father's rifle and rush to the girl's side.

The young boy desperately wanted to console the girl but had no experience to draw upon in this situation, so he stood silently at her side. In that awkward moment, he remembered another time that he had stood unprepared in front of this same girl and the advice his father had given him, "Sometimes nothing is the kindest thing you can say," and so the boy stood. After a few moments, he reached over and touched the girl's hand; it was as if she awoke from a bad dream, turned to him, wrapped grateful arms around his neck, and wept. He held her as tightly as he dared and had decided that he would stand there the rest of his life if it would help the girl. It wasn't necessary, though, as shortly, his grandfather rode out of the grove of trees on his mule.

CHAPTER 46

When the old man had ridden out of the yard gate at the Strider cabin, he was returning to his mountain hideaway. He missed his self-imposed isolation and couldn't wait to return to it. This excursion into the world of people reminded him why he had gone there in the first place. He was glad to have met his son's family but knew that there was no place in it for him. The woman's hatred of him, even though he was sure she realized it was misplaced, would never allow her to accept him into their circle. Better to spend his days alone, remembering the good life he had lost, than growing bitter at being rejected trying to regain it.

He hated leaving his son and grandson in such dire straits but knew that the tensions between him and the woman would only distract the family from possibly sharing and appreciating the last days of their loved ones' lives. Losing his entire family so abruptly had left him hollow, cheating him of experiencing grief for the individuals he had lost. His mind had been overwhelmed with the flitting images of their faces and memories too numerous to count. As he spiraled down into depression, these recollections merged into one entity that became his dead family. Depression became despair, which he later recognized as self-pity at having been left behind. Perhaps if he didn't see his son and grandson's dead bodies, they would not join the others haunting the dark corners of his mind. He knew that he was much better prepared to live with that bit of self-deception than to deal definitively with their deaths.

The mule plodded along at her own pace and volition, leaving him to distract himself with his inner thoughts, for she knew her way home as well as he did, and so he was left to consider life without even his one son in it. Perhaps no life at all would be preferable to the one he now contemplated.

Suddenly he realized that the rocking motion of the mule's stride had stopped. As he focused on their surroundings, he saw them standing before a fork in the road. To the right, the trail would lead them up to his mountain home; to the left was the direction of the soldier fort. "Clever girl," the old man whispered to the mule, then without hesitation, he nudged her toward the fort. "There might just be one last worthwhile thing for us to do," he said aloud to no one, or perhaps he said it to himself. Whichever it was, it boosted his sagging spirits.

With a new purpose, the old Indian pushed the mule into a comfortable trot that would not slacken for two days and two nights. Occasionally, he drew jerked deer meat from his saddle bag and drank water from his canteen; he slowed only to allow the mule to grab a mouth full of grass or drink from a mountain stream. When he rode through the perpetually open gates at Three Forks Army Station, he was greeted with curious stares by everyone he passed on his way up to the Army hospital. He eased himself gingerly from the saddle and held on to the mule's bridal while he stretched the stiffness from his legs before stepping up onto the wooden walkway.

A man he didn't recognize from his previous visits sat on the bench in front of the big glass window of the hospital, napping. The man jumped and sat upright in a mild daze when he spoke.

"I need another bate of that medicine that you all give my son for his leg," said the Indian.

The man on the bench, not a doctor but a second assistant to the actual doctor, glared blearily up at the Indian standing in front of him. Had it been a soldier, a string of curse words would have ensued to cover his embarrassment at having been caught in his compromised condition. Instead, the embarrassment turned to anger when the soldier realized that he had been startled by nothing more than an ordinary red Indian.

"I don't know who you think you are, Chief!" said the man, "but this is an Army hospital, and there ain't no Indians allowed here, so you best get back on your donkey and skedaddle on out of here before somebody shoots you for trespass!"

The old Indian man, who was tired and had little patience with army soldiers to begin with, recognized the same type of disrespectful bigot that he had been so unfortunate to have to deal with his entire life. His first inclination was to reach down and cut off the man's left ear and stuff it into his shirt pocket, but he could imagine the ruckus that it would raise, and besides, it would surely damage his chances of getting the medicine he was after. While considering alternatives, the man rose from the bench and stood menacingly above him, a good foot taller and fifty pounds heavier than him.

"We was here a few days ago," explained the Indian, "and the other doctor patched up my son's leg and give us some medicine to take. I ain't askin for nothin free; I got money to pay."

"Yeah, I know who you are now," said the assistant, "All I can say is, you were lucky that I wasn't on duty when you come. Doc Howard has a soft spot for curs and Indians, but I ain't got no such affliction."

It was apparent to the old man that this conversation was going nowhere, so he reluctantly switched to plan B.

With no apparent emotion or threat, the saddle-weary old Indian took a step toward the disagreeable young man. Instead of standing his ground, the assistant involuntarily retreated an unbalanced step back against the bench. The Indian peered up into the startled man's eyes and smiled his toothy smile. While he held the man's stare, he deftly slipped the razor-sharp skinning knife from his belt and slid its point up past the man's ribcage and into his left armpit. At the same time, he hooked his left arm securely around the soldier's midsection. As the man struggled to free himself, the Indian applied pressure upward on the blade; he felt it slide easily through the material of the man's shirt and just enough into the flesh to demonstrate his seriousness. The sensation of the blade entering the soldier's body caused the assistant to stiffen. A small whimper escaped his throat; he closed his eyes against the sharp pain and then moistened the front of his uniform pants.

"How much medicine do you figure using your left arm is worth?" asked the old man.

The assistant to the doctor opened his eyes enough to look down into the face of the man who had impaled him. The cold determination that he read there sent chills up his spine. At that instant, the realization came that anyone willing to ride into the middle of an Army post and stick a knife into a soldier would probably not leave before getting what he had come for. They both knew that the old Indian's actions thus far had already earned him an execution, so any subsequent violence could be carried out for the sheer pleasure of it without accruing further consequences.

Displaying an entirely new attitude, the assistant swallowed the lump in his throat and said with humility, "If you allow me, sir, I will be glad to get that penicillin for you now."

The old Indian didn't speak, but he did lower the knife enough for the man to turn and stumble through the hospital doorway. They encountered no one, for there were no patients, and the second assistant's job was to keep a presence at the hospital while the doctor was away.

After accepting a sack containing enough medicine to cure ten people, the old Indian tied the assistant to a chair and placed a gag in his mouth. Before he left, the Indian shook a leather pouch in front of the man's eyes and opened the top enough to see that it contained many shiny yellow metal objects. He cinched the top and shoved the pouch into the man's pocket.

"This is for your trouble," the old Indian winked.

The assistant began to feel much better about the encounter and spent the next couple of hours waiting to be freed, imagining what that bag of treasure might be worth. You could never tell, thought the man, for what do Indians know about the worth of gold anyway? When he was finally released from his bonds, he vaguely described his assailant, not even mentioning that he had been an Indian. He would be just as happy if the old man were never found or questioned. When dismissed, his first act was to sneak away and open the leather pouch to discover that he had been rewarded with a hand full of brass Army trouser buttons. By then, it was too late to amend his account of the abduction, and he threw the bag of worthless buttons into the dirt.

The old man had to temper his want for speed on his return trip, as the mule was dead tired from their forced march to the Army post, so they soon made camp for the night on a bluff overlooking the wagon trail. He was anxious to know if a troop of soldiers would be out looking for him, so he slept lightly in case they should pass in the night. By morning the mule had recovered, and the Indian felt they could push on. The fact that no one had followed them in the night gave him confidence that they would be safe to continue on the road.

On the morning of the second day after leaving the soldier fort, while making his way up a canyon only a few miles from his son's cabin, a series of shots rang out that the Indian immediately recognized as having come from his son William's long rifle. He slapped the tired mule on the rump with the reins and urged her forward as fast as she could manage.

Coming through a grove of trees, he heard someone scream and the roar of a bear. The sound was very close, and he didn't trust that he would be able to control the mule if confronted by the fierce beast ahead of them, so he dismounted and pulled the assassin's repeating rifle from its scabbard and ran forward on foot. He knew that the shots couldn't have come from his ailing son, so the next most likely person would be Miguel. As soon as the trees began to thin, and he could see into the meadow beyond, it quickly became apparent that it was too late to stop the tragedy unfolding there. The shape of a person that he couldn't immediately identify was lying face down on the ground, mauled by a huge black bear. He stopped long enough to steady his gun against a gum tree and fired into the head and chest of the animal who reared above its victim. It took five rounds before the huge creature would tumble backward onto the earth.

The old man walked hesitantly forward to discover the identity of the bear's victim. Should it be his grandson, he wasn't sure how he would cope. Visions of carrying the boy's mangled body back to his mother and father caused him to choke back the emotion as he made his way through the tall grass.

He was only a few paces away before he was confident that the body didn't belong to his grandson. The victim had been a full-grown man, so instead of moving closer, he went down to one knee, struggling to recover the breath he hadn't realized he had held through the encounter. It was as if the clouds formed in his mind at the thought of losing Miguel had parted, and he felt an intense moment of joy. In his mind, he said a silent apology to the dead victim, but at that moment, he was incapable of feeling sorrow.

It was a few moments before he heard the drumbeat of hooves

coming rapidly across the meadow. His first thought was for caution, as a man alone in these mountains was vulnerable to those like the assassins who had attacked them before. He crept back through the grass to the trees and made his way to where he had left the mule; no use taking undo chances considering that his rescue attempt had already failed. Before revealing his presence, he would wait until he knew who he was dealing with.

CHAPTER 47

When he recognized the riders as Miguel and Natalie, the old Indian deduced the victim's identity. After waiting a few moments to observe the young people's reaction, he rode from his concealment into the open. His eyes met with his grandson's as the boy held the girl in an awkward embrace. There was surprise and relief in the boy's look, for this was the second time he had found himself out of his depth in consoling this young girl for the loss of a parent.

The sound of the mule's approach caused the girl to peer back over her shoulder at the old Indian, but as soon as she recognized him, she turned back to the comfort of Miguel's shoulder.

The Indian dismounted and checked the bear and the man for signs of life before speaking. "What were you three doing out here in the mountains anyways?" he asked.

"The two of us were looking for…," and the boy hesitated, nodding toward the girl's father, "he decided to go back to the soldier fort for more medicine. When I found out, I was afraid he might get lost finding his way through these passes, so we came after him. We had just about caught up with him when we saw the bear attack."

"Then that was you that fired your poppa's rife?" asked the old man.

"Yessir, it was," replied Miguel. "I was trying to warn either him or the bear off," said the boy, looking again at the fallen victim and attacker.

"It must have been you who killed the bear," the boy said distractedly.

A pang of guilt struck the old man as he realized that if he had ridden back to the cabin to tell them that he was going for the medicine, the Mexican man might still be alive. He realized that it had been his selfish pride that had prevented him from doing that simple thing. Without confessing his failure, he told the girl he was truly sorry. When she didn't respond, he was compelled to explain further.

"I have the medicine; I was on my way home when I decided to get it; I don't know why it took me so long to think of it. I wish I had taken the time to ride back and tell you all that I was going; I just thought every minute might count."

Natalie released her hold on the boy and wiped her eyes on the sleeves of her heavy shirt. "I think every minute does count," she said, taking a deep, shaky breath. "If you and Miguel dig a grave, I will prepare my father for burial. I want to ensure that his good intentions are not wasted, so we should get the medicine to Mr. Strider and his son as quickly as possible."

They all looked at one another in agreement, and Miguel said, "I'll get the shovel and a blanket, and we can get started."

It was hard for the girl, but she was determined to see the job through. She cleaned her father up as best she could with water from a canteen and a kerchief given to her by the old Indian. She then laid the wet cloth over his face, wrapped him in the blanket Miguel had retrieved, and sat waiting while the man and boy finished the shallow grave. This was by no means the first time she had helped to prepare a relative to be laid to rest, as injuries left from the war were still a significant cause of death in her country. In the short time between leaving their home in Mexico and today, she had lost her mother, father, and brother, leaving her unsure of her future. She was sure her aunt would want to take her to her home in San Francisco, but while watching Miguel dig with his grandfather, she wondered if there might not still be a place for her in these mountains.

After the hastily dug grave was deemed adequate, the Indian and boy lowered the Mexican man into it. Miguel and the girl helped gather stones to cover the body as the Indian explained that they would provide a barrier against digging animals. They pushed the earth atop the rocks and placed a larger stone as a marker at the head of the grave. There would be no inscription, but should they want to, they would be able to find the grave again. The bear was left to the scavengers and vultures as it was too warm for the hide to be of value, and besides, they were in a hurry to get back to the cabin.

Surveying the area, the Indian man thought to himself, here in the middle of nowhere stands an old Indian, a half-Indian boy, and a young Mexican girl. The most unlikely participants were at an unexpected funeral arranged by a hapless Mexican man and an unlucky Sierra Nevada black bear. They were all players in a ritual as old as man himself, one that could be described quite simply as the entombment of a body in a shroud of earth. None were here by choice; all were just victims of happenstance. He suspected that the procedure held no special meaning for the dead but seemed a necessary token to be performed for the living. It has always required an awkward period of silence, during which people are encouraged to contemplate the mysteries of the universe and their tiny place in it. He was reminded of the last time he had stood thus, looking down upon his young daughter's grave. There had been no one to stand by his side at that event, for she was the last to be taken by an illness he neither understood nor had any power to defend against. He remembered looking at the mounds of earth to the left and right, trying to picture those he had placed there. He had been horrified that the only countenances he could bring to mind were the shrunken masks painted by death upon the face of each of them. Were these the images that would come to him in the night for the rest of his life? If so, he might never sleep again; thankfully, this had not turned out to be the case. When he thought of them today, they stood together in bright sunlight, eyes shining with life.

Miguel stood in support of the girl, acutely aware that this was the fifth in a rash of burials in which he had never participated before their excursion into the desert. First, there was Natalie's mother and brother, then the two assassins, and now the girl's father. His feelings were a mix of sorrow for the girl and dread for himself because the next one was likely to be for his father or brother.

Natalie was still processing her father's demise, she had always thought more of her mother, but it turned out that her mother was responsible for taking her brother's life. She had loved her father after a manner, but he had taken her mother's life. Had they never left Mexico, her mother and brother would be alive, but her father would probably still be dead. It was too much for the young girl to process, so she wept for them all and then wept for herself.

When the Indian thought enough time had passed to respect the dead, he said, "I think we should try to get started."

The other two agreed, so they gathered their gear and headed back up the valley.

"What about the horse and donkey?" asked Miguel.

The old man said, "Let's spread out, and we will watch for them on the way home."

Miguel rode nearer to the girl than was practical to the search for the missing animals, but he wasn't willing to let her out of sight in case there was another bear.

It wasn't long before they heard the old man's whistle, and he came riding to them, leading both the Mexican man's horse and the donkey.

"They was happier to see me than I was to see them," the Indian reported as he rode up. He handed the lead rope from the donkey to the young girl, slipped from the tired mule's saddle, and remounted on the still-saddled horse. As soon as they were lined out, leading the extra animals, the old man put his heels to the horse and established a mile-eating gallop to take them to his son's home.

As they rode side by side through the meadows, Miguel asked his grandfather, "Did you have any trouble talking them out of more medicine? Cause when we left there the last time, it sounded like that doctor wasn't interested in giving us any more help."

"No trouble at all," the old man smiled, "it's all in how you ask."

The boy nodded in agreement but had severe doubts about his grandfather's diplomatic skills.

The day was still young, so they hoped to reach the cabin before dark. They stopped to water the animals as they crossed the willow tree stream, then increased their pace as they acquired the wagon road leading them to the cabin. Despite the day's events, all three felt their spirits rise as they grew nearer to their goal.

When they finally reached the steep incline in the lane that led up onto the plateau where the cabin was situated, the old man brought his horse up short in the fading light, causing Miguel and Natalie to stop along with him. He tugged on his mule's reins to bring her up alongside him where he could reach into the saddle bag, and when his hand came out, it was holding the paper bag that contained the penicillin; he handed it to the girl as she was closest to him.

"This is as far as I go," said the old man.

The boy was confused and asked, "but aren't you coming up to see Poppa?"

His grandfather said, "No, give the medicine to your momma or the nurse and tell your poppa; I hope he gets well. You know where I live, and I will keep an eye out for you. I'll keep this horse for a while till I can find another mule; then, you can have him back."

The old Indian reined the horse and started back the way they had come, still leading the tired mule.

Miguel's impulse was to follow and try to change the old man's mind, but when Juliet started up the road toward the cabin, he was reminded that they needed to get home with the medicine.

CHAPTER 48

The interaction between his mother and the old Indian was of grave concern to the boy; he wasn't sure exactly what, but he knew that something had to be done about it. It seemed that the two of them were both content to go their separate ways, as had been the case for the past dozen or more years, but not so for Miguel. It was like six people living on an island; one of them was being forced to live apart, even though a blood relative. Before this, he hadn't known that he had such a thing as a living relative, but now that he did, he was determined never to be deprived of his company again.

When Miguel and Natalie reached the cabin, they had to push past Juliet, who stood staring into the darkened doorway. No one had bothered to light the kitchen lantern, and the bedroom lamps hardly produced a glow in the hallway. When the gate to the yard had been closed behind them, they let the animals wander as they wished and hurried inside with the penicillin the old man had provided them.

"Mother?" called the boy cautiously when they entered the kitchen door. The darkness threw his voice back at them, and the two young travelers stood for a moment in reverent silence. It was as if they had entered a tomb and were reluctant to disturb its occupants.

Miguel walked to the kitchen table by the fading daylight coming in through the windows and reached up to push the lever that raised the globe on the smokey lantern. He selected a wooden match from the bowl that sat forever at the table's center and struck it alight on the metal bail from which the lamp was hung. He pushed the match near the blackened wick and waited while the guttering flame grew longer as the coal oil warmed to its touch. He lowered the soot-smudged glass back into its seat and backed away, letting the light fill the room, making the darkness outside complete. The last glow in the western sky made the pines seen through the kitchen windows stand out black against the dying light.

They heard footsteps from the back of the house, and Maria and Margarita emerged from the hallway. Both looked worn and haggard as they squinted against the intense light of the lantern.

"Weren't you able to find your father?" Maria asked, looking at the young girl. The women had discussed it and agreed that Natalie and Alejandro would probably return to the cabin, and Miguel would continue to the soldier fort.

"We found him," said Miguel, answering for the girl. "He was attacked and killed by a mountain bear; we had to bury him where we found him."

At this news, the nurse walked quickly to her niece and offered her a hug, but the girl merely took her hand and held it in silence.

"Darling, I'm so sorry," said Margarita, "how did it happen?"

"First," said the girl, as she set the paper sack she had carried into the house onto the table, "we brought the medicine back with us."

The news about the much-needed medicine surprised the two women almost as much as the bear attack had.

Miguel picked up the bag, dumped its contents onto the table, and looked at his mother, "You should get a dose of this into Poppa and Raphael, you know to crush them, right?" he asked. "I have a chore to do, and I might be gone for a day or two."

"But how did you get this medicine so quickly?" Maria asked her son.

"Grandpa," was the boy's short reply, turning to walk back outside into the dark.

Natalie looked at her aunt and said, "Father made a mistake and lost his horse, and the bear caught him on the ground. There was nothing we could do."

To Margarita's surprise, Natalie gave her a 'let's don't argue about this look' and marched through the door, following Miguel.

"Where are they going?" the nurse hurriedly asked Maria, hesitating before going after the girl.

"They are going to find that old man," was the mother's disappointed reply. "Now, if you would, please help me with the medicine." It was as if the tragic news about the girl's father were folded in with the rest of their ongoing ordeal and failed to stir in them any heightened grief.

Miguel walked down the steps toward the barnyard where the animals had collected; ten steps away from the porch, he heard Natalie's footfalls behind him. By now, the boy had learned the futility of arguing with the girl, so he marched on, caught both their horses, and stood holding her reins. He waited for her to take them, and when she did, he looked around to see a victorious smile spread across her face. He gave her a token scowl in return, admitting his acceptance of his lack of control over her, then turned to capture Leah, who was still loaded with their supplies.

"Juliet!" the boy called, and the dog met them at the gate to the yard, and they were on their way to find the stubborn old Indian.

"Do you think he will come back with us?" asked the girl as they followed the lane down from the plateau.

"I don't know," said the boy, "I am afraid it might seem like crawling to him, and I don't see him ever begging her to forgive him for whatever she thinks he did to her."

"What do you think happened between them?" asked the girl.

"I don't know and don't want to know," said the boy, "I just want to get them together and make them settle it. I found out that there is a village of people my poppa grew up with, and I want him and my grandpa to take me there to meet them someday. I might belong to a whole world outside these mountains and want to see it."

"What about your father and brother," said the girl, remembering the reason for the medicine.

"They will get better or worse without us, and besides, if my poppa dies, my grandpa is the only one who can help us survive out here," replied the boy.

They urged their horses into a fast gallop hoping to overtake the old man, for Miguel was sure that he could find his grandfather's camp with the help of Juliet.

They rode late into the night by the light of a waxing moon and only stopped when it slipped over the mountains to the west, and it became too dark to navigate the woods. They made a small fire and pushed two potatoes into the glowing ashes to bake while they removed their saddles and set the animals up for the night. They made their beds near the fire and sat waiting for their supper to cook, talking about unimportant things, and avoiding the serious subjects that occupied their minds.

"Miguel, how did your mother and father happen to get together? Her being from Mexico and him an American Indian and all?" asked the girl.

The boy had a ready answer, "Well, Poppa always says that he went looking for a girl who used coal oil for perfume and cracked walnuts with her teeth, but he settled for our momma. She said all the marrying aged men in her village died, and she swore she would marry the first man who rode in, not knowing it would be a wild Indian. She guessed they both just got lucky."

They had a welcome laugh together, and Miguel started to ask about her folks but thought better of it.

Finally, the girl asked, "What would you think if I stayed with your family instead of going home with my aunt?"

Miguel's heart leaped at the suggestion of the thing he hadn't dared entertain for fear of the disappointment he would feel when it didn't happen. "I think it would be a good idea!" he blurted, "even if my poppa gets better, it will be a long time before he's fit enough to help with things. I know Momma could use the help, and I will be busy keeping up with the place and putting food on the table. Heck, I could teach you to hunt and fish, trap, and no end of other things." He finally stopped his runaway talking long enough to smile an embarrassed smile at the young girl who sat before him, enjoying his enthusiasm.

"I guess we can talk to your mother and my aunt when we get back," said the girl. She suddenly had hope for a better future than her present circumstances would have suggested.

Miguel dug the potatoes from the ashes with a stick, then pulled two forks from his shirt pocket and speared the steaming morsels so they could handle them until they cooled. They sat nibbling cautiously, trading ideas on how best to approach their elders with their plans. Their conversation became a guilty pleasure, having committed to a secret plan together.

When the potatoes were gone, and the fire burned down, they rolled up in their wool blankets, slept until early dawn, then quickly returned to the trail.

The old Indian was in no particular hurry to return to his lonesome homestead on the mountain, and they overtook him by the time the sun was high enough to chase the chill from the morning air. When they found him, nothing was said as if everyone had expected them to meet in just this way. He acknowledged them, and they him as the young boy and girl rode up from behind to stations on either side of the old man. Juliet ran ahead and then sat watching them until they came up to her; when they didn't stop, she barked and remained seated as if expecting some interaction between them to resolve the question of where they were going.

The Indian pulled up and sat looking down at his hands, holding his reins. After a few moments, he said, still looking down, "If you two will ride with me to my place where I can get a few things I need, I will come back with you. I will help care for the place until we know how the sick ones make out, but I won't stay at the house; I will make a camp nearby."

Miguel, satisfied to have gotten everything he had come for without saying a word, felt a deep connection with his grandfather, whom he now hoped would always be a part of his life.

Despite the woman's displeasure, the old man had already resolved to return to his son's home and care for them. Sometimes a man has to put his feelings aside and do what he is expected to do for his family.

Natalie knew that everything would work out regardless of all that had happened, and a sense of joy and belonging filled her from the top of her head down to her toes.

The two young people rode back through the yard gate at the cabin and turned their horses loose in the barn lot. They had left the old man situating his campsite by the mirror pool on the back side of the plateau. When they walked through the kitchen door alone, Maria and Margarita looked up in surprise at the absence of the old Indian.

Natalie went to the table and found a seat beside her aunt, and Miguel walked over to help his mother, who was preparing a round of medicine for her husband and son. Without a word, Maria finished crushing the pills, and the boy raked the powder into two cups and then splashed water on top to create a paste.

"I think your father and brother are better," said the woman, trying to draw her son out. She wanted to ask about the grandfather but was afraid her satisfaction with his absence might show on her face.

Miguel had decided to say nothing until he could get his mother alone for the talk he was determined to have, so he picked up the cups and headed toward the bedroom.

Maria followed her son with a frown of unanswered questions remaining on her face. The boy was stubbornly silent, and she thought she could guess what was probably on his mind.

Left alone with the girl in the kitchen, the nurse said, "Now tell me about your father." She scooted her chair closer to the Mexican girl; for now, she wasn't concerned about anything but consoling her young niece. She was thinking only about her own family for the first time in a long time.

Natalie gave a quick, dispassionate account of the events that had led up to her father's death, for she had already put that tragedy behind her, just as she had the others, and was now thinking more about her future than her past.

"I wish we could leave this place today," said Margarita, "but someone will have to take us back to the Army depot so that we can make arrangements for transportation to California. The penicillin seems to be working marvelously, so it shouldn't be long now."

Natalie sat in silence, waiting until she and Miguel had a chance to present their case in front of her aunt and his mother.

In his absence, Miguel saw that the women had moved Raphael into his father's bed and had turned the headboard toward the wall so that they had free access to both patients. Having them both in the same room allowed one of the women to be with Gabriella while the other stood vigil over the man and boy. He had noticed Gabby asleep in his bed as he passed by his room.

After they administered the medicine, first to William and then to Raphael, and, they both lay dozing, the boy stood back to watch his mother tidy up his brother and tuck in his covers, as neatly, Miguel thought, as preparing him for a long winter's nap. He wiped away an unwelcome tear before his mother could see it as the random nursery rhyme flitted through his head. That one had always been the twin's favorite, and he hoped they would all get to share it again this Christmas.

When they were finished, Maria began to gather the things to take back to the kitchen, but Miguel put a hand on her arm to stop her.

"Stay here a minute," he said awkwardly, sensing that he was about to enter unexplored territory. He had never thought to or attempted to tell his mother to do anything. On the contrary, she had been the one always to tell him exactly what to do. The words were familiar, but the flavor was somehow foreign to his tongue, as if they belonged to an unfamiliar language. He didn't realize it, but he was learning to speak the language of grownups.

Maria sat on the side of the bed next to her husband, feeling like a child who had been caught saying naughty words, and she was about to be dressed down for it. This entire ordeal had been one extended test for her, and she knew that in so many ways, she had failed. When Raphael had needed her most, she had panicked, had it not been for Margarita, she might have run screaming into the woods. When she was convinced that he was dying a horrible death, she was ready to give up on her faith and deny God. When confronted with the truth about her Mexican family's deaths, she clung to her hatred of the old man she had blamed for half her life. Now, she thought, her son, who was nothing more than a boy, had somehow seen through her carefully constructed camouflage. All the doubts and fears she had hidden, even from herself, seemed to be written plainly on her face. It made no rational sense to her that he knew anything that had happened while he was gone, but her guilt told her that he did, and he was now compelled to call her out for her every weakness. She was ashamed and was now ready to be shamed.

"Momma," the boy began, and she had to force herself to meet his eyes, "Momma, I'm sorry, but I need to ask you a favor; I need you to forgive my grandpa for whatever it is that he has done to you. If you can't do it for him, please do it for me. When Poppa was shot, Grandpa saved his life; I know that he did. When we all thought Raphael had rabies, Grandpa knew he didn't. When Poppa and Raphe needed medicine, Grandpa rode day and night to get it. I can't imagine how he got the soldiers to give it to him, but if he had to kill someone for it, I don't even care. He has lived alone all these years, and now I want him to live nearer to us. I want him to be a part of our family."

Maria's face was a waterfall of tears when the boy stopped talking. She was so beside herself with relief, grief, and pride in the boy who stood before her that she couldn't speak and could hardly breathe. To think that she and William had raised such a son in the middle of the wilderness with no church or schools or family outside the walls of this house was unbelievable to her. Instead of scolding her for her faults, he had shown only his love and respect. She realized that she had been so busy being the all-knowing parent that she had failed to stop to appreciate the people living in those small bodies that were her children. Now that she was forced to face this fact, she realized that somehow, she had missed the time when she should have stopped being the parent to become the friend. What she saw for the first time was the man her son was becoming, all without a word of encouragement from her.

These thoughts came to her as would a revelation, this was God's plan, and it happened without the need for either her knowledge or approval. She thought there was indeed a force in life greater than mere mortals can comprehend, and knowing it brought her overwhelming comfort. She knew the world would continue to turn with or without her help or interference.

She felt her husband stir beside her as he placed his hand on hers next to him on the bed.

"What do you think about what your son said?" asked the man weakly.

The woman and boy both looked with surprise into the cloudy face of the husband and father.

"I think he may be brighter than I gave him credit for," said Maria smiling through her tears.

"I noticed that too," replied the man, "but don't ask him to whistle." He then coughed in an attempt to chuckle.

Sierra Sunrise

The woman looked mildly confused, but the boy smiled a broad smile; he was elated that his father could speak at all, and the fact that he had the energy to make a joke brought happy tears to his eyes.

Raphael, moved to wakefulness by all the talking, rolled over and placed his chin on his father's shoulder. "Hi Willie," he croaked up at his brother, then closed his dark brown eyes tiredly.

Not to be outdone, a small voice from the doorway said, "Hello, Willie," and they all looked up to see Gabby leaning sleepily against the door jamb. She walked over, and her mother picked her up and sat her on her lap.

"Tomorrow," Maria told her son, wiping the tears from her cheeks, "I want you to go find your grandfather, and I don't care if you have to drag him; I want you to get him back here. Tell him we need to talk."

The boy smiled, "She won't have long to wait," he thought.

When Miguel left the bedroom, his mother was still sitting at his father's side; she and the tiny girl were leaning over, petting the recovering man and boy. He fairly floated down the hallway, "Everything is going to be ok," he said with satisfaction, "the future couldn't be brighter."

Afterword

I want to take a few moments of your time to tell you how this story came about; My father and mother were married in 1939 and raised nine children on the red dirt plains of Central Oklahoma. They lived through the Dust Bowl and the Great Depression and for a time as Okies in California on McDonald Island in the Sacramento-San Joaquin River Delta. They experienced lives that few today can imagine, let alone appreciate. I was the skinny, sickly number five child my father carried on one arm to work with him at the grain elevator as I was recovering from Scarlet Fever (later Rheumatic Fever). How they were able to pay my medical bills and still feed the family is still a mystery to me.

I am sure my extended illness earned me an advantage over my parents in the competition for attention in such a large family, a gift I shamelessly exploited over the following years and even into their later lives. When my father was in his eighties, he was struck down by a stroke; this was when I realized that my parents would not live forever. He recovered to a degree, but the big, strong, quiet man I had looked up to and admired my entire life was now incomplete. Hard work had taken its toll on his body over the years, but his mind had remained intact up to this point. After he was sent home and we all sat with him for extended periods, I and others realized that we would never again see the happy, humorous man who had always been our anchor. He began to sleep more and more, and when he was awake, he spoke of what we initially thought were his dreams, but over time we realized that his mind was compensating for the loss of the life he had so enjoyed for over eighty years. It was being replaced with one created from his imagination. We became frightened and disturbed when we realized that we were losing him to this sleeping fantasy, but slowly, it occurred to us that he was coping with a world over which he had lost all control and had reached a point in his life where there was nothing to look forward to but these dreams. When I finally got over my selfish wish to get my father back at any cost, I realized what a gift God had given him, the ability to create a reality from thin air where he could be happy even in the face of actuality.

In his new world, my father had become the man the government hired to find lost souls in the desert. I suspected a childhood in the country with its hunting and exploring and several trips across America were the roots of his fantasy, but now I think that he may have been unconsciously seeking the escape from harm that William described in the story as, "A kindness meted out by God, which is death."

I sincerely hope that he is living out his best dreams at this very moment in Heaven.

Made in the USA
Monee, IL
31 January 2023